# The Fool
# Arises Dreaming

## Book 2

# Books in this Series

- *Dreaming Wakes the Fool* (Book 1)
- *The Fool Arises Dreaming* (Book 2)

# The Fool Arises Dreaming

## Book 2

Jan Bear

A WORLD OF SPECULATION PRESS

Woodburn, Oregon, USA

# Contents

# The Story So Far

In Dreaming Wakes the Fool, Book 1, Echo found a job that seemed to solve all her problems. Ignoring advice that what seems too good to be true probably is, she took the job and entered a world she had never known existed—where everything is what it means and nothing is what it seems.

On the verge of success, she discovered that she was helping to murder a man. She destroyed a friendship to end the mission, and in Book 2, *The Fool Arises Dreaming,* she sets out to make things right.

CHAPTER 1

# Squat and Stretch

ECHO ALREADY MISSED GALYNN as the sound of her car engine joined the humming, howling river of traffic going past in utter darkness.

She tried to imagine her former companion beside her, the six-foot-tall raven in Doc Martens boots, beautiful and terrifying, street-smart and sarcastic, entitled and beneficent, but for some reason what came to mind was a sad, angry girl, whom Echo had hurt as deeply as her own sister had hurt her.

In the two days of traveling from Portland to Ashland and back to Salem, navigating the journey through the dream of Ytilaer and helpless in the physical world, Echo had come to like, trust, and depend on the raven to get her through every situation.

And now she was gone, sent away, cruelly, like kicking a puppy to save her from the danger of what Echo's quest had become. The pain Echo felt on Galynn's behalf mingled with her own loss, and she wondered if she had done lasting, even fatal, damage to them both.

But Echo's quest continued. She had been tricked into betraying a man who had never done her—or possibly anybody—any harm, and she had to stop it. She had to stop it.

She took a deep breath and stood in the blackness listening for sounds that would tell her where she was and where to go. The traffic noise told her there would be lights around, as well as shadows, but in this world blackness surrounded her like a fog, and the loudest noises were voices from inside, shouting: *You're all alone. You can't see anything. No one cares where you are.*

The aloneness was more terrible than anything she had yet experienced in Ytilaer. She felt marooned on a dark and empty planet, where no one would ever find her.

She went into her esuoh, the inner house of her psyche, decorated with the colorful chaos of a Romany traveler's wagon, and sat on her porch, a place that usually gave her calming perspective. Even there, the fog was as black as smoke, and its billows and streams danced like ravers at a concert.

After a while, nevertheless, her breathing returned to normal, and her fear retreated. She went back out into the world's darkness and listened. When panic came creeping up again, she squatted on the ground with her hands on the concrete, feeling the rough and dirty surface like a familiar friend. She became conscious of the mechanistic river of traffic on one side and post-apocalyptic silence on the other. She stood up.

Navigating between the traffic noise and the silence, she shuffled along, feeling the way with her feet so she wouldn't trip. She made slow progress across the barren wasteland. After what seemed like hours of walking through a lightless cave, finally her foot struck a curb. It was a step up. A sidewalk. She had reached—something. Assuming Galynn had dropped her at the right place—she had to assume Galynn dropped her at the right place—she had found the train station.

She ran forward to the building, banging her leg on a metal thing and hitting her face on a wall of concrete or stone. On further exploration, her hands identified the object she had run into as an electric meter with metal posts on each side. Crying for joy, she reached out and embraced the scratchy bricks and the metal downspout. She felt more than saw a lessening of the darkness, as if a crack in the cave let in a distant hint of twilight.

She had crossed the parking lot without Galynn.

Walking with renewed confidence, she swept her hand along the building's surface of bricks and windows until she came to a set of columns and a step up to a locked door. The porch was raised above the surrounding sidewalk, so she sat down on it to wait for morning.

She fished out of her bag the sandwich that Galynnhad bought for her that afternoon at the truck stop on I-5. Even though it was lukewarm and slightly squished, she ate it gratefully. She promised herself again that she really would get in touch with Galynn after all this was finished. But she didn't have Galynn's number, and she didn't know what "finished" would look like. And maybe Galynn wouldn't want to talk to her again anyway.

After the sandwich, she stashed the wrapping inside her bag and went onto the porch of her esuoh and watched the swirling fog, now a purplish-gray.

She felt a jostling and a sense of invasion. She came out into the world and saw two people made of twisted balloons shining like glow-in-the-dark toys. One was tall and thin; the other short and round. The tall one was pawing through Echo's bag while the short one stood by.

"Hey! What are you doing?" She grabbed the bag and held it tight against her abdomen. "Did you take anything?" *Lazar's key.*

"We wanted to borrow your phone," the tall one said, his hands on his hips. His voice was nasal and piercing, like wind through a closed airway.

"I don't have a phone."

"She said she doesn't have a phone," the fat one said. His voice was deeper, with a liquid quality, as if it had burbled up from the swamp.

She named them Stretch and Squat. "You must have something." Stretch came closer again. "Or you wouldn't be afraid for us to see it."

"It's my stuff." She held the bag tighter. *Lazar's key.* She had to give it back to him to protect him. "It belongs to me. Get your own stuff."

Echo went into Stretch's esuoh. The furniture was cheap—fake chrome and peeling pleather. A huge black-velvet painting of a rainbow with a pot of gold at the end of it dominated one wall, along with four-leaf clovers, rabbits' feet, horseshoes, and dice showing sevens. A shiny red plastic seven, on a platform of plastic gold, stood on his rickety table of memories in front of a bowl of poker chips, mostly white, red, and blue, with a few green and black sprinkled among them. On a shelf of trays where more chips were stored sat a plush toy made in the image of Squat, the balloon man. It was the color of grape soda with googly eyes and an explosion of brilliant red hair on its bulbous head. It buzzed with meaning. *A key.* Before she could inspect it further, she felt tugging at her bag again, her body being lifted off the ground with the force of it, and she shouted at him to stop. The tugging ceased.

Through Stretch's eyes, she saw him look around the lighted parking lot. He took in the fat, soft face of Squat saying, "C'mon. Look at her. She's got nothing."

The view swung back to Echo, her scarred face, her tunic and tights dirty and deranged. She clung to her bag like a life ring in an empty ocean.

"She must have something." Stretch took a step closer to Echo. "Or she wouldn't hold on so tight."

Squat sighed. He turned toward Echo. "You're going to have to give him something, or he won't go away."

Echo's pent-up sadness and fear suddenly transformed into fury. *You want to take my stuff? Let's see what matters to you.*

She stormed into Squat's esuoh. Heaps of bags and boxes, broken furniture and discarded toys, dirty clothing and foul blankets, intermixed with discarded fast-food plates and trays, all filled the space to the point that there was no room to move. Partially obscured by the jumble, Squat's window showed Stretch like a figure from the cover of a romance novel, with a strong jaw and a torn shirt revealing rippling abdominal muscles.

On the top of what stood out as a special mound of knickknacks—dolls, baby toys, Hot Wheels, stuffed animals, antique kitchen tools, pencils and pens, silly erasers, ripped photos in broken frames, shiny rocks and marbles, and too many other things to count or identify—sat a stuffed toy, in the shape of Balloon Man Stretch, presiding over the chaos. It was longer and slimmer than the one in Stretch's esuoh, golf-course green, with googly eyes and fluorescent orange hair. It was a perfect counterpoint to the other—down to the buzz of a key.

She reached across the pile to pick up the toy and found it soft as a stuffed animal and heavy as a heart on Jupiter. A memory poured from it into her: the back of a lanky boy running joyfully as a deer, Monster drinks stuffed in the pockets of his light jacket flopping at every step. In the foreground of the vision, battered handlebars shivered in the juddering progress of a bicycle that at top speed could barely keep up with the runner. "Wait up!" Squat shouted in a boy's high tenor.

Pain pulled Echo back into her own esuoh, and she found herself being lifted by her hair. She came out into the deep and empty twilight and found the skinny balloon man reaching over her, smelling of rage and will and hopelessness. Clutching her bag with one arm, she strong-armed Stretch away and dived into the darkness, searching for a column to put between herself and him. When her hand brushed it, she embraced its scratchy bulk, then went into Squat's esuoh, where the scene seemed frozen, except for a silver glint at the end of Stretch's balloon arm.

She screamed in rage, "Stop it!" It surprised her to hear her words coming back to her in the high, panicked voice she knew was Squat's.

Stretch turned from Echo to Squat, wrath answering in his eyes.

Relieved at having delayed Stretch, she went into his esuoh again to look for a solution. The only thing that spoke to her was the plush key, the companion to the one in Squat's esuoh, and she reached for it; its pulsing energy made her fingers tingle. But instead of waiting for her grasp, the goofy little guy bounced onto her fingertips like a silken balloon, delicate as a soap bubble and so light it could float away.

A memory flowed into her from the figurine: an over-the-shoulder look at a little fat guy riding a bicycle too small for him, his knees pumping up and down like oil wells. It was Squat, elementary-school-aged, grinning and shouting, "Wait up!" but pedaling with all his might, stolen bags of chips stuffed under his T–shirt.

The plush key trembled on her fingertips.

 Outside the window, Stretch turned back to Echo, growling, a knife flashing in the streetlights. She felt his anger boiling and her own fear. He would kill her for her stupid bag, and at this point probably even if she gave it to him.

What if she broke the plushy? Even if it were possible, it might not make any difference. But the complementary memories suggested a link between the two. And whereas Squat's key seemed indestructible, this one seemed . . . .

What happened next was not deliberate, she would tell herself again and again—it was an unavoidable response to a random thought. But wherever the blame might fall, the toy broke, its fragments scattering like ice bubbles on a summer day.

Squat howled in fear, and Stretch in rage. Through Stretch's window, Echo watched his outlook swing from Echo to Squat and back in tense indecision. His peripheral vision still held the knife. In desperation, Echo grabbed a rabbit's foot, the lucky seven, and a framed photo of a queen of diamonds and carried them to his front porch.

Below the porch, a city of casinos blazed with light—so far below that she could see it laid out like a map but close enough to explore like a doll's house. A cacophony of noises rose from the city—traffic, the clickety-click of roulette balls, lounge singers hitting the climactic finale as trumpets wailed, and the ding! ding! ding! of slot machines. She took in all this in an instant as she tossed the lucky objects over the railing and watched them fall. Her breath came hard in fear and rage.

From far below, she heard cries of excitement as people received emblems of luck from the sky.

She went back into Stretch's esuoh, hoping the loss would frighten him away or at least distract him. Her head hurt where Stretch had pulled her hair, and her heart was still pounding.

The world spun crazily as Stretch staggered and nearly fell. But instead of running away, he turned on Squat and ran toward him.

Squat looked at him, horrified. "Warren! No!"

And in less than a second, Squat was holding his abdomen, with blood running through his fingers.

"You asshole!" Echo shouted, heaving the painting of the pot of gold over the porch railing.

Stretch deflated, and out his windows, the parking lot, sidewalk, trees, and road, sped by in a blur as he ran away. Before she recovered from the shock of what had happened, distance forced Echo from Stretch's esuoh into her own, and he was gone.

IN THE EMPTY WORLD OUTSIDE, Squat lay on the ground, whimpering in pain. "Call an ambulance."

"I don't have a phone. Give me yours and I'll call."

He handed it to her. She couldn't see anything. Her hands felt a glass block with a crack across it.

She kneeled down beside him, held out the phone in front of him, and went inside his esuoh.

Closed blinds blocked his windows.

"You need to open your eyes." She spoke to the clutter, willing the man to hear.

"But I'm dying." His voice came to her, clear but from a distant place.

"If you don't open your eyes, I can't call for help."

Outside the window, his phone appeared. Echo dialed 911 and went out of his esuoh to speak to the glass box. "There's a dying man in the parking lot of the train station. He's been stabbed."

At the end of the call, Echo put Squat's phone back into his hand. He lay with his eyes closed, but he said, "You were—in my head?"

*How did he know? What could she answer?*

"Come back in," he said weakly. "I want to talk."

She went back into Squat's esuoh and found a man in a champagne-colored suit with a purple satin cummerbund. He lifted his white Panama hat to her and put it back on his head. He walked with the easy confidence of a film-noir villain.

He moved some junk off a chair and sat down, his hands stacked atop a silver-handled cane standing between his knees, as if his hoard were the way the debonaire set lived in Paris.

"I probably ought to be going," Echo said. "I think you're going to die."

His image shivered, and she glimpsed a frumpy man with wild hair wearing a dingy blue sport jacket over too-large blue jeans. "I don't want to die alone," he said. But then he was the tall, portly, sophisticated villain again—like the old-time actor, Sydney Greenstreet, Echo knew from Aunt Doris's classic movie nights.

It would have been easy to say no to Sydney Greenstreet, but knowing the pathetic figure that lurked beneath? "OK."

He sat there, smoking a cigarette in a long holder that had suddenly appeared in his hand. He didn't ask her to sit, and there was neither a clear chair nor space to create one, so she waited, standing.

"Do you know what happens next?" he asked.

"I've never died before."

"That's too bad." He said it casually, as if sympathizing with her for never having visited Prague. "If you had, I wouldn't be in this position."

"You would be in this position sooner or later. You picked a bad friend."

"Ah, Warren." He spoke as if Warren were somebody long ago and far, far away. "Not much of a friend, really, but the heart wants what it wants." He sighed, looking away into the middle distance. A shelf full of knickknacks faded and disappeared.

"Are you losing your memories?"

"What?" He looked at her, surprised. Apparently, she was one of the memories he had lost. "Are you here to take me to the land of the dead?"

"I don't know where that is."

He pushed himself out of the chair. He seemed older than when he had sat down. "Will you walk with me?"

Wait. Sitting here to wait for DEATH to arrive on a white horse with a witty remark was one thing. Walking to the land of the dead and leaving someone there was something else. She'd heard the stories, and they didn't end well. But she was—partially and indirectly and accidentally, she protested—responsible for this man's death. It was his last journey. And possibly her last chance to see death before it became uncomfortably relevant.

He put on his hat and lifted his walking stick. He stood in the pathway that wound through his hoard, turning this way and that. As he looked around, piles of things melted away. He went to the outside door, but it wouldn't open. He went onto his front porch and came back inside. "Where am I supposed to go?"

"Your memories are upstairs."

"I'm done with that." At his word, the entire hoard disappeared, leaving shabby furniture that might have been good quality at one time. He ignored the change. "Where else?"

"Your basement is all that's left."

He shivered. "A nasty hole in the ground?"

"I've been in one. It's bigger than I expected."

He took a long look at her, then led the way to his basement door. He stopped at the barred and locked door and looked back at her with peeved helplessness. "I can't get in."

She went around him and pushed against the door. "See? I can't open it without a key. You're the only one who can. Put your hand on the door. I'll follow."

He held his hand there a couple of inches away, as if gauging the heat of a wood stove, then took a deep breath and pushed. The locks fell away, and the door opened.

Darkness loomed. He stepped back.

"Maybe there's a light switch by the door."

He reached around and a dim light came on, barely piercing the darkness.

"Watch your step," Echo said.

He crossed the threshold. "There should be handrails," he said. And then, "Oh, look. There are." Grasping the rail, he took his first step into darkness, and Echo followed.

At the first turning of the stair, there was a closed door, battered metal with a heavy doorknob and a peephole. Behind it voices of two women screaming at each other and a baby crying. He turned back to Echo as she waited a couple of steps behind him. "Is this it?"

"We have a long way to go."

"Why is this door here?" Squat looked at the doorknob as if it had teeth.

"An event that matters to you?"

"I told you I don't want memories."

"I didn't make this place," Echo said. "I've been in someone else's basement, and what was behind the door was important to her."

"Do I have to go in?"

Echo shrugged. "I don't make the rules, but it's probably there for a reason? Maybe it would help you understand something."

He pulled himself up to his maximum height. "You can't make me go in there."

"It might be your last chance."

He looked at the door again. Reached for the doorknob. He jerked his hand away as if at an electric shock. "No. You can't make me." He continued to walk down the stairs. Another fifteen steps down, he turned back to Echo. "Did I need to go in there?"

She stepped aside for him. "If you want to go back—"

"No. I made my choice. Don't try to change my mind." He continued his downward course.

At the second turning of the stair, another door and more shouting. A boy, whose voice occasionally broke with impending manhood, and a man's voice with the lugubrious slurring of the chronic drunk. Echo couldn't make out the words.

Squat gave a dismissive wave as he walked by.

At the door on the third turning, he didn't even pause. Echo stopped at the eerie silence with her hand raised over the doorknob. Squat turned back and said, "Come on." The doorknob disappeared.

Echo followed him downward.

When they arrived at the bottom of the stairwell, Squat led the way onto the dry sand at the bottom, then stopped and turned for a backward look up the stairway. It was still dimly lit by the bulb at the top—there had been no others—even past all the turns and the distance they had come. When Echo followed him out onto the sand, she heard the noise of a door slamming behind them. When she looked back, all evidence of the man's basement stairs had disappeared, leaving only an expanse of sand and the distant sea at very low tide. Fear took her for a moment, but this wasn't the Land of the Dead; it was just the beach.

They stood in the half-light of a November day, with neither sun nor cloud in the sky. There was no breeze—odd for the beach—but a chill in the air seemed to rise from the cold, dry sand. A thumbnail of a crescent moon hung over the ocean, white against the clear gray sky. Mild white-caps, barely visible in the distance, marked the beginning of the ocean. Far up the beach, colored lights searched the sky.

Squat stood a long time looking in that direction, until Echo finally asked him, "Do you want to go that way?"

When he turned to her, there were tears on his face. "Warren—he was a terrible person, cruel, and he hated me. But I loved him so, and now he's gone." Tears rolled down his face as if he were the living, grieving for the dead. "But, no, I don't want to go there. I need to go this way." He turned away from the surf and began trudging through the dry sand.

There was no track in the sand. They kept the moon behind them and walked.

After hours and hours, Squat began to throw things away. First to go was the Panama hat. "I'm never going to need this again," and he flung it like a Frisbee across the sand. It immediately began sinking where it fell.

Later, he sat on the sand and took off shoes and socks and left them there. He hopped across the sand, complaining about the cold, but he left the shoes sinking away. He continued walking, and she followed.

Then the cufflinks and cane. And then his jacket, vest, and cummerbund. Then the stiff shirt, leaving him in pants, undershirt, and suspenders.

With each item of clothing, he lost some of the elegance he had carried.

At last, he stopped and walked away from the non-trail they were following. With his back toward her, his arms worked on something in his front. With effort, he pulled off the body suit of the tall, portly gentleman-villain. He threw it aside on the sand and came back to Echo as the short, frizzy-haired, overweight man in the dirty sport coat and overlarge blue jeans. "Surprised?"

"I knew the other guy wasn't you. I like the real you better."

He shrugged.

"What's your name?"

"Chandler Siskin. Yours?"

"Echo Shearwater."

"I can't say it's nice to meet you. I know you made Warren kill me. But coming with me here at least partly makes up for it. Warren wouldn't have done that."

"No, he didn't."

He scrutinized her for a couple of seconds and turned to continue walking.

Before long, the beach gave way to trees and impenetrable salal bushes. He stopped and looked back at her like a dog who had lost the scent.

Echo stopped and took in their surroundings. "I've been to a place like this before. There was a lake with a little building on an island in the middle of it and a formal garden around it. It's different here, though. Do you see an opening?"

"I don't want to go in there."

"I don't know what to tell you. I'm not an expert."

"I need my suit." He looked around his feet, as if expecting it to appear there. "I shouldn't have thrown it away."

"Let me try. Maybe I can find a way through."

He stepped aside and let her lead the way.

Echo walked along the sandy woodland edge until she came to a slight break in the bushes. Not much, but more than anywhere else. "Come on. I'll pull you through."

She stepped into the gap and felt the salal twigs pulling on her clothes, their larger branches pushing her back. She held out her hand, and Chandler grabbed it. He complained about every scratch and scrape, and with every complaint the distance grew longer.

Echo turned back to him. "Listen. You've got to shut up. You're making it worse."

"How could it possibly be any worse?"

His question released her irritation. "How about if I left you to navigate it yourself?" Would she really abandon him here in the forest to fend for himself? She thought not, hoped not, but he seemed to be trying to push her to it.

He gave her a reproachful glare, and she kept going. To his credit, he didn't utter even another "ouch" until they came to the end of the salal and into a wetland clearing in the dark fir forest.

Backlit ahead of them, in the middle of the marsh, was a metal railing, a concrete porch, and a door. "Come on." Echo started walking toward it, and a causeway appeared under her feet.

"I told you I don't want to go through that door." Fear shone from his face and came from his mouth as anger. "Why did you bring me to it out here?"

Echo's heart pounded. She had agreed to walk with him, assuming it would be straightforward. But here was a door looking like the first one in the stairwell, even the same dents and scratches. "Maybe you should have gone through the one in the stairwell."

"Just get out of the way. If this is where we're going . . . ." He headed out over the causeway like a freight train, with Echo following.

As they came closer, walls grew out around the door, and a window appeared in the wall, with a concrete walk between the door and the  metal railing like a second-floor apartment, the whole thing isolated from any neighbors like a picture that ends before the edge of the page.

Chandler turned back to Echo. "I told you I didn't want memories."

"This is your place. I didn't make it."

He opened the door and then tried to slam it after a short glance inside. It wouldn't shut. He swung the door several times, but it kept bouncing off an invisible doorstop.

Echo stepped past Chandler into the room. It had stained green carpet, thrift-store furniture, and a strong odor of musk and perfume. It was neat but dirty, with dust on the furniture and a couple of glasses on the coffee table that looked as if their contents had evaporated. "Come in. It's an apartment."

Chandler stood at the doorway. "I swore I would never go back there."

Echo sighed. "Have it your way, but I don't know what—"

"Hey!" A high-pitched voice came from somewhere in the room. "Hey!"

She searched around the couch, behind the TV, under the dinette table, and around a shelf of miscellany, into the empty maw of a hallway, where lurked a small grubby person, the size of a four-year-old with the stubbled face of a man.

"Bring him back here," the little man said. He wore shorts and an overlarge Portland Trailblazers T–shirt. His hair was cut short over his chubby face, and his arms and legs showed bruises new and old—finger-shaped marks on his arms, stripes on his legs.

Echo shivered at what that must mean about the man she had volunteered to escort into death. Was this his soul? It was so small, so young, despite being old. "Chandler, you need to come here a minute."

But Chandler's voice came to her from outside. He was on the porch conversing with a bird, seven feet tall, with black feathers and a bald, pink head with red eyes. A California condor, and the sight of it with this dying man didn't bode well.

Chandler turned, smiling. "Oh, Echo. This is—" He turned back to the creature.

"I didn't give my name." The condor spoke in a deep hoarse voice.

"He's telling me I don't have to die," Chandler said.

That gave her a deep chill. "Are you going to cure him?"

The bird squawked. "How is that going to help? He would just die later. I'm promising him indefinite existence with eternal pleasure and no problems."

"I'm going to live on a beach." Chandler sounded like a pilgrim who had been promised paradise. "I'll sit in a lounge chair, and waiters in Speedos will bring me drinks with umbrellas all day."

"Wouldn't that get boring after a while?"

The bird squawked. "It's a perfect equilibrium of happiness—no past, no future."

"Chandler, please come inside with me. I'd like to talk to you."

He turned away from the condor and folded his arms in a willful gesture. "What about?"

For a reason she herself didn't understand, she didn't want the bird to hear. "Please."

"If you can say it to me, you can say it to my friend."

Echo sighed. "There's a man in there, and you need to talk to him. It's important."

"Oh, good." The bird brought its wings around and came as close to rubbing them together as it would be possible to imagine. "You found it." It hopped closer to Echo. She stepped back. "Tell you what. Since you found it, you can have it."

"What?"

The bird was now between Chandler and Echo with its back to the frumpy man. "His soul." The bird's tone called her Captain Obvious even if his words didn't.

She stepped back again. "Have it? To keep? Why would I do that?"

It lifted its head toward the sky again and flapped its massive wings. "Power. Have what you want. Do what you want. Go where you want. Live as long as you want."

"I would get that from Chandler?"

"His soul. Looking at *this*"—he gestured to the fat man beside and slightly behind him—"I would guess there's not much to it. But it's a start, and it's easy. Just make a cage over him"—he gestured behind him with his beak—"and the soul will follow. Give him a scene that makes him happy—he seems to like the one I suggested—and he never has to die."

"I don't mind," Chandler said. "No past, no future, just sitting on the beach with nice scenery. I give you permission."

Echo went inside the apartment again. "There's a bird out there who wants me to put a cage around Chandler."

"Don't do it," the little man said.

"Chandler seems to want it."

"He doesn't know what he's asking for. It's slavery, not freedom."

"But why is he so afraid?"

The little man gave her a *well, duh,* look. "The Light brings everything out of hiding. That—*thing*—will maintain the lies until we're used up."

Two different views of what was happening, and Echo had to make a choice. Chandler could be happy and *comfortable* indefinitely, or he could face ultimate reality. Which would she want, if the offer were made to her? In the daily world, she would probably take comfort. But taking the side of the carrion-eater filled her with an instinctive revulsion, and she wondered if it was rational to be so influenced by the bird's appearance.

"Why are you offering him to me?" Echo called out to the condor.

"I've got plenty, and I'm impressed with your progress."

*Progress?* She shivered again. "I'll take you out to Chandler," she told the child-man. She held out her hand to him.

"Don't touch me. You'd be taking me to *him*. Just leave us. Maybe the portal will open before that monster wins."

Outside the door, the condor was doing a sort of dance while Chandler watched in fascination. Golden cords formed in the air and drifted around Chandler.

A blinding light broke like dawn on a planet of a blue star.

Then she was alone in the featureless wasteland of the outer world, hunkered down beside Chandler's body, which lay on the concrete like the carcass of a prehistoric beast. He was entitled and annoying and a bad judge of character, but she mourned him as if he'd been a friend.

CHAPTER 2

# Awaiting the Dawn

SOMETHING CAUGHT ECHO'S ATTENTION, and she stood like a wild animal listening for the hunter. A siren? Her journey with Chandler seemed to have taken hours and hours, but she had called 911 before he died, and no one had come yet. They must be still on the way.

They would find her, a poor blind girl, sitting next to a stabbed man, having been an earwitness to murder.

They would ask her questions whose answers they wouldn't understand or even believe. She would be put somewhere for her protection, and that would keep her from getting to Lazar in time to warn him. She got up and moved away from Chandler.

Echo shuffled through the barren wasteland, now featureless gray on gray and as empty as if millennia lay between the last and the next human habitation. Galynn would know what to do.

Echo squirmed at the memory of how she had botched that relationship, and a small inner voice suggested that her friendship with Galynn might not be the only relationship she had destroyed.

A siren, definitely a siren, broke the quiet. She ran in response to it and almost fell over a barrier that a touch of her hand revealed to be metal rope. She ducked under it and walked, hands extended, along hard, flat concrete. Her knee found the bench before her hand did. Ouch.

Sirens wailed.

That would be police, ambulance, a search for the culprit. She would be arrested, interrogated, tried, weighed in the balance, and all the while Jeph and Cain would be free to carry out their evil plans for Lazar. All because of her. She had to get Lazar's key back to him if there was any chance to save him.

She kept walking. Her feet felt the rift of the railroad tracks through concrete and then where the concrete ended. Then, even though she saw only twilight and emptiness, the noise her feet made communicated twigs and dead leaves, and her arms felt the scratchy embrace of a copse of trees. At a noise from behind, she stopped, frozen, breathing through her mouth for silence.

She went into her esuoh and sat on her porch, trying to calm her pounding heart.

She couldn't escape the sense of being the prey of wily hunters, so she came back into her esuoh and watched out her window. Two dogs—police taking the form of long-eared hounds in Ytilaer—sniffed the ground and stopped, ears alert, listening with wary curiosity. They faced her, eyes wide closed. Did they see her? She had to find out.

She went into the esuoh of the closer of the two. Through his window she could barely make herself out in the line of bushes, and that only because she knew where to look. He took out a flashlight, its hard bright beam piercing the night, and she willed him not to flash it across her form, frozen and trembling among the trees.

"What about there?" The other officer pointed to the space in the hedge where the light hadn't shined.

She exerted her will, guiding the flashlight.

"Where?" The policeman flashed in a circle around her again.

She went into the second hound's esuoh. *Nothing there*, she whispered.

"Nothing there," the first policeman said.

She went back into her own esuoh and watched them through her window.

The hounds looked at each other with their ears perked and their foreheads wrinkled in confusion and turned back. Echo waited until she felt alone again to breathe and creep further through the trees to a place where it would be safe to sit. She felt her way through the trees, and when she passed one with a larger diameter than the rest, she planted her body on the far side of it and sank to the ground. She went into her *esuoh* and made a chair from which to watch through her windows.

Through the night, shivering, she listened to footsteps, voices, the crackle of radios, and the occasional siren. When dogs came close, she went into their *sesuoh* and guided them away. Gradually the activity ended, like a retreating tide. She permitted herself a sigh and a regret for the way her ham-handed management of Stretch and Squat—Warren and Chandler— had gotten one of them killed. "Live and learn," Aunt Doris would say, but when the outcome is death, what is the lesson?

In the stillness after their absence, she came back into the world and felt around her neck for Lazar's key. It was gone.

After a moment of alarm, she remembered. Galynn had said Echo should put it into her bag for safekeeping. Of course. She had zipped it into the pocket with Jeph's credit card and her ID.

The pocket was still zipped, and the key wasn't there. She pulled out her ID and the credit card, flipped through them again and again as if they were a deck of cards instead of only two. She felt in the bottom of the pocket. Warren would have taken the cards and been uninterested in the key.

Panicked, she dove into her bag, like Alice on her way to Wonderland, falling through all the things she kept in there. The light was dim but enough. Plastic coins in pastel colors. A huge, crazy hat, with an extraordinary feather in the band. Flags of imaginary nations. A toddler's teething ring with plastic keys on it. A rock that looked like a hitchhiking hand that Echo had lost when she left Pennsylvania to live with Aunt Doris in Oregon. A bottle with a golden liquid labeled, "DRINK ME." A rain of confetti. When she landed at the bottom, all the things she had seen on the way down landed on top of her.

She sighed at her own forgetfulness. She didn't have to dive into her bag; she could just bring the key into her awareness, and it would be there. She concentrated. And waited. Listened. Lazar's key was not there.

*Lazar's key was not there.*

She was falling again. The plastic coins were now rocks, the flags were cicadas, the bottle held the waters of Lethe, and the hitchhiking rock had become a boulder rolling down an incline.

Galynn had taken the key.

What would Galynn do with it? Take it home for a souvenir? A yarn-wrapped chip? No. It was the key to what Galynn wanted most—connection with Jeph, who could give her entry into the dream world and guidance in using it.

Echo had broken Galynn's trust, and Galynn had broken hers.

She sat in a swirl of anger and fear, with hope and despair battling like Titans over her head. She had hoped she could save Lazar by returning his key. But if Jeph got Lazar's key, Lazar was defenseless. All she could bring was a warning.

The key was long gone, and Jeph could be on his way to Depoe Bay right now. But would Jeph drive down there in the middle of the night? He was unlikely to take on that inconvenience. She hoped.

She had helped set all this in motion. But the casino bus that Aunt Doris had told her about would take her halfway to Depoe Bay. She would do what she could do.

CHAPTER 3

# The Man on the Beach

GRAY FLOPPED OVER ON THE BED. Had he been sleeping? He must have, because the last time he looked around, Travis was scrolling through his phone, writing notes in that little notebook of his. Now Travis snored in the other bed like a truck backfiring, and the room was lit only by the red numbers on the alarm clock—3:33—and the yellow glare of sodium streetlights slipping in under the window curtains.

Gray got up and opened a window to let some fresh air into the room. Then he stepped outside and leaned on the balcony railing, barefoot in jeans and T–shirt, with I-5 like a river of lights and the rolling hills around Ashland faintly visible against the dark sky.

*Where's Echo?* It was a constant refrain in the back of his mind. In Ytilaer, he could *feel* her existence in the world, but in Oge everything deep and true was hidden by hard, reflective surfaces. State Senator Cali Zielinski, who had sent them here, had seemed strangely terrified at the visit of two—*Two? Who was Echo traveling with?*—young women asking uncomfortable questions about her past. Somehow, from that encounter, Travis—the retired police detective who was only supposed to be Gray's driver—had reached the conclusion that Ashland was the next stop. It was either Ashland or home to defeat, but Gray had no confidence they would find Echo here. It nagged at him that she was in danger and he had the luxury of sleep.

He sighed and went back inside. He got a drink of water and lay on the bed again, certain he would lie there fully conscious until morning.

And then he was riding in Travis's car on the highway along the beach. It wasn't just any beach; it was the edge of the Eternal Ocean. The ocean thrummed with life and death, and the soughing of the waves sounded like whispers. He had been there before with parties of Srelevart, traveling to the beach and as far as the carnival and the town, but—he turned in his seat and saw the lights of the carnival behind them—never this far north—north in Ytilaer having nothing to do with a physical direction on a physical globe. Instead, north was where disaster came from—marauding barbarians, famine, plague, and the cold death of winter's embrace.

Mitch, a member of the Srelevart who studied the far paths, said there were great cities, separated by vast swaths of nature, red in tooth and claw, and somewhere out there an upside-down world of chimera, walking gargoyles, and strange creatures such as warrior snails and man-eating monsters. Mitch sought those places in lonely forays through the unknown Underground, but the rest of the Srelevart gave him the side-eye, keeping to the established paths.

Gray had never been anywhere. But now, Travis drove through the beachside town with the ocean out of sight on their left, although present in every breath.

The further Travis drove, the more anxious Gray became.

Down the empty residential streets, the ocean peeked at them, flashing under the setting sun. All around, the town was empty as a movie lot after the cast and crew have finished the film, and far ahead, the road disappeared into dense coastal forest encroaching on the beach. Gray had something he needed to do, but he didn't know what. Echo's danger was imminent, and he had to find her, but where? Travis was driving, driving, driving, and at any moment it could be too late. He looked over at Travis, who drove with his eyes closed, facing the roadway, both hands on the wheel, like a sleep-driver.

"Stop!"

Travis looked toward him, eyes still closed. "Is this it?"

Gray fumbled. "I thought you knew where we were going."

"I told you this isn't my world. I'm following what you say."

*Crap. Did I stop too late?* "Let's park here. I want to get out of the car."

"Good thing we're stopping." Travis pulled into a parking lot that let onto the beach and parked the car higgledy-piggledy across the marked spaces. "It's the end of the road."

Before Travis could cut the engine, Gray was already opening the door to get out. But he was weighed down by stuff—heavy, clanking, and off-balance. He tripped on his way out the door, but recovered and stood there, looking down at himself in wonder.

He was wearing medieval armor, but it seemed to have been put on him by a blind person—or an idiot. He had stumbled over a helmet, in which his foot was encased like a shoe. Arm pieces were slung around his shoulders; leg pieces on his arms. And his sword belt circled his waist, with the sword hanging straight down between his legs.

He kicked the helmet off his foot and tucked it under his arm, then walked forward. He left the parking lot and slogged through deep dry sand. The weight of the armor pulled him down, and the awkwardness made it hard to move. But he had a sense that Echo was on the beach, and he needed to get to her.

A man came walking up beside him, taller than Gray, around Quig's age maybe. He had dark hair cut close to his head and a horizontal scar on his cheek under his right eye. "I think you need some help." There was laughter in his eyes that didn't mock but encouraged.

Gray stood in the sand as the man took the pieces of armor off him and then patiently and calmly helped him put it on again, starting with the lower legs and working up to the helmet. The last step was to belt the scabbard in the right place. He handed Gray a silver sword.

Gray inspected its rich lustre and admired the fine workmanship. He raised it to the sky, where it shone like fire in the light of the setting sun.

"Thank you," Gray said. Other than the man, the beach was empty. Gray couldn't see the carnival now, nor any of the town, just the two of them and the beach and the whispering ocean. "I'm looking for Echo. Do you know where she is?"

"Your paths are converging." He started walking away to the north, toward a rock formation that jutted out into the ocean, the end of the beach and possibly the end of the world. "Meet her here at sunset tomorrow."

"Wait!" Gray shouted after him. "Who are you? How do I get here? I'm not in Ytilaer anymore."

The man turned back. "Remember God's Thumb. It's at the end of the road." He turned and kept walking.

A voice spoke. "We need to check out and get breakfast before we talk to Newton Zielinski."

Gray was lying spread-eagle over the covers on the bed, the pillows on the floor.

"I've taken a shower already." Travis stood across the room holding his duffle bag. He was already dressed and his hair combed. "Better get moving if you want one."

Gray groaned, more at the loss of the dream than at the idea of getting up, and went to get ready for the day.

GRAY AND TRAVIS CHECKED OUT of the fifties-style budget motel around 8 a.m. and drove to a nearby diner for breakfast.

"I hope the service is fast," Travis said, opening the door. "Our appointment to see Newton Zielinski is at nine."

Over a plate of eggs and toast and melon, Gray jumped every time a dish crashed into a clean-up tub.

"You're on edge this morning. What's the matter?" Travis asked.

"We need to get to the end of the road by sunset."

Travis calmly spread butter on a biscuit. "End of the road. By sunset."

"A man told me in a dream."

"Oh, a dream." He didn't say "just" a dream, but he might as well have. Gray saw it in his eyes and the shape his mouth made. "Eat up, and let's get out of here."

"Ytilaer changes your dreams, even when you come back to Oge. This one was real."

"Real. Like the black monster."

"Do you have to keep bringing that up?"

Travis put his fork down and looked Gray in the eye. "It's a perfect illustration of two ways of looking at the world. I'll give it to you that it's probably true about Cain. And it might even be true about where you need to be. But we also need facts. The end of which road? Where? Sunset when?"

Gray put his head in his hands. "He said sunset tomorrow. But for all I know, we may already be too late."

Travis picked up the check. "I can't speak for your—Ytilaer, but it would be pretty stupid to give specific instructions like that if you couldn't possibly follow them. Let's stay on the path and watch for the end of the road around sunset. For now, we've got an appointment with Cali's father at nine."

CHAPTER 4

# Ride to Mystic Mountain

Echo waited in the barren wasteland, squinting in the bright morning light and wondering if she would even see the casino bus when it came into the parking lot. An old-style Portland city bus drove out of the nothingness and pulled up near her. It was orange, white, and silver, with rounded corners, and the route number and destination in the black bar over the windshield read "11 Labyrinth." She shivered at that, not sure if it was the right bus, but the ad on its side was a light-sucking black, with a Native coyote figure painted in glowing red. It had to be the bus she was waiting for.

The driver—a gambler in a purple velvet suit with a black satin collar, big floppy black bow tie, and a black trilby hat with a red lucky seven in the band—climbed out and stood at the door to the bus taking tickets. Four men and four women dressed in red, white, and blue square-dance costumes appeared out of nowhere and lined up at the door of the bus, holding out golden tickets.

Echo fished her ID from her bag and got in line.

The driver looked her over carefully. "You're not a member."

"The first time my aunt went, she came with a friend, and she joined when she got to the casino."

He pointed over his shoulder with his thumb. "These people are going to gamble."

"I'm going to try to win back what I lost."

"That's usually the last step before losing everything." But he shrugged and stood aside to let her get on board.

It was dark inside and unbearably hot, filled with steam and smoke. There were no bus seats, but a fire smoldered in the center of the floor. Someone poured water from a gourd cup onto a rock in the fire pit, and clouds of steam filled the air. Echo coughed and stumbled to an empty space near the fire. There was a mesmerizing singing going on, but she couldn't understand the words.

She sat cross-legged on the ground with her bag between her knees and turned to look out the window. Although she knew she was on a Mystic Mountain Casino tour bus, and she could feel its vibration as it moved through the city toward its destination, an opening in the wall of hanging blankets revealed black sky and a glimpse of the Milky Way.

"What is your quest?" The voice came from out of the darkness, a very old voice, and she couldn't tell if it was male or female.

"I had a quest," she said, "but now I've discovered it's evil and selfish, and I'm trying to undo it."

A sudden flash of firelight illuminated the end of a long gray ponytail draped over a shoulder in a faded denim shirt. "A worthy quest." There was a long, long pause. "But more difficult than the first."

Echo listened to the singing, trying to sort out words. The effort made her sleepy. She snapped awake.

"How long does it take to get to Mystic Mountain?" she asked.

"If you're going for fun, it takes an hour, which is too long. If you're going for a vision, it takes a lifetime, and you won't be ready at the end."

"My aunt goes to Mystic Mountain with her friends sometimes."

"Here's where you make a joke about Indians scalping white people."

Echo tried to smile but couldn't quite pull it off. "She likes it. She enjoyed the Elvis impersonator a few months ago."

"Elvis is dead, but Lazar is still alive."

The turn of the conversation unnerved her. "I wasn't trying to get him killed."

A movement outside the firelight indicated a nod. "Then make his life matter."

"I want to stop them from killing him."

"The river flows down the mountain in a headlong rush to the sea. Nothing can stop it. A beaver can dam it. A boulder can divert it. An animal track can reshape the channel. Still it reaches the sea."

Echo reflected on those words, repeating them again and again in search of comfort or encouragement, but finding neither. She focused on the beaver, the boulder, the animal track. She wanted to believe her efforts weren't entirely futile, but the effort to believe in belief was as useless as the effort to believe in her efforts. Believing in believing in believing . . . a pointless circle making her dizzy but leading nowhere.

The old person's words merged with the singing, which she still couldn't understand, but then the song became the background for many voices and she understood some of those words. "Last time we were here," a woman said, "the food was good. You really liked your steak, didn't you, Bud?" A noncommittal grunt. "I had the salmon, and—" her voice faded out and a high and querulous voice faded in— "I don't know why this always takes so long. I told you we should—" followed by a man— "I won seven hundred fifty dollars last time, and damned if I won't double it tonight" —and then farther away— "Still a mile to the gas station." Echo's bubble of attention seemed to encompass a wider distance, and a child far off woke from a nightmare crying.

Someone was shaking her shoulder. She was in a old-style city-bus seat with the gambler standing over her. "Wake up. It's time to get off."

She sat up and looked around. There was no fire pit and no fire. All the other seats on the bus were empty.

She rubbed her eyes and reached for her bag. It was gone.

"My bag is gone." Maybe she just couldn't see it. She felt around, reached under each of the seats. "It had everything in it. My money, my debit card, my ID."

The driver set his hat on a seat to help her look for it. "You lost your ID?"

"Everything." She went to every seat, crawled around looking on the floor, pulled on the cushions at the back of the bus.

The driver stood up, done with his search. He put on his hat and watched her. "This is inconvenient."

She turned to look at him, then flopped on the back bench. "More than you know."

"You need your ID to join the Coyote Club. Your free ride."

She stood and looked up and down the bus aisle again. "I can't help it. It's gone."

"Nobody carried it off the bus."

"Are you sure?"

"Let's go file a police report."

"I can't! I need to get to Depoe Bay to change the course of the stream."

"You're not a boulder. You're a coyote who thinks she's better than a raven."

That snapped her attention to him. He walked up the aisle toward the front of the bus.

"Who was the old one sitting next to me?" she asked him. "Could he have taken my bag?"

"Over-55 day is Monday. I could get in trouble for bringing you here without a Coyote Club sign-up. You need to file a police report."

"What are you going to do? Drive me back to Salem?"

He examined her face with a skeptical gaze. "You're not going to find what you're looking for here. You can get a ride west if you head to that exit."

CHAPTER 5

# Newt's Tale

NEWTON ZIELINSKI, ATTORNEY AT LAW, had office space on the second floor in an old-fashioned building—not old but "old-fashioned"—in the historic part of Ashland. Travis and Gray went in through the side entrance to the second-floor hallway upstairs, where office suites opened left and right like doors into memories upstairs in an esuoh.

Zielinski's office was small, with simple furnishings and old magazines on the table for waiting clients. His receptionist was professionally dressed—black jacket over a stiffly pressed white blouse—and had a nose ring and butterfly neck tattoo. "Can I help you?"

Travis did the introductions. "Travis Rankin and Gray Birdsong. We have an appointment with Mr. Zielinski."

"Yes. I remember. Have a seat, and I'll tell him you're here."

Newton Zielinski was, like the building, more old-fashioned than old, sitting behind a huge, scarred antique desk with shelves of law books behind him. On the wall to his left was a poster-sized closeup of the moon in a night sky. To his right, a display of four swords: broadsword, rapier, katana, and scimitar. He had a bulging file organizer on his desk with papers sticking out of it. His office had a sense of intimacy like Travis's home, as if Gray was seeing the inner person reflected in the physical world. Gray tried to piece together the meanings of the swords, the moon, and the many files, but it was like reading a poem in an unfamiliar language.

The lawyer looked over steel-rimmed glasses at Gray and Travis. "What's all this about?"

"We're looking for a girl who might have come by here yesterday," Travis said. "Tall, with a scarred face and short hair. She had her eyes closed."

"And?"

Gray didn't know how to answer that question. He could open his mouth and begin his life story, or Echo's life story, what he knew of it, or why he wanted her back.

But Travis got it. He pulled his ID from his wallet. "I'm a retired police detective, and this young man is concerned about her welfare." Travis gestured with his eyes, and Gray also brought out his ID.

The attorney compared them to their photos, wrote their names and addresses on a yellow pad, and handed their IDs back. "She was here yesterday with another girl, and they both seemed fine." There was an "end of discussion" quality to that statement that worried Gray.

"Did she say where she was going next?" Gray asked.

"She didn't say, but I have a guess. Persuade me to tell you."

Travis frowned, more confused than angry. "An exchange of information?"

"You can call it that."

Gray just hoped he had the right information to get Echo back. "What do you want to know?"

"For starters, why did you and those women frighten my daughter?"

Gray was taken aback. "I have no idea why she should be frightened. All we did was ask about my friend, and she had armed security escort us out."

Travis took a more conciliatory tone. "Did she tell you what frightened her? We didn't threaten her in any way."

"What are you people up to? Prank video? Political hit job? Cali was quite upset." He stood at his desk, a demand for their exit hovering over his angry face.

"We don't mean any harm to your daughter—or anybody," Travis said. "We're worried about this young man's friend."

Gray spoke before he knew what to say. "Lazar Kyrillovich." It was a wild leap, but it was the name the woman had mentioned in her "statement" for the cameras that didn't exist.

Zielinski fixed Gray in a piercing gaze. "What do you want with Lazar Kyrillovich?"

"Nothing," Gray said. "Your daughter mentioned him; I don't know anything about him. I'm concerned about Echo working for Jeph Blackthorne—"

"I knew that son of a bitch was at the bottom of this somewhere." He pointed to the door. "Get out."

Gray spoke fast. "I don't like him either, and Echo has only been working for him for a day. I'm sure she doesn't know his real plans. She just believes everybody."

He leaned forward over his desk. "You don't know why Jeph wants Lazar." It was a question in the form of a statement.

"I'm sure it's nothing good."

"That's nice, but it's nothing I don't know already." He straightened and turned toward the door. "I'll see you out."

"Wait." Gray was begging. "Ask me something you don't know."

He was standing now, but he smiled in a way that didn't reach his eyes. "I have a tough one. Why are Lazar's eyes closed?"

"Lazar's?" Gray was confused. "I know why Echo's are, but I told you I don't know anything about Lazar."

"OK," Zielinski said. "Then why are her eyes closed?"

"You won't believe it."

"Is that because you haven't perfected the story yet?"

"Experience. I was like that from the time I was seven until yesterday. When I try to tell people, they never believe me."

He looked at Travis. "Is this true?"

Travis shrugged. "I haven't been with him every day since he was seven, but yeah."

Zielinski sat again. "Tell me the story, then. If it fits, we'll talk."

"It's a different view of the world. We call it Ytilaer. If the world is a tapestry, Ytilaer is the side where the picture shows. Oge—what we're seeing now—is the side where the threads seem to go in random directions and you can only guess at the patterns." He hoped that was enough description. It could be an all-day rabbit trail. He went to the reason Echo's eyes were closed. "If you're in Ytilaer, people in Oge see you with your eyes closed—and vice versa."

Zielinski covered his face with his hands and leaned back in his chair. "Well, damn me for a dragon. Lazar tried to tell me. I just didn't believe him. Couldn't believe him."

"You believe me?" Gray was astounded.

"It's the only thing that makes sense. He wasn't crazy, at least after they got the drugs out of his system. But he was in another world. What he said wasn't rational, but it was true." He leaned on his desk again. "He was innocent. His mother knew it even when he didn't. I didn't know what to believe. But now I know."

"What was the charge?" Travis asked.

"First-degree manslaughter. He had party drugs in his system. Cali thought Jeph put them in his drink, but there was no proof."

Travis looked puzzled. "I thought the sentencing on first-degree manslaughter was closer to ten years."

"There were two small children in the car, as well as the other driver. All dead. Apparently the driver—Lazar, they said—lost control of the car going ninety on a twenty-five-mile-per-hour curve."

"Couldn't he get a plea deal?" Travis asked. "Or even a GEI?"

*GEI?* Gray wondered, but the attorney answered before he could ask the question.

"With his eyes closed like that and the change in his—perception—I thought 'guilty except for insanity' was a good option. But his mother had lost a relative to the Soviet psychiatric system, so that was out."

"Why did she get a say?" Travis squinted at him. "Wasn't he tried as an adult?"

"He was over eighteen all right, but the mother and son deferred to each other in everything."

"No plea deal?"

"The DA didn't offer much. All the evidence was against the kid, and he couldn't—or wouldn't—say with any conviction that he didn't do it. So we went through the trial because his mother asked."

"She sounds like a witch."

The attorney smiled sadly. "She does, doesn't she? But she's exactly the opposite. She's the kind who bends the world with a look and a word." He sighed. "He was found guilty, of course. She's still paying the trial expenses, a hundred dollars a month. I've told her it was pro bono, friend of Cali and all that, but every month the check comes."

Gray had been watching Travis and the attorney talk about *his* matter of concern like a couple of adults with a child in the room. But they weren't getting any closer to Echo. "What was your last memory while Echo was here?"

The question seemed to surprise the attorney. He paused for a moment, gazing into an upper corner of the room. "The day I talked to Lazar's mother in my office. I didn't give them the address or anything, but there are ways to find it." He looked it up on his computer and wrote on a notepad. "I shouldn't do this, but I'll save you the time." He ripped it out and handed it over.

Travis took it.

"I would tell you to be kind to her, but you're the ones in danger. More likely she'll ask you to do something that will almost kill you but make you better for it." He smiled sadly; then his face hardened. "And I hope you get that son of a bitch Jeph Blackthorne out of circulation."

"Thanks." Gray and Travis got up to leave.

"I'll call her and let her know you're coming."

In a few minutes, they were on their way to Irina Simon's house.

## CHAPTER 6

# One Road Ends, Another Begins

IRINA SIMON LIVED IN A SMALL RANCH-STYLE HOUSE on a street without sidewalks. Travis knocked on the door, and around his shoulder Gray got his first glimpse of a woman a few years older than Travis, petite, with amber eyes and gray hair tied back in a bun.

"Irina Simon?" Travis spoke, but Gray squeezed into the space between him and the doorjamb.

"We're looking for a girl you may have met yesterday," Gray said.

"Echo and Galynn came to visit me." She studied Gray's face. "I can see in your eyes that Echo is the girl you're looking for. Is everything all right?"

"I'm Travis Rankin, and this is Gray Birdsong. We're friends of hers and just want to find her, make sure she's okay."

She stepped back, holding the door open. "Please come into my house." Gray felt a chill at the wording of the invitation, but they were all in Oge, and in Oge, a house was just a physical thing—or so he had thought before he began this journey.

The house was small, its furniture old but well made. An Oriental rug with most of its pile worn off lay on the floor. A huge cabinet with glass-doored shelves above and many drawers below stood against the wall; it was intricately carved in a wood so dark it was almost black. It seemed to hold everything from books to teacups to writing materials, all neat and well dusted. If this were Ytilaer, it would hold her short-term memories.

There was no TV. Instead there was a wall full of religious pictures in vibrant colors, and below them on a low table, candles, unlit.

"Can I get you some tea?"

"Yes. Thank you," Gray said. Travis gave him a hard look then glanced at the clock next to the kitchen door, but Gray gestured toward her with his eyes.

Travis gave a terse nod.

When she went into her kitchen, Gray got up from the sofa to look at the pictures. Two large portraits of a man and a woman, looking quiet, ancient, and ethereal. One that seemed important was a large image of a mummy emerging from a cave. A man, the same one in the portrait above it, stood outside the cave making a hand gesture, and other people in the picture reacted with joy, anger, or shock. Two women kneeled at the man's feet, and two servants scurried to remove the mummy's bandages.

"You like my icon?" She had come quietly into the living room and was setting a tray on her coffee table.

Gray went back and sat down. "It looks like it's telling a story, but I don't know it."

"My son, Lazar, is named after the man coming out of the cave—Lazarus, you say in English. Jesus brought him back from the dead a week before his own crucifixion. I felt this joy when my son came out of prison after twenty years."

Travis picked up the cup. It was tiny and delicate, and he seemed afraid of it. He took a sip and set it down. "So you had some visitors yesterday, a couple of young women?"

"Yes. Echo had her eyes closed like my Lazar. Not blind, but not seeing what we see. Galynn was helping her."

"Did they say where they were going next?" Gray asked. "I'm worried about Echo."

"Lazar asked them to go home, but I think your friend Echo had other plans."

Travis looked surprised. "Lazar asked? Is he here?"

"No. He is with his father in Depoe Bay. But he spoke to me in a dream and gave me a message for Echo. She was to take the key and go back to Portland and give it to Jeph."

Her words disturbed Gray. A man who travels in dreams and delivers messages—could he have been the man who told him to go to the end of the road? "Take the key and give it to Jeph?" He heard incredulity in his own voice.

She gave a little shrug. "Lazar said that was the way it would be. But I think your friend Echo doesn't always do what she's asked."

Gray shook his head. "You've got that right."

She opened a drawer of the cabinet and brought out a shiny red flyer. It had a photo of an inflatable boat with two men standing beside it. One looked like the man who had helped him in his dream down to the horizontal scar under his right eye. The headline read "Krill's Whale Watching Tours." She handed it to Travis. "Lazar is working here with his father."

"How was Echo traveling?" Travis asked.

"The other girl, Galynn, was driving."

Travis drove to a gas station and quick mart at an entrance to the interstate before he said anything. Before leaving, he parked and went inside and came out with two cups of coffee. "Black, right?"

Gray didn't answer, because he sensed it wasn't really a question. He took a sip and found it as bitter as the pain of regret. *Do things mean something in Oge?* he asked himself again. *If so, how do you find what's meaningful out of the multiplicity?*

Travis took a sip from his cup and made a face. "What's next?"

Gray picked up the Krill's Whale Watching flyer from the console and handed it to Travis. "There."

Travis turned it over to get the address. Punched it into his map app. "Five-hour drive and another day. We're going to go over your five hundred dollars. Are you sure?"

Gray asked himself that question. He answered truthfully. "No. But I ask if the Echo I know would go back home as she was told or try to stop this."

"Stop what?"

"Whatever Jeph has planned."

"You're sure she's not in league with them?"

"I never doubted her. But she's still in danger, even if I don't know what it is."

"She could just hand off the key and go home, right? Then she'd be safe."

"Safe." Gray had to laugh at the idea of Echo valuing safety. "In my dream, the man told me to meet her on the beach."

"Right. The dream."

"And the coffee is bitter."

"I'm sorry you don't like it—"

"Not that. In Ytilaer things have meaning. Maybe in Oge, too. It stood out as a warning."

Travis sighed and put his phone away. "Those are interesting reasons. In our world, if you get a message in a dream or from a bad cup of coffee, you can just say your gut tells you." He put the car in gear and pulled out of the parking lot. "And my gut tells me we need to go to Depoe Bay."

CHAPTER 7

# Hitchhiking

THE CAR THAT PULLED UP ALONGSIDE ECHO looked familiar. At first she thought it was just because she was seeing a car, rather than the various bizarre modes of transportation she had used since being in Ytilaer.

But then the window rolled down, and Echo's mother looked out and asked if she needed a ride. It was the same make and model as her family's car that had been totaled, and she stared at the woman for a long time, wondering if she was a ghost.

"Miss?" the woman said. "Are you all right?" It wasn't her mother's voice, but the car and the woman's appearance brought back Echo's last ride with her family so powerfully that she almost turned down the ride. But her need to save Lazar was strong and persuasive.

She overcame her last objection when she jumped into the woman's head and found out she was not, in fact, Echo's mother. Her face in the mirror showed her to be about Aunt Doris's age, with short silver hair and perfect makeup. She turned to her husband, the driver, at Echo's bidding and showed him to be around the same age, also silver-haired. The two were handsome enough to be AARP models.

Not her parents.

Echo said thanks and got into the back seat. Her hands felt empty without her bag, and her life felt bereft without it. *Another thing lost on the journey.*

"Where are you going?" the man asked. His voice was very different from her father's, but the dream world kept attaching her father's face to him. This was going to be hard. She tried to concentrate on Lazar.

"Depoe Bay," she said.

"We're going to Lincoln City," the man said. "That's most of the way."

"That's fine," Echo said.

The woman turned to her husband. "Don't be silly. We don't have to be there at any particular time. We can take an extra twenty minutes and run her on down to Depoe Bay."

"You don't have to do that," Echo said.

"We insist, don't we, David?"

*David.* Her father's name was David.

David turned and caught her eye. He gave her a we-have-to-do-this-now smile, just like her father used to do. "No problem at all."

Echo went into her esuoh and discovered her twelve-year-old self sitting on her bench looking out the window. "What are you doing here?" present Echo asked.

Twelve-year-old Echo looked at her with fury. "This is *mine.*" Her hair was messy, and her teeth were too big for her face. Echo felt a surge of pity for the gawky girl, but it was washed away by the shame of having been that girl. "You always blame me for it, but I'm going to show you. It was Diana's fault, not mine."

"Can't you let it go?" Older, wiser Echo had more important things to attend to. "Diana is dead—along with everyone else."

"Dead. Damn her. Her last act of vengeance, and she'll never apologize."

Echo tried to go to her porch. Her heart was pounding, but the door wouldn't open. She went back into the world and found Diana sleeping on the other side of the back seat.

Diana was beautiful, smart, popular, talented, and her little sister was awkward, unattractive, and at the middle of her class. Every report card was a celebration for Diana, a solemn "You could do better" for Echo. Every school year was a parade of triumphs for Diana and a walk of mediocrity for Echo.

And here they were, on the road to California to take Diana to Stanford. She had been the princess on the pedestal for more than a year. Choosing a college, preparing to leave, saying goodbye, worrying about the distance from home, planning for the money. Whenever Echo wanted something, they couldn't afford it because Diana was going to Stanford. Whenever Echo wanted to go somewhere, they didn't have time, because Diana was going to Stanford.

Echo wanted to be like Diana. She wanted to *be* Diana, but of course, Diana had already taken all the gifts from the genetic smorgasbord, and what Echo got was Echo. These were the feelings and memories that flooded her as twelve-year-old Echo took over the chair facing out the window in her esuoh.

The real, present Echo sat down beside the young version of herself, explaining her desperate and vital mission, but the twelve-year-old ignored her, instead making furious faces at Diana, who slept with her head lolled to one side, beautiful even with drool coming out of her mouth.

Echo went into David's esuoh to watch the road. But she still heard twelve-year-old Echo whisper from the back seat: "Hey. Shut up. You're snoring like a garbage truck."

Echo went back into her esuoh and tried to push twelve-year-old Echo out of her seat. The younger girl was scrappy and fierce. She screamed that Echo didn't understand; she even bit older Echo's hand. It didn't hurt, but it did rattle her.

Their dad spoke from the front. "Leave her alone, Echo. Why don't you go to sleep, too? You girls have a big day tomorrow."

Young Echo turned on her older self. "That's wrong. That's not what he said. He said *Diana* has a big day tomorrow."

"Maybe you heard it wrong."

The twelve-year-old who had taken Echo's place in the back seat of the car said, "*I* have a big day tomorrow. I lose my toxic sister forever."

Diana woke at the gibe, smacking her lips and wiping her face. She turned on Echo, her expression wrathful and her voice so low that only Echo could hear it. "Once I'm gone, no one will want to be around you, and you'll be alone forever."

Echo screamed, grabbing Diana's hair, and the fracas so startled their father that he drove off the road into a concrete barrier.

And it was happening again. The car swerved right and left. The woman in the front seat gave a cry of fear.

Darkness like a bottomless cave, a whoosh of air past her ears, noisy machinery. Then screams, squealing brakes, spinning and whirling like a carnival ride, crunching metal, breaking glass—

The car flipped over a couple of times and landed on its roof.

Echo knew what would happen next. She had experienced it thousands of times after the first. She steeled herself, always steeled herself, but it never worked. The experience never stopped until the drop of blood slid down her face in the moment preceding the sight of her dead sister.

She remembered pain, but she didn't feel pain anymore, only anguish and despair and a loneliness she never expected.

"Echo?" A voice in the darkness, familiar but not very, sounded delighted to see her. "You're on my favorite ride!"

Ride? She felt around herself. Found her knees. Found a metal bar fixed in place across her lap. The one-person cart she was riding in jerked around a ninety-degree curve, then emerged into the lights and motion of the carnival. The wall next to her had pictures of broken glass and words in garish type: "What You Did." It was the ride she had seen at the Eternal Carnival on the night before she began her journey in Ytilaer.

Death, looking as dapper as he had in the game that distant evening, in his black three-piece suit with the little black skulls on his red tie and holding the tall scythe, was standing on the platform as the cart slowed and stopped. He unlatched the door for her to walk out. A long line of people waited patiently to get on.

"You won't like it," Echo told them.

"Don't bother. They're dreaming. They can't change their minds about riding it." Death smiled at her as they stepped down from the platform. "Didn't you love it? It's the hinge point of your life so far."

He and Echo were walking uphill, toward the highway.

"So far?" She turned to him, but he was gone. She was walking away from the accident where her parents—who were not her parents—stood next to their wrecked car, with no Diana in sight. The car had run off the highway and down the embankment, fortunately without flipping over.

Twelve-year-old Echo's screams in the here and now had caused another crash.

She went into her esuoh to rebuke her younger self. No one was there. The door to her basement lay open. How had that happened? She closed it firmly and made sure the locks were in place. She checked the door to her porch and found that it opened easily. She looked out with longing, but no eagles floated on the air currents across the chasm. She closed the door again and came out of her esuoh.

The couple watched Echo leave, their faces showing a changing display of confusion, concern, and anger. "Where are you going?" the woman who was not her mother called behind her.

Echo turned to walk back toward them. "I— I'm sorry. Are you OK? Can I do anything to help?"

The man, who had a phone by his ear, scowled and waved her away. "You've done enough damage. Just go."

"I'm sorry," Echo said again. She watched them a few more seconds, but they didn't look at her again. She began walking south on the highway toward Depoe Bay.

A TRAIL PARALLELED THE HIGHWAY. Walled on both sides by salal bushes and wide enough for two people to pass easily, the path meandered along on the ocean side of the highway as the wide pavement veered off into mist. Something about a "road not taken" slid through Echo's mind like the refrain of an old song, and soon she walked alone through a dark forest where ravens sat in the trees shouting, "Murderer!"

A noise behind caught her attention, and a barefoot man came toward her, carrying a battery-powered camp lantern and wearing a long robe of some coarse brown cloth, cinched at the waist with a rope belt. Although he moved at the speed of a car on the highway, his robe showed no ripple from his rapid movement. She stepped off the path to let him pass.

He stopped beside her.

"You going to see Lazar?" It was more an accusation than a question.

Echo took another step back, pushing into the salal along the trail. "Who are you?"

"A friend."

"I don't have any friends." She started walking.

He came up beside her. "Lazar's friend. He called me at work and asked me to bring you to him." He leaned down to look at her face. "He wouldn't do that if it wasn't important."

"I'm not sure that's a good idea. I seem to be dangerous to have around." She started walking again.

"You know he's going to die, right?"

That stopped her again. Through her efforts, Jeph now had Lazar's key. Irina had said Jeph planned something worse than death. What was worse than death? She turned to the man. A teardrop was tattooed at the corner of his closed right eye. "What do you know about it?"

"He said goodbye to me."

Echo took in a breath and released it. Maybe Lazar could escape. "Is he getting away?"

"Not that kind of goodbye—not, 'Feed my cat; I'll be back in a few days.' It was the kind of goodbye where you say what there was never time to say. before" There were spasms in the muscles of his mouth and cheeks, and she thought he might cry, but he recovered. "Lazar knows things."

Echo absorbed his words. Her knees felt weak, and her breath left her. She staggered forward on the path.

He caught up again. "If you've got something to say to him, you'd better come with me. They're on their way."

Go with him? He was tall and powerfully built, his brown robe emphasizing rather than hiding his heavy muscles, a spiderweb tattoo on his neck. "Who's on their way?" she asked.

His voice rose in frustration. "The guys coming to kill Lazar. There's not much time."

She compared the value of her safety to the value of Lazar's life. She couldn't have explained why she chose the latter, but she did. Anyway, although the man was massive, the danger he presented seemed to be more a warning than a threat. She went into his esuoh and found it clean and sparsely furnished: A small bed with a tiny table beside it holding a kerosene lamp and a book. A straight-backed chair faced the window, looking out at an ugly girl with her eyes closed, leaning down to look in a car window beside a busy highway.

She came out into the world. It was still the forest. He stood beside her, his expression more anxious than angry. "I wanted to warn him," she said.

He leaned over and pushed at something invisible. She felt the car door bump her hip. "Get in."

Echo stepped inside. She closed the car door, and then they were walking side by side in the thick coastal forest, with the ocean peeking at them through the Douglas firs on the beach side. "Are you and Lazar good friends?" she asked.

He ignored the question. "Why you?"

"Why me what?"

"Pardon me for thinking you don't exactly look like a powerhouse." He walked looking forward for a while, then spoke without turning to her. "Why did he want you here instead of me? I told him I'd protect him." He rubbed his face with his hand. "But he said I had something else to do for him." He looked over at her, brows tight, mouth a straight line. "Bring you. Why?"

"I chose this road," she said. "I didn't know I was choosing it. It's not going where I thought it would, but I'm still responsible for the decision. I want to change the outcome."

"I don't believe you can. I could stop them."

"Then why don't you?"

Now he looked at her. "You don't know him, do you?"

She shook her head, knowing her voice would be unsteady.

A little puff of disgust came out of his mouth. "I trust him more than I trust myself, because he came to me in a dream and showed me my soul." He glanced over at her. "Don't bother asking: I wouldn't explain it if I could." He faced forward again. "But now if he says, 'Stay away; you've got other things to do,' I stay away. But some people"—he turned a piercing gaze on her—"go against his wishes and get a last conversation with him. Makes me want to break something."

She looked up at him, fearing the fury in his voice, but he had turned his attention forward again. "What do you know about the guys who are coming to kill him?" His voice was calm and level now, the anger fenced off.

"I didn't know they planned to kill him. I was trying to help." *Irina said something worse than death.* She didn't tell him that. "Didn't he tell you anything?"

"He only tells you what he thinks you need to know," the man said.

"Then why should I tell you?"

"Because maybe he doesn't know what I need to know."

Echo was silent for a while, thinking about the bad effects of secrets. "Jeph is a guy he knew in high school, the one who got him arrested and put in prison."

"Oh." There seemed to be a lot behind the "oh."

"The other one is a guy named Cain. He's in it up to his elbows, but I don't know how he knows Lazar."

"Cain! Cain Timrod?"

"I think that's his last name. I wasn't really paying attention when I met him."

"Son of a bitch."

"You know him?"

"The important thing is that Lazar knows him. Tell him that Cain is in it."

"Okay."

"Make sure you tell him that."

"Okay. But why is it so important?"

"Lazar will know."

Echo sighed.

"I get it." He sounded more sympathetic than angry now. "It's mysteries within mysteries with him. I'll tell you what I know. Maybe you can put it together."

"I'm listening." Had she gained an ally?

"Lazar and I were cellmates for about five years starting a couple of years after Lazar went inside. There was a guy named Arthur, who liked to be called Deadwood. He was mean and crazy as shit, and he started picking on Lazar as soon as he came in.

"Lazar took it and took it and took it, and then he didn't take it anymore. He made the guy think the shower water was boiling hot. Deadwood said he didn't believe it, but he came out of the shower screaming, with blisters all over his body. He spent two weeks in the infirmary, and when he got out, he stayed far away from Lazar."

"What happened to Lazar?"

"Nothing. Everyone else said the water was normal—not quite warm enough for a good shower."

"Wow." That story Jeph told her was about Lazar.

"Yeah. People didn't mess with Lazar after that." He walked on for a while. "Here's where Cain comes in. He arrived around that time. Kept to himself. Looked like he could kill you by looking at you."

Echo saw Cain in her mind, smiling his predator's smile.

"We had an old guy, a lifer everybody called Gramps. He used to sit on the bench in the exercise yard, snoozing in the sun. One day Cain went over and sat beside him. Both of them had their eyes closed, and Cain had a little smile on his face. We thought he was asleep, too. Time's up, and Cain gets up and goes inside, and Gramps is still on the bench. Dead."

"Heart attack? Stroke?"

"That's what they said. Lazar told me not to go to sleep around Cain because he had kidnapped Gramps's soul."

"What? That sounds insane," Echo said. *Something worse than death. Is that what was happening to Chandler?*

"I knew Lazar well enough then to take him seriously, not as seriously as now, but even so. That was a leap for me. One old guy with no obvious cause of death is a pity. Two, three, four—start looking like a trend."

The condor had danced around Chandler, and it threw golden cords over him. The condor promised power, and Chandler's soul was afraid. *Is that what Irina was talking about?* The condor said Echo was making progress. Cain or Jeph? Jeph or Cain? *Progress.*

"He asked me to warn as many people as possible without raising the alarm," the man said, "because most people wouldn't believe it."

A chill ran down her spine. How much did Gray know?

"They couldn't charge Cain with anything, because he hadn't 'done' anything. He went through three cellmates before they put him in a cell by himself."

"Did that stop him?"

"Slowed him down. It seemed like the victim needed to be close and sleeping."

"You're sure Cain was doing it?"

"Lazar was sure. He must have seen something. I got a hint or two, but he wouldn't confirm or deny. Cain started hanging around him."

"Like—friends or—?"

"Friends? Never Cain. Friendly, like, but there was always something else. Maybe he was trying to get Lazar's soul, and it didn't work. Maybe he was trying to form an alliance. Maybe both. There was always a sense that something was going on between them that nobody else could see. Neither one talked about it, but Lazar was always focused on something else when Cain was nearby. He didn't tell me everything."

They continued in silence, and a break appeared in the forest like the opening at the end of a tunnel.

He turned and caught her eye, speaking urgently. "You tell him Cain is coming."

"I'll tell him."

A look of pain crossed his face; the tattooed tear glistened under his eye. "He's going to die today."

"If I can stop them, I will."

He laughed an angry, sad laugh.

Echo sighed. "I'll do what I can." They arrived at the opening in the trees.

They stopped walking, and he turned to her. "This is where we stop. Do you need help getting out?"

"I can find it." She felt around the door for the handle and got out of his car. "Thanks for the ride."

He lifted one hand and walked away as fast as a hummingbird's flight.

## CHAPTER 8

# Crossing the Bar

Echo stood in an open field of yellowish-green grass bounded mostly by thick forest. The beach side, beyond a thicket of salal bushes, dropped off to reveal the ocean, still hiding the line where water met the shore. The trail where she stood veered down to the beach, with no sidetracks continuing down the coast or off into the woods.

The man, Lazar's friend, had disappeared, leaving her utterly alone, isolated, and exposed under the wide sky, where not even a seagull flew. The only way out was forward. She followed the path toward the sea.

The blacktop trail made a channel through the waist-high salal, and as soon as she crested the embankment, a lighthouse appeared, sitting on a basalt foundation in the wet sand of the low-tide beach. She tried to gauge its distance, but the featureless sand and limitless ocean made it seem far away.

The trail made a mostly gentle descent, punctuated by concrete steps where the slope grew steeper.

The size of the lighthouse became clear when a door opened, and a man, barefoot, in wide-legged white pants, white T-shirt, and a Greek fisherman's hat, stepped out and came toward the path she walked. It was too far to see him in any detail, but he walked like a young man, upright, with a spring in his step.

By comparison, she now saw that the lighthouse was the size of a tiny cabin, two stories tall, with a streetlamp in its attic.

The man arrived at the far end of her path long before she did and looked up at her with a friendly wave, then turned to look out to sea as he waited for her arrival. As she descended stairs that extended like the horizon on a Midwestern highway, a man came from the other direction on the beach and met the man from the lighthouse. She recognized the new arrival from her foray into Irina Simon's Underground as Lazar's father. And the first man was Lazar—who else could it be? The two men spoke briefly, then shook hands, and Lazar enveloped his father in a hug, slapping his back. The man went back the way he came, becoming a bear as he walked away, and entered a shack on the sand that became an opening into a cave as he walked into it.

Lazar continued to wait, facing the ocean, until her steps hit level ground. He turned then and gave her an open-faced smile. He had a horizontal scar on his cheek under his right eye, and his eyes were open. "My mother said you would come."

"I had to warn you."

He turned with her, and they walked toward the ocean. Just as the blacktop path disintegrated into the sand, a boardwalk appeared under their feet that became a boat dock as they walked forward. A single beat-up dory was tied to the dock, rocking in gentle waves, with pools of water in the bottom of it.

He stepped down into it and turned to offer his hand to help her into the boat.

"Where are we going? You need to get away from here. Jeph and Cain are coming. The friend you sent? He told me to make sure you hear that Cain is coming, too."

He was still holding his hand out to her, still smiling. Now he made a little "come on" wave with his hand. "We need to talk, and we don't have much time."

"We can't go anywhere in that boat, and you've got to get away."

He sighed and put down his hand. He came back up onto the dock and stood beside her. "Please come into my house, and I'll show you what I see." A door appeared beside them on the dock. He opened it, and she followed him into a white circular building, with a wrought-iron spiral staircase leading up through the ceiling.

"Your esuoh is a lighthouse?"

He held out his arms in a welcoming gesture. "My home sweet home." He walked over to a pair of windows with a chair sitting in front of them.

"But I saw this on the beach."

"You were looking for me, and I wanted to be seen."

His esuoh had a high table with a stool tucked under it and neat shelves of logbooks on the wall above it. A tiny black-iron woodstove in the corner held a tea kettle, and next to that was a small table with two chairs. A winding stairway led to a floor above.

"Come." He motioned to the place where two windows looked out, separated by a narrow section of wall. He stood with the light shining on his face.

She walked over and stood beside him. Out one window was open ocean with neither land nor ship in view anywhere. They stood in a lifeboat half covered by canvas. He turned in place, and the view in the window was endless sea. As he completed the circle, the canvas moved like an ocean wave.

At the same time, out the other window, his rotation revealed the lively summer face of Depoe Bay, Oregon, the way most people see it. In the harbor were dozens of cabin cruisers, sailboats, fishing boats, and other vessels. Encircling the bay where the boats lay at rest, basalt cliffs rose to the level of Highway 101, where a steady stream of cars, trucks, RVs, and bicycles crossed high over a graceful bridge. Condominiums were stacked like Legos on the green hillside. In place of the lifeboat, or even the leaky dory Echo saw, was an inflatable boat like the Coast Guard uses with "Krill Whale Watching Tours" painted on the side.

Echo wasted several precious seconds taking that in. "You're seeing the real world."

"Physical world. Consensus reality. But not all there is."

"No. I mean you're seeing both worlds at the same time."

He shrugged. "It's easier in sequence."

"And you don't have a mirror?"

"I never did. I think Jeph forgot to give me one when he changed the direction of my life." He changed position again, and now, looking up from both the whale-watching boat and the lifeboat, his windows showed Echo—in the physical view wearing dirty clothes, untamed hair, and the scars on her face; in the dream view, her clothes were even dirtier and torn in various places, but her scars were hardly visible. In both views her expression held a hint of madness.

His movement disturbed whatever was under the canvas in his dream world, and a low growl answered. He held himself very still.

"What was that?"

"That?" He sounded partly casual, partly scared. "I call him Richard Parker. He won't hurt you."

The canvas moved again, and a huge head revealed itself, a hypnotic pattern of orange and white with black stripes arrayed around an arresting stare from amber eyes. Another move, and a pink nose appeared, followed by a muzzle, white with black stripes and orange dots punctuated by sharp white teeth.

"It's that lifeboat? Are you crazy? Why don't you change it?"

He seemed to think about that, standing barefoot in clothes more ragged than hers, alone in a lifeboat with a hungry tiger. "I suppose I could. But if he's here, I need him. When he's taught me everything I need to know, the dream will change."

Echo shivered and left his esuoh and went back into the world as she saw it. He stepped into the empty dory again, smiling, his hand extended.

"We're wasting time," Echo said. "You've got to get out of here. Did it ever occur to you that the tiger might be a warning that death is coming?"

"Death is always coming. You and I need to talk, and whatever is coming won't wait." He waved the waiting hand at her.

She took it. It was firm and strong and roughened by work.

"Step down." He guided her to a seat and steadied her until she was secure. "There's a rope behind you. Hold onto it. It may get rough going out of the bay."

"Where are we going?"

He pulled a life vest out of a half-rotted chest at the other end of the dory and handed it to her. "A few miles offshore so we won't be interrupted."

She put it on and sat down in the boat, finding the rope and looping an arm through it.

He set the oars in the oarlocks, and the boat began to vibrate. "You may want to cross over into physical reality—you can come back into my esuoh again if Jeph left you stranded, too. Crossing the bar is quite an experience, and you'll understand why I don't do it in the dream world."

She went back into his esuoh and looked over his shoulder as he prepared to depart. In one window, the tiger peeked out from under the canvas, its eyes full of fear and hunger.

Echo turned away from Lazar's dream and moved closer to the window looking out on physical reality, where he stood before the boat's dashboard, with its throttle and wheel and electronic dials. A flexible plastic window surrounded them. Echo saw herself sitting near the front of the boat, staring into space.

Lazar's hand picked up a radio microphone. It came close to the window, and he said something she didn't understand, to which an answer came, low-pitched and scratchy, like a message from outer space. He returned the microphone to its place, and the boat moved slowly among the other boats until it caught the current of what looked like a white-water river, then plunged into a narrow channel toward a wall of rock. The rock loomed like a ship graveyard, and spray splashed off the windows around them. Echo felt more exhilaration than fear—her hands gripped her knees, and she gave a squeal of half fear, half delight—and then the boat turned, and the tiny harbor spit them out into the ocean.

She went back into her own esuoh. Out her window, Lazar was rowing mightily, and she was sitting on a seat too far forward to ask any questions. She got up to move closer.

"Relax and sit down. We'll drop anchor in a little while and we can talk."

"But Jeph and Cain—"

"Won't be able to find us, unless we capsize and the Coast Guard has to rescue us."

"Capsize?"

"Unlikely. But please sit still and let me get us to our destination."

A destination. That sounded promising. She sat and turned forward in the boat to watch the ocean swelling gently around them, while Lazar's powerful strokes pushed them forward into what seemed like infinity. She looked for an island.

And then he stopped. Noise, clanking of a chain, splash that rocked the boat a little.

She turned to see what he was doing. Dropping an anchor.

"What are we doing?"

"Having our talk."

"Out here? I thought there'd be an island."

"We're the island. Come into my esuoh. I want to introduce you to someone."

Lazar was waiting for her beside the windows. Through both, she saw a sunny day and calm water. Richard Parker had gone quiet, and in physical reality, other boats were scattered around—fishing, touring, whale-watching—marking the distance to the horizon.

Lazar led her up the winding stairway. Once they had passed the ceiling of the first floor, they continued climbing, with windows alternating the reality they displayed. From above, the lighthouse seemed to float on the water.

Lazar pushed open a trapdoor and climbed out. Then his hand reached down through the opening, reminding her of the hand reaching down in his mother's picture of a woman taking her risen son back to the grave.

She expected to step into a hallway of many doors, but instead, it was a circular room with a small table and a couple of chairs, one of which was occupied by an old man who sat quietly, with bright eyes watching them enter. The room had windows all around it, and the glass had the property that when you looked through it, you might see one world or the other, sometimes briefly both, like those pictures where you see different images depending on the angle. She moved her head back and forth for a moment, trying to figure out the principle—degree of angle, placement in the room, what direction she was facing—but couldn't work it out. After a few seconds of silently experimenting, she brought herself back to the matter at hand.

"Is that your grandpa?"

Lazar smiled. The old man stood, and Lazar merged into him. That was the only way she could describe it. There were two, and then there was one, the way the worlds merged outside the window. The man who stood there now was Lazar and yet more than Lazar—taller, stronger, with white hair and only a hint of the scar on his face, which now looked more like a decoration than a blemish. He—they—sat in the chair "Grandpa" had occupied and motioned Echo to sit in the other.

She did.

After a space of silence, he turned to Echo. "Give us your message."

Echo had forgotten her urgent message. "Who are you? What are you?"

"I'm a man. A human being. Like you."

"I've only been here a couple of days, but this doesn't seem—normal."

"What is normal? A jungle? A luxury apartment?"

"No." Although that was kind of what she meant. "Aren't your memories up here?"

"They're in a room off the main floor. I rarely use them and spend most of my time up here."

"OK. I guess architecture isn't essence." Her head was spinning. "But what about him? Who is he? Where did he go?"

"You met my mother in her chapel?"

"In the middle of the lake where I talked to her soul? That man is your soul?"

"It would be more accurate to say I'm his ego, but close enough."

"But you and him." She held out two fingers and closed them together.

He held out three fingers and closed them together. "Body, personality, and soul. We have ended the animosity, at least part of the time. That's a gift from Jeph, and in every moment of awareness, I ask God to bless him for it."

"But he got you arrested for a crime you didn't commit."

He nodded.

"He broke your mother's heart."

"She will see the light burst forth in her chapel."

"And your father?"

"He's both weak and strong. I can't change his past, and only he can change his future."

"Why is your esuoh so different from everyone else's?"

"Long story. Tell us what you need to say."

"Jeph and Cain are coming to kill you—or worse."

"That's it?" Lazar stood and slid out of the combined person, and now there were two again. "I'll take you back to shore."

"It's my fault. I got the key from your mother because Jeph sent me to do that. I told Galynn about it. I think she stole the key, and if she did, they could be here at any minute. We can't go back to Depoe Bay. You need to get away from them."

"There's plenty of time." Old Lazar's voice was deep and resonant. "Tell us the rest of it."

Lazar pulled another chair up to the table, and she told them all of it. Jeph and Gray. Cali and her dad. Galynn and Irina. Losing the key. Killing a man. Almost killing a kindly old couple. Riding with Lazar's friend. Time lost and Lazar's danger. "People keep telling me I'm a fool. I didn't mean to get anyone killed. And before any of this happened, I promised to stop it."

Lazar looked to the old man, who nodded as if in answer to a pending question. He turned to Echo. "Let's go."

"Finally. Are you going to get away?"

"No. Do you remember what my mother told you to do?"

"Take the key back to Jeph and go home. But—"

"But you couldn't, because you felt responsible."

"It was my fault."

"Partly. But you changed the outcome. Responsibility is a big mantle to take on yourself."

"You mean I shouldn't have?"

"I mean you did, and now you need to be prepared for what comes next. I had thought I would finish this, but it doesn't work out that way."

"Wanted," the old man chimed in.

"Wanted to finish this." Lazar smiled a rueful smile. "But now you'll take over."

"Me? I'm the fool who got you into this. Remember?"

"The fool is the one who goes forward without taking risks into account. Promise me you'll humble yourself to ask for help."

"I'll try." She spoke with hesitation, because the only one she could think of to ask was Gray, and she didn't know what Gray thought of her now or whether he would be willing to help. The older and younger Lazar stared at her intently, waiting for a more complete answer. "If he's willing."

The old man nodded.

"We've got work to do." Lazar stood and asked solemnly, "May I come into your house?"

She was afraid of his judgment, but she said, "Please come in."

Lazar stepped into her esuoh.

It was dusty and messy. Things she had collected on her journey were scattered around. Shreds of broken glow-in-the-dark balloons, along with unfiled notebooks of memories. One sketchbook was open to the page where Chandler stood terrified outside the apartment door.

She would have offered the template apology for the mess, but Lazar walked through without looking, straight to the trapdoor to her basement. He waited there, like a dog asking to go outside.

She stopped, fearing that twelve-year-old Echo was hiding in a corner, planning mischief. When she held her hand near the trapdoor, she felt an electric charge and expected her inner troublemaker to jump out like at the surprise party she'd never had. Lazar stepped back to give her room. Why was it so hard to go through her own door when going through others' was so easy? She forced herself to press her hand against it. She hoped she would need a key, but of course she did not.

When the terrified Chandler was about to step into the darkness, she had told him there was a light switch. Now she felt his terror, and only Lazar's presence kept her from slamming the door shut and locking it.

She turned, looking back at Lazar, as she took the first step down the ladder, then the second and third, the darkness rising up her body like water. When she sank below the surface, her hand found an old-fashioned oil lamp, of the kind miners would once have carried, hanging from the ceiling—floor, whatever—and when she touched it, the fire lit, creating a bubble of light in the ocean of darkness. She took the lamp and finished climbing down the ladder.

Chapter 9

# Echo Journeys to Her Soul

Echo's basement was a flat area that smelled of earth and silence. Aside from the ladder, free-standing in the sphere of light, there was nothing. The lantern illumined only a small, empty space, with no indication of any limit to the darkness. A basement should contain something, right? Washer, dryer, rumpus room, junk, lost tools, forgotten toys, or even a wine cellar with a fabulous cask of Amontillado. "Creepy crawlies," Jeph had said. She would be less terrified if she saw a ghost.

Lazar came down the ladder and stood beside her.

"Where to?" she asked him. If the sound had bounced back, it would indicate boundaries, but it didn't.

"You're the only one who knows," he said.

She held up the lantern and turned again, proving that the light revealed nothing. "There's nothing down here." She knew it wasn't true, or rather that the abundance of "Nothing" was exactly what frightened her. She would accept any excuse to climb the ladder again into her cheerful— if unkempt—esuoh with its familiar furniture and decorations.

"Start walking from where you are, and the way will come to you."

"But I was told there were monsters down here."

"Not if you bring them out and let them live aboveground."

"Like the tiger?"

He didn't answer. She was stalling, and he knew it. She took a deep breath and walked forward. This darkness was where her path had been leading from the time she stepped onto Jeph's polished table and picked up the small key she had tripped over. All the quaint and charming personalities she had met that evening and their funny, *interesting* sesuoh. Every one had a basement, but could any be as horrifying as this emptiness?

A door appeared in front of her, standing by itself in the small light of her lantern, with no walls to hold it. She walked around it. The two sides of the door were the same. *Would they go to the same place?* She went back to the side where Lazar was standing and turned the handle. It opened to a stairway descending into deeper darkness. She looked back at him, caught his almost imperceptible nod, and went through the door.

Down the interminable stairway with the flickering light and shadow from the lamp. She looked back a couple of times to see if Lazar was with her. He was always a step or two behind, but never seemed to be walking at all. He gave her an encouraging smile, but didn't say anything.

She stopped and turned back to Lazar. "I've been on two of these stairways before. Why is mine longer?"

"It's exactly as long as you know it is."

"So if I *know* I can walk to Florida in a day?"

"Florida is outside. This is inside."

"You mean if I want it to be shorter or I believe it's shorter, it will be shorter?"

"That kind of *wanting* and *believing* are the ego's way of warring with the soul. The ego only wins if it's satisfied, and it never is. In this case, you win by losing. Accept that it's as long as it is, and you'll get there when you get there."

"And all the time, Jeph and Cain are coming to kill you."

He smiled and gave a little half shrug. "Time here is disconnected from time in the other world."

"You're not taking this seriously enough."

"We need to do this before we go back."

Echo sighed with frustration, the anxiety of what was going to happen roiling through her. She continued down, down, down, until she forgot she was walking.

And came to the door at the first turning.

She stopped in front of it. It spoke to her. Not in words, but in pain, anguish, and regret. She turned to keep walking.

"You need to go inside." Lazar stood behind her.

"It will take extra time."

"Even if wolves were chasing us, you can't get there without going through these doors."

"Then Chandler—"

"You can't get there without going through these doors."

"Oh, hell." She pushed through the first door.

She was bored and restless and too tired to sleep, riding in a darkened car on a featureless interstate. Her sister and mother were sleeping, and her dad was staring at the long highway ahead. His head nodded, and he stretched his arms one by one and slapped his face. The car kept rolling between fields of nothingness. Diana was snoring softly, her head twisted to the side. Her perfection irritated Echo, who had always been and would always be in Diana's shadow. And when they left Diana at Stanford, Echo would go home and be nobody.

Anger, sadness, and envy rose up in her like a monster, ready to kill. Diana woke in that moment, as if Echo's pain called to her pain. Their separate pains snarled at one another like two cats on a fence. Their screams of anger startled their father into running into a concrete barrier. The car flipped over, and the sounds became screams, shrieking metal, breaking glass.

Watching now, Echo didn't have the luxury of passing out and waking up to the face of an EMT pulling her out and saying, "This one is alive." She saw them all dying. The broken bones and the cuts that later became scars on her face were outward manifestations of the anguish that she had stamped out, squashed down, pushed aside so that she could keep on living. She had thought she would die if she felt this again, and the death was a burning fire of guilt and sorrow that flared up and died down, and she was still there, with her hand on the doorknob and the interminable steps before her.

She didn't want Lazar to see her face, so she turned without looking at him and kept walking, wiping away her tears.

It seemed like the number of stairs in an ordinary house before she came to the next door. She hesitated before opening it, but didn't wait for Lazar to urge her to go in.

Circus music in a minor key, and mannequins in a bank lobby doing normal things in a jerky way, dancing around like marionettes. Everything was slowly spinning, merry-go-rounds within merry-go-rounds, and Gray was in the middle of it, seeing it all, held on a leash by a kid with a bully's face.

She watched from above, an omniscient observer, and also saw herself through a fisheye lens, from Gray's point of view. "Now I understand about you," she had told him—as if she had understood anything in those first few hours of being in this world—and as if she understood anything now. She had popped into his esuoh, his private space, when she wouldn't have had the gall to pop into his physical house. And he had pushed her out.

The fury on his face—his open eyes, as if he was seeing who she really was for the first time—shallow, frivolous, presumptuous. And now here she was, in a boat on the Eternal Ocean, trying to stop a murder she had set in motion, with no prospect of getting home. His eyes snagged her heart, and her breath caught in her throat when she thought she might never see them again.

A weight pressed down on her like a rock the size of the world. Gradually it dissipated, until it was light enough that she could move, and she felt the doorknob in her hand.

The last turning was only a few steps away. What could it be, if they were chronological? Curiosity overcame her fear and drove her through.

Deep fog, white and thick as smoke. And voices coming out of the fog: Jeph and Cain. A voice behind her, Lazar. They were all talking, but she didn't understand them. Guilt. *No! No! No!* She screamed but no one answered. It was as if she wasn't there. The voices rose in pitch and volume.

*It's my fault! I caused this! I can't let it happen!*

The fog turned red as blood. Jeph and Cain kept talking, and Lazar was silent.

*I came here to stop it!*

The fog cleared, and Echo was alone on the beach watching the sun slip over the horizon. The reds and pinks in the sky looked like scraps of the bloody fog that had turned into clouds before passing away over the earth. She wept, disconsolate, feeling the crushing weight of responsibility. She stood up and began walking toward a high spot on the coast with intention and purpose. She didn't know the next destination, but she knew the next step. Lazar spoke. "Go to God's Thumb."

Then she was outside, with her hand on the doorknob. She walked the last few stairs before arriving at a door that opened to sand and sky.

She was alone. The sky was streaked with red and gray clouds, the same colors as behind the third door. Was she caught in that reality forever? She looked back for the door she had just left, but it was gone, leaving only sand and a dark forest punctuated by deeper shadows. Ahead, the sea tossed gentle waves against the beach. To her right were the lights of the carnival and town; to the left, empty shoreline as if on an unsettled planet. The moon, not quite full, shone through a film of mist above the forest like a white smudge in the sky.

And then she caught a presence over her shoulder, and it was Lazar, as if he'd only escaped her notice. "Where to?" she asked him.

Lazar looked around as if he'd been there before, a long time ago. "Tell me what you feel."

"The beach is a long journey with no end in sight. Like the stairs but more so. The carnival is crazy-making. But that forest—" She turned and stared into it, remembering what Chandler found. "Death lives there."

He gave a wry smile. "Guess which way we're going."

"Is there a place along this beach for everyone?"

"Let's focus on you for now." He gestured to the unmarked sand. "After you."

She started walking away from the ocean. The sand, rust-colored as if in the light of a dying star, had already released all its heat from the day, and a chill was descending. "There was a trail through open sand to your mom's house."

"That's because she spends a lot of time there."

"But she wasn't in this world." She turned back to answer and tripped over driftwood and nearly fell. *Watch where you're going.*

"More than you would know."

"Does she have a mirror?"

"You don't need a mirror."

"But—" She stopped, turned to look at him. He was alive and vibrant, smiling slightly, but under the light of the red sky, his white T–shirt and sailor's pants seemed to have been washed in blood and not fully rinsed. "No. Jeph used a mirror to push you through. You may not have it now, but you used it to begin with. And your mother . . . ?"

He shook his head. "No. She doesn't see a tiger on her lifeboat or even the chapel where her soul lives. But she sits in the darkness, listening, and waiting for the one who waits beyond the screen."

Echo started walking again. "Why?" They were coming closer to the woods. There were roots and rocks and sticks under the sand, and only now did Echo perceive that she had lost her shoes.

"Why does she wait?" Lazar was still barefoot, too, but didn't seem to notice.

"No. That's not it. I mean, that's a good question, but it's not my question. Not now." She came to the trees, standing with their limbs locked in a silent game of Red Rover, and she felt that if she got caught there at the entrance to the forest, she would become a member of the tree team and never leave. Silly idea, of course. She kept walking, looking for an opening. "Why the tiger? No. That's another good question, but not the right one. Why am I here? Ever since I met Jeph, I've felt like this world called me, sent the help I needed, brought me to this place for its own unfathomable reasons. Why me? Is this world too stupid to realize I would mess everything up?" She found an opening she could slide through and dived into the darkness.

"Because fools like us—" his voice came to her over the sound of twigs breaking and branches squeaking "—get lost in the multiplicity and don't see things as they are without help."

They crashed through the forest, threading among the trees. She had forgotten she was barefoot again until she remembered and felt the sharp points under her feet. "Maybe that's you. Your only fault was that you were 'lost in the multiplicity.' But I'm a special kind of fool, carrying pain and terror everywhere I go."

He didn't answer.

She looked back at him, and he was struggling not to laugh. "What?"

"The ego holds its specialness the way a baby holds its blankie. It alternates between special hero and special villain. When you meet your soul, you will understand."

She pushed past a branch, and it slipped out of her hand and snapped back, hitting Lazar in the face. "I'm sorry!"

"You *really* don't want to be here, do you?"

"You think I did that on purpose?"

"Everything that happens here has a purpose. It's OK. I was more terrified than this the first time. It was right after I almost killed Deadwood with shower water."

"I heard about that."

"From Logan or Cain?"

"Logan and Jeph, so both, I guess. That was amazing."

"Amazing. Yes, that his mind was powerful enough to fool his body that way. That I could be driven to such cruelty by fear? Not as amazing. Later that night I heard wolves howling in the basement. I went down planning to kill them, but they welcomed me as one of their own, and we went down to the beach together."

"Did you open the doors off the stairway?"

"Not then. They said I could be a wolf, too. I liked the idea. I had served five of my twenty years in prison for a crime I didn't commit. I was tired of the monotony. I was tired of being bullied. They invited me to join them. We ran to the city and found an old man sleeping. The wolves showed me how to take his soul from his body."

Echo didn't realize she had stopped. The forest had cleared around them. She sat on a log, and he sat on another one nearby.

"They said I could own the world, live forever, control everyone I met. I could taste the desire for it."

"And?"

"You know that deep rumbling sound that comes from my mother's chapel?"

"Like an earthquake in music."

He nodded. "I heard it. She didn't know it, but she stopped me. I ran from them, becoming a man as I ran, climbed out, and slammed the door to my basement."

She waited. That couldn't be the end of the story.

"The next night I went back. The wolves were waiting. They thought they would win this time, but I opened the doors on the stairway. My mother's soul was beyond one of them, preparing me for this day. When I came out onto the beach, the wolves were there, but different."

"Different how?" Echo asked.

"The wolves were men. Cain, Deadwood, some of the others. Fearful, dressed in rags, and begging like hungry dogs. I woke up." He stopped.

Echo wanted him to get on with the story. "You woke up?"

He said it again, looking directly into her eyes. "I woke up. I saw the cell, the bars, Logan sleeping on the bunk below me. I also saw the sand and the dogs running away from me. I found my soul, sat with him for a while, and came back a free man." He stood up. The log disappeared, and the woods closed in around them. "Let's keep walking."

"Why does your soul live in your lighthouse and mine way out here?"

"As you spend time in your soul's company, the path gets more pronounced and the way easier. One day I went to the upper part of the lighthouse, and he was there."

"And now you just—walk into him?"

"Not always. There are good reasons to be a personality in the world. But when I have a deeper question or need to rest from the glitter, I go into my soul and know things from the inside that I can only glimpse from the outside."

"Does everybody do that?"

"Is that your real question?"

She pondered that, noticing at the same time that the trees were becoming further apart, and blue-gray light was filtering through the branches. "No. I don't think it is. What I want to know is if I have to do that."

She broke through the trees and found a grassy hillside with woods surrounding it. A cemetery where gravestones, moss-covered and crumbling with age, were scattered like seeds flung from a sack. The grass was vibrant green against the cold gray of the sky and fir trees. There was a half-fallen hut at the far edge of the clearing.

"Are we here?" she asked Lazar, but he didn't answer. When she turned around, he was gone.

A chill ran through her. She remembered she was barefoot, and the grass felt icy against her feet. She ran back to the woods and called him, but she couldn't find exactly where she had entered the field. She ran along the edge of the forest, peering through the trees. Pru had sentenced her to the Dungeons of the Labyrinth. Edward had warned her of dead ends from which she could never get out. What did she *know* about Lazar? Only what he said about himself—and that he had almost killed a man using the man's own mind.

And here she was, lost in a forest, with no one around except dead people. She longed for the comparative warmth and friendliness of the mannequins. She despaired of finding a way out and ran to the nearest gravestone. The letters were hard to read until she kneeled at the stone and traced them with her fingers. "Lazar Kyrillovich." The date was undecipherable.

The tombstones looked like they were hundreds of years old. Where was this? *When* was this?

The next grave read "David and Clara Shearwater." "Diana Shearwater." "Chandler Siskin." Then "Doris Shearwater."

No! Aunt Doris wasn't dead. She was at home, working in her garden, talking to Clarice on the phone, watching *Magnum, P.I.* Aunt Doris was a fixture in Echo's world; she couldn't die.

Or maybe it was Echo who was dead, forgotten, eternally disconnected from the life she knew.

She sat on the hillside and wept over the eternal separation of death. The evils done, the good undone. Her lost opportunity to tell Gray—

She stood up to distract herself from that thought.

The only thing she hadn't examined was the shack that looked like a gardener's shed, and just outside it was another stone, calling her to identify her loss. Kneeling down like a servant, she read the words "Gray Birdsong," and burst out sobbing. She collapsed on the wet grass and mixed her anguish with the earth's moisture.

The world was utterly quiet, and after a time, her voice seemed to be an offense to it. She rose, wiped her face on her wet sleeve, and went on to the shed.

It terrified her. She didn't feel a monster here; she felt no presence here but her own. But its dilapidation spoke of long abandonment, and if she went in there, she was sure, she would accept her fate on this hillside and never leave it. She would die and become one of the graves.

She had thought she would sacrifice everything to fix what she had broken. But now that she knew what sacrificing "everything" really meant, she was not so sure.

Her phone, the key, her bag. Things she had thrown away or lost through carelessness. Dross. Trinkets. Nothings.

Even death was trivial compared to this eternal loneliness.

She walked into the shed and closed the door behind her.

A FAINT AND FILTERED LIGHT came in through a window in the back of the shed. It revealed a couple of battered chairs, a table with one leg broken off halfway down, and a wooden crate the size of a bed—or a coffin—filled with straw.

She stood there, choosing between the bed and a chair, and sat in the chair. She didn't know what she was doing here, but she would do it awake and with her eyes open.

Then it seemed the shack was bigger than she had thought. Someone came out of the darkness carrying a candle. It was an old woman, much older than Aunt Doris, wearing tattered clothes but smelling of flowers.

The woman sat on the other chair and put the candle on the table. Miraculously the candle stood as upright as if the bottom half of the table's leg was not broken but just invisible.

"Are you my soul?" Echo asked.

Instead of an answer, the woman reached beneath the table, brought up a huge wooden salad bowl and set it on the table. In it were two other empty wooden bowls and probably a gallon of seed beads, so tiny they could hardly be distinguished from each other and glimmering like sunlight on water. When Echo picked up the two empty bowls, one had "Diana" written on it in a beautiful script, and the other, "Echo," in a plain sans-serif type.

"Sort them," the old woman said.

Echo stared down at the beads, in various shapes and colors—some as small as a grain of dust; the largest the size of a mustard seed. The largest even had marks like writing on them, but it wasn't either of their names, as far as she could see. "How can I do this?"

"Start, and you'll know," the old woman said.

"But it will take forever," Echo whined.

"Best to start sooner rather than later, then."

"I have things to accomplish."

"You need to sort the beads," the old woman said with a finality that carried an undefined threat.

Echo sighed and picked up the first bead. It was so small that she could hardly feel it, but as she rolled it between her thumb and forefinger, she felt *something*. She couldn't define it. It was a memory of dead leaves ruffled by a breeze on an uncharacteristically warm day in late fall. Sunbeams glinted off a few shiny surfaces. And that was all, but the tingling sensation that flowed from her fingers through her spine and down to her toes told her it belonged to her. She dropped it into the "Echo" bowl. And so on, bead by bead—a glimpse, a musical note, an intuition. Echo, Diana, Echo, Diana, Echo, Echo, Diana, and on and on for hours, days, months. Once she fell asleep at her task and woke to find the "Diana" bowl spilled and beads embedded in her cheek. She looked up at the old woman in chagrin, but the old woman stared back without sympathy or amusement or impatience. Echo began again.

In a hundred years or maybe forever, the bottom of the bowl appeared through the pile of unsorted beads. By now she knew where a bead would go almost before she picked it up. As she sorted the last dozen, she realized she had a different view of Diana, not a shining, unapproachable star, but a talented girl whose life ended before she and Echo could bring their sisterhood to its fruition of friendship. The sadness she felt was less about herself and more about the two of them. She dropped the last bead into its bowl with a sense of triumph and turned to the old woman again. She no longer needed to ask the question. "You are my soul."

The old woman nodded and said, "We belong to each other."

"Okay, then." Echo brushed her hands together. "I'm glad we got that straightened out." She stood up. "What am I supposed to do next?" She waited for instructions to save Lazar, stop Jeph, get the world back on track.

The old woman picked up a box from under the table. It was made of cardboard and cube-shaped like an Amazon box for shipping a basketball, except its logo smile shaded toward malice. The woman hefted it like a heavy thing, and it jingled as she set it on the table and ripped off the packing tape. "Sit down," she said.

"I've got to rescue Lazar. He's been waiting for me all this time, if he's still waiting."

The old woman opened the flaps of the box, revealing a jumble of metal pieces, loops and twists. "Make the chain."

"What?" Echo picked up a handful. They were like entrapment puzzles, but disconnected and made up of two metal puzzles to be joined at each end. And they were all separate. "This is impossible."

The old woman looked pointedly at the two bowls of beads and back at Echo. She said, "Only if you don't start."

"But I've been here forever already. I can't sit here for *another* eternity doing the next set of puzzles." She got up and looked out the doorway at the gray winter sky, the frost on the grass, the bare trees. She didn't see Lazar waiting. She didn't see any way of returning to her home reality, only the gravestones looking older than they had when she came in. *Sacrifice everything.*

She sat at the table again. Pushed the box aside, and started laying out the pieces end to end, to see which ends would match and join.

After bringing out a few handfuls from the top and finding no matches, she thrust her hand down into the box and closed it around some of the shifting pieces. When she brought her hand out, some pieces magnetically attached themselves to her fingers, her wrist, and the back of her hand. Each joint was a puzzle in itself to connect the link, and each link accessed a memory, this time of Gray. An old T-shirt he used to wear. Mismatched sneakers he wore to school sometimes. His closed eyes looking at her. A sly half-smile at something she said. The way the kids called him Eleven after a character in some TV show they were watching. His habit of disappearing into his esuoh, which she partly understood now that she knew about sesuoh. All the things.

Link by link, she constructed a chain, and the thousands of pieces in the box gradually grew into coils on the table. When the last link connected the last two coils into a circle of chain, Echo pushed them across to the old woman, who scooped them into the box again and slid it under the table.

Echo stood up, sighed and stretched, and looked out the window. A dusting of snow lay on the hillside, and the gray-green trees looked hard as ice. "I suppose I'm not finished yet," she said, still looking out the window.

The old woman didn't answer, and Echo turned to her, half expecting—half hoping—she would be gone.

But she wasn't. Instead, the table now held three river rocks, shaped like potatoes.

Echo glanced out the window again. She had been here months, certainly, if not centuries, so perhaps the next task would bring her around to good weather again. She sat at the table and tried stacking the stones on top of one another, trying different ways of ordering them, adjusting the balance.

The woman watched like a patient scientist. When Echo looked to her after the tower of stones collapsed for the umpteenth time, she pushed a wooden yoke with two buckets tied to it across the table and tossed the rocks into one of the buckets. "Take the path to the river and bring back stones like these. You need to shore up the walls."

"Shore up the walls? Of this house?"

The old woman nodded.

"I'm not a stonemason."

"Easier than trying to stack them on the table," the old woman said, "and more useful."

"Just start," Echo said in bitter mockery, unwilling to hear it from the old woman again. She took the buckets and stomped out into the cold day.

She followed a path she hadn't noticed before—*Of course I didn't notice it before. It wasn't here before*—that led through a patch of blackberries—*It* would *go through a patch of blackberries; it can't possibly be a simple path over a grassy slope*—and even though the vines weren't in their luxuriant and impassable summer state, and it was, in fact, possible to see the path, she remembered she was barefoot again—*Ouch!*—and the thorns pierced her feet and sliced her legs and arms and ripped her clothes. At the end of the briar patch—*Too bad I'm not a rabbit*—she came to a riverside trail, and a steep drop-off down to the river itself.

The way down to the river was a sharp gully formed by human feet and the workings of water. She could climb down only by using both her hands and feet. *How am I ever going to get back up here with two buckets of rocks?* "Just start," she told herself, stepping into the winter-swollen stream to gather river rocks.

The water was cold and the rocks slippery, and the way back up the bank would be harder than down, so she loaded only a few rocks in each bucket, climbed the bank, traversed the blackberries and arranged the seven rocks she had brought on the nearest wall of the shed and went back for more.

She had intended to count the trips to the river and back, but soon she didn't know if she was on number three or four, and later if it had been a hundred or a thousand. The wall grew, slowly at first. Sometimes she would rearrange the rocks already placed to stabilize them, but usually she just set the rocks she had brought before going back for the next load.

The rock wall rose in a slow spiral. Walking toward the cottage—for it was becoming that, rather than a broken-down shed—she admired the way the stones fit, and walking back to the river, she considered the size and shape of rocks she would need next. The wall became more important than the tenaciousness of the blackberries or the frigidity of the water. And then she noticed that the blackberries had retreated, leaving a clear path to the river. Steps cut into the dirt of the gully gave easier access to the water. The water level had gone down, revealing a beach covered with the rounded river stones, and in the river's fast current they made a cheery clackety-clack sound.

Echo was so eager to shore up the walls that she no longer noticed the overflowing buckets across her shoulders, even though she occasionally dropped stones along the trail.

When she had slid the last rock into place, she walked around the building again, adjusting a stone here, shifting one there, and feeling a sense of beauty similar to what she had felt at Irina's chapel in the Underground. Not more or less beautiful, not even the same kind of beauty, but she felt it as a *right* place, cozy and secure and even more *hers* than her esuoh. She stepped back and looked around the clearing again, where the grass was vibrant and the trees wore their spring cloud of green, promising leaves and fruit.

She went back inside through the sturdy door, now painted yellow, and found well-built, well-cared-for furniture inside, along with a black iron woodstove, so clean it almost shone, and a steaming teapot with three cups on the table. Echo took her seat across from her soul and waited to find out what would come next.

A knock at the door. "May I come in?" Lazar's voice.

The old woman rose to open it, and Lazar came in, ducking under the lintel and creating a chair to sit at the table.

"I thought I'd lost you," Echo said to him.

"You had to come here alone." He turned to the woman. "What do you think?"

"We will do."

When Echo and Lazar left the old woman, only one grave remained on the hillside. Fresh flowers were propped against the headstone, and Echo ran over to see whose it was. She was expecting Lazar's name, but when she kneeled next to it and moved the flowers to see the carving, she was surprised to see her own name. Fear shot through her like an electric current, and she looked around the clearing, but everything was still there—the stone cottage, the path to the river, and Lazar waiting at an opening in the trees for her to join him.

She was leaving something important behind, but she didn't know what it was and wasn't sure she would miss it.

Chapter 10

# Return to History

Lazar allowed Echo to lead the way through the forest.
When they came to the sand, she looked back and saw a definite opening in the trees. "Why is it so clear already?"

"You made the path today. Keep using it, and it will get clearer. But you'll have many reasons not to use it—fear, distraction, a feeling of your own importance—and it might slip into chaos again, and you'll have to find it. But it's always there."

"But your soul—"

"I had fifteen years after I found my soul, when I wanted distraction from the fear outside, when I had no illusion of importance. The inner house and the outer house became one house."

"Like moving your grandpa in with you?"

"In the language of this world, age is not helplessness, but wisdom and authority."

"I like my house, even though it's messy right now."

"My house was a hut on the beach. I liked it, too. My memories were in the loft, and my basement door was a trapdoor into a hole dug in sand. It changed over time, preparing for my grandpa," he said, smiling. "It became a lighthouse gradually, like the changing of seasons. When I noticed, it was already there."

"And your eyes are open in both worlds?"

"To both you and my father, who knows only the world of reflected light."

They had arrived at the place where their footprints stopped, so where they had come out from the stairs onto the sand. There were a couple of beach chairs in the sand, and he sat in one. "I need to tell you some things."

She sat down beside him.

"Events will happen very fast once we reach the shore."

"Can't you—"

"The wheels are set in motion and can't be stopped. But you can affect the outcome." He looked out at the ocean, his eyes half-closed as the wind caressed his face. "After it's over, put the ocean on your left and travel along the beach until you come to God's Thumb. Climb to the top, and help will meet you there."

"God's Thumb?"

"It's a landmark. You'll find it. Do you know how to make yourself invisible?"

"I've been invisible before. I didn't like it."

"Well, now you need it."

"I don't know how I did it. It was when I first got into this world. All the other people were mannequins. It was terrifying."

"Navigate through your front windows and don't engage with anybody."

"I can't do that. It's just not me."

"People who can change the outcome of your journey will be looking for you. If you do as I tell you, no one will see you, even if you walk right past them."

"Will they look like mannequins?"

"Maybe. They're real people, but you don't want them to see you." He stood up. His chair disappeared.

Echo stood up. Her chair disappeared as well.

"Last word. Can you swim?"

"Yes."

"Good. Let's go then."

They turned from the sea, and now a door stood on the sand with no walls around it. She led the way through, and after only a few steps, they came to the ladder and climbed up to her esuoh. It looked as if a maid had come in and tidied while they were gone. Lazar left her, and she felt the vibration she knew as the boat engine. She went into Lazar's esuoh to watch through the window to the physical world.

When she had gotten her bearings, she left his esuoh and went back into the world of dreams. She got up from her seat to stand beside him.

"You need to sit down," he said, holding their destination in his gaze.

"Please don't do this. This boat can land anywhere. We can go get the police. Something."

"Sit down." There was a fierceness in his manner that was unlike the easy-going smile she was used to. "Do you think I want this? There are bigger issues at stake here than our convenience."

At that moment, a monster rose out of the water like a shining tower, and fell with a splash that soaked both of them.

"What was that?" she said, tasting the sharp saltwater as she gasped for breath.

"Orca. My father calls them money in the bank; for right now, it's the reason you need to sit down." He looked out over the water, and Echo returned to her seat.

THE DORY BUMPED AGAINST THE DOCK with a sound more like a bouncy house than like a wooden rowboat. The engine sounds had stopped seconds ago, and Lazar leaped into action, tying ropes and pulling them secure. He held out a hand to her and said, "Don't watch your step; feel it." Her feet found a sort of stepladder, and she left the rocking boat for the sturdiness of the dock.

As they walked away from the boat, Echo practiced being invisible. Lazar stood out, very real and present; it was impossible to see him as a mannequin or, she presumed, to make him unable to see her. But two mannequins strode toward them on the dock, their heavy steps ringing like wooden bells.

As they came closer, their identities broke through. They were mannequins, then something else, then mannequins again, changing back and forth at first so quickly she couldn't make out what the something else was, and then they were Old West characters, one a cowboy court judge—black suit, white shirt, string tie. The other wore a black rodeo shirt, black leather chaps, and a red bandana around his neck. Blood-red boots. Both wore black hats and long leather range coats—black for the judge, tan for the cowboy—flipped back over their sidearms.

Jeph and Cain.

*Jeph and Cain.* Fear gripped her guts, threatened to freeze her arms and legs. Lazar walked in front of her. His shoulders stiffened, but he kept walking. She wanted to tackle him. Grab him by the knees and throw him into the water. To run past him and push Jeph and Cain out of the way. She didn't have the physical power to do any of that. Maybe to knock Lazar down with her advantage of surprise, but that would only put him at a disadvantage against the monsters walking toward him.

She went into Lazar's esuoh and shouted at him. "Make them stop. I know you can do it. You have powers nobody else has. Make them stop!"

He turned to her with firmness like fury in his eyes. "You need to leave now."

She found herself outside his esuoh.

The cowboys came closer, the boards of the dock ringing under their boots.

Echo pounded on Lazar's esuoh door, wanting to see what was happening. He glanced at her, concerned, distracted. "I want to be here," she said.

He nodded and turned toward the cowboys.

Entering, Echo saw them through the window of physical reality. They were just Jeph and Cain in their regular clothes, Jeph's business suit that brought out the blue of his eyes; Cain's black jeans and rumpled Oxford shirt and of course the red cowboy boots. Aside from the clothes, they were changed from the last time she had seen them, especially Jeph. In both realities, they had a lean and desperate look, like hungry wolves on the hunt.

Lazar stopped as they drew nearer. "It's been a long time, Jeph. Want to try a little whale-watching?" He turned to Echo inside his esuoh. "Remember what I told you."

She nodded, but she was so full of terror and sorrow she could hardly remember anything.

Jeph and Cain walked calmly into Lazar's esuoh, filling the small, neat space with their aggressive presence.

Jeph turned to Echo with a predatory smile and held up a tiny cross on a string, swinging it like a movie hypnotist. "Thanks for sending your replacement. Ravenne's daughter is more cooperative than you are." He winked at her and dropped Lazar's key into the inner pocket of his suit coat.

Cain looked out the windows, a glance turning to a stare. He prodded Jeph with his elbow.

Jeph followed his gaze, taking in the twin views of sunny Depoe Bay and Richard Parker's massive feline head poking out from under the canvas, teeth bared in hunger. Jeph's eyes widened, then narrowed, and then he set his face in a neutral arrangement before turning to Cain again.

Echo wanted the tiger to attack Jeph and Cain, but he was Lazar's death, not theirs. She was watching a movie filmed from a script written long ago; her part was over, and she couldn't change what happened next. It was too much to bear. There had to be a way to change what would happen next.

Having taken in the ground floor, Cain climbed the spiral stairway and pushed open the trapdoor at the top, turning to talk to Jeph below. "His old man is up here." He sounded surprised.

Jeph turned to Echo. "You've been a big help," he said in a taunting tone. He turned to climb the stairs.

Guilt and rage rose in her. She lunged at Jeph, but he pushed her to the ground.

Lazar stepped forward between them. "Still pushing girls around, Jeph?" His eyes spoke to Echo, a warning to stop or leave.

She turned to the window to hide the tears welling up in her eyes.

Jeph spoke to Lazar. "Echo and I are good friends, but she tends to be—passionate."

Lazar made a door in the middle of the room and walked through it. Through the door, Echo saw Lazar in the upstairs room, moving to stand next to his soul.

Cain muttered something under his breath and moved his arms and legs in a dance like the condor had done over Chandler. Cords of gold light flowed from the fingers of one hand toward Lazar.

The cords of light attached themselves to Lazar's head, neck, and shoulders. There was pain in the crinkles around Lazar's eyes and the set of his mouth, but a deep serenity overall. He held out an arm, and his soul walked to him. They merged, becoming a shining man in a white robe and a simple silver crown, like a king who didn't need to prove anything. Gold light flowed back from Lazar to Cain, filling Cain with light, like a front-yard Christmas decoration.

At first Echo thought Cain was winning, but then she wasn't sure. His face showed more fear than triumph. He cast side glances at Jeph, desperation encroaching on his arrogant face. But Jeph stood with his arms folded, like a spectator at a traffic accident.

Cain's movements grew less coordinated. He seemed to lose focus on his dance. "God damn you—Blackthorne," he said, the phrases punctuated by gulping inhalations. "We had—a deal."

At that moment, Lazar grasped the crown and threw it onto the floor, where it clanged like a gong, the sound growing louder and longer until it became a vibration that shook everything and set Echo's teeth on edge. A rift appeared, like a rip in the wall of a tent that seemed to run from the sky to the center of the earth, and blue light poured out of an almond-shaped portal.

The cords Cain held broke like a spiderweb on a child's slide and disintegrated into sparks that flew away. Cain howled and covered his eyes, bent over double and panting hard. He collapsed to the ground in a fetal position, his face red and contorted in pain.

The crown returned to Lazar's hand, and the portal disappeared as if it had never been.

Jeph pulled something out of an inner coat pocket. "You said you were the expert." His tone was between disappointment and *I told you so*. "I'll finish it."

Cain pushed himself to his feet. "I said *we* had this, you son of a bitch."

A movement out the window into physical reality caught Echo's attention. Jeph walked toward Lazar with cold fire in his eye and something shiny black in his hand. His movements were quick and determined, but time slowed to a crawl. His hand came forward, and then a blade exploded from it, thrusting toward Lazar—not the inner Lazar, whom Cain had failed to destroy, but the soft and fragile body standing on the dock.

Still using Lazar's window—thus, clumsily—Echo maneuvered her body between Jeph and his prey, but Lazar put his hands on her shoulders and pushed her sideways into the salty brown water.

The shock ejected her from Lazar's esuoh and into her own view of the world. She struggled to figure out which way was up. She reminded herself that she really was in water, so she didn't breathe in. Her feet struck the muddy bottom, and she stood up chest deep, seeing two massive sharks gathering around a pool of blood.

They weren't her sharks. They were the tiger's replacement.

She leaped into Lazar's esuoh just in time to see the portal open again, and Lazar's silhouette walk through the doorway. A blaze like blue lightning burned her vision. Then she was outside again, and there was no inside to go to. Lazar was dead.

She went into her esuoh, waiting for Jeph and Cain to come after her. When nothing happened, she went back out into twilight darkness. She was in black water, and on the dock lay a dead man, giving off a faint and fading light. A hyena and a bird that looked like an old man in silhouette spoke in Cain and Jeph's voices.

"What the hell?" Cain yipped like he was in pain as well as out of breath.

"You were letting him get away." The bird pecked at the body. "Look at you. You're a mess."

The hyena growled. "I showed you everything. I told you we needed to work together." His tone shaded into a rising yip. "We had an agreement." It howled again and pushed in to rip at the flesh.

The bird gave a hoarse squawk. "That sounds like a 'you' problem."

The hyena spoke with a furious growl. "I get the girl, then."

The bird lifted its head and flapped its massive wings, and in the movement, she recognized his silhouette. He was indeed the condor that had tried to take Chandler's soul. The smothering inevitability of this moment fell on her like a lead blanket. "Try it," the bird said. "I've got her key."

The hyena bared its teeth toward the condor, its eyes glowing red with rage.

The bird flapped and lifted itself into the air above the hyena's reach. "We don't have time for this. Someone's coming." It flew away up the embankment.

A bear came loping along the beach, its clawed feet kicking up little clouds of sand at each step. When it reached the wooden dock, it shouted, "Hey! What are you doing?"

The hyena followed the condor up the path Echo had come by.

A bird with an electronic call chirped twice from the level area above; doors slammed, an engine roared.

"Lazar!" The bear kneeled beside the body. "My God!" He pulled a small wooden plank out of its fir and spoke to it. "You've got to come. They've killed my son. On the dock at Depoe Bay."

Echo hesitated, then walked through the water toward him. "I saw it."

The man looked at her, surprised. Then, "You're like my son was."

"Jeph Blackthorne did it. The same one who put Lazar in prison the first time."

He gave a cry of rage and grief. "It's not enough to take twenty years? He has to take the rest of his life!"

"Do you want me to stay and tell the police? Lazar told me to go to God's Thumb."

"Police." He spat into the sand. "They'll come when they come, and they won't believe you. Do what Lazar told you to do."

She swam across the calm and sheltered waters of the circular bay, then climbed through a rocky forest toward what she knew only by sound was the highway.

## CHAPTER 11

# Echo Walks to the End of the Road

The stone steps up the cliff took Echo away from the teacup of a harbor where animals of various species congregated with hoots and yips and howls. The tiny white lighthouse that had been Lazar's esuoh was gone. Heavy clouds gathered, and wind-driven rain fell like arrows from the sky.

Near the top, a German shepherd dog came trotting down the steps, a brother in arms to the ones she had evaded in Salem. Echo entered her esuoh and watched out her windows. She slowed her walk and concentrated on being invisible. The dog, now a mannequin that might be used as a display for dog clothing, gave her a passing glance and kept walking. Several others followed—two more large dog-mannequins, growling as they walked, a penguin-mannequin, and a man-shaped mannequin passed her in the same direction she was going—but she stayed in her esuoh, and they walked by as if she were, indeed, imperceptible.

When she reached the top of the cliff, salt rain streamed down her face, and the raindrops stung like ice crystals. Putting the ocean on her left, she took a forest path where the wind's blast pushed her backward, lashing her with rain. The limbs of trees danced in rage.

Inside her esuoh, where she stood in front of her window guiding her course, the colors of the shabby, gaudy wagon had faded into dreariness. Her radio was playing again, something classical, slow, and minor key, appropriate to the occasion.

The path turned toward the ocean and then paralleled the beach, threading among the misshapen pines at the top of a bluff that gradually descended to sea level. The rain stopped, but the sky and water were the same shade of gray, meeting seamlessly at the horizon. The path eventually delivered Echo onto the beach among mannequins teasing the waves, throwing and catching, or flopping playfully in the sand. She turned up the mournful music in her esuoh because their joy offended her. Lazar had told her to walk to God's Thumb, but even if he hadn't given her a destination, she would walk here in the open air, anonymous, with only grief for company.

Echo walked between the water and the dry sand. The beachside carnival appeared up ahead, its lights faint but visible against the gray sky. She stopped to look out the windows of her esuoh to orient herself. Where was God's Thumb? Was it a physical place, like Ashland, or a dream place, like the carnival?

She flipped through her sketchbooks, looking for a memory of a map. She found one of the Oregon Coast, a rectangle unevenly divided between blue on the left and green on the right, with various dots and print she couldn't read. Tossing it aside, she discovered another map half buried in the books spread on the table, this one with "Eternal Ocean" marked in pirate script, where shifting clouds allowed quick glimpses of "Carnival" and "The City." At the top of this map was a green "like" emoji marked "God's Thumb."

Stripped to essentials, that's all there was: The City, the Carnival, the Ocean, with Echo creeping along the border, alone through her own choices.

She walked again. Gray sky, gray ocean, gray sand, gray colors in her esuoh. The music took a darker and more aggressive tone. Guilty, guilty, guilty. She embraced it, immersed herself in it, as her feet took her over the cold wet sand toward the offensive carnival.

She stopped at the edge of the jetty and sat on one of the boulders. She went out onto her porch and watched the eagles for a while. The mournful music still played at the edge of her hearing, but the eagles soared and swooped, their flight paths diverging and intersecting like dancers. After a while, she left her esuoh and climbed the jetty to walk through the carnival.

The lights that had seemed so bright and cheerful on her first visit to the Carnival, back before she began this journey, were now lurid against the gray sky. The music of the rides took on the minor key of the music playing inside her, making it feel macabre and dangerous. The juggling clown was menacing instead of funny. The food booths smelled rotten, and their signs held secret symbols indicating poison. The unfeigned screams of the What You Did ride and the falling ride filled her with horror at what had passed and terror of what was to come. She thought of turning off the music, but it was appropriate, and she refused to retreat from reality.

The people at the carnival—mannequins now—waited in line for food or rides or walked hand in hand through sawdust pathways, taking photos of their faces through holes in boards painted with comical fat people in old-fashioned swimsuits. They all seemed shifty, dangerous, unknown and unknowing. She maintained her distance from them even as the crowd grew thicker.

But they weren't all mannequins. Death came out of the last turn of the What You Did ride with his hands in the air and laughing like a child. Echo kept walking. She was surprised only moments later to hear his familiar but out-of-breath voice behind her. "Here you are again."

She turned to him.

He still wore the black vest from his three-piece suit and the red tie with black skulls. He carried the tall black scythe she had seen in the umbrella stand in his esuoh. But he had left his jacket and shoes somewhere and walked barefoot with his pant legs rolled up past his calves. He ran his free hand through his hair to push it back off his face. "Great day, isn't it?"

Echo sighed. "Not the way I would describe it."

"You were kind to me. Is there anything I can do?"

His eyes were open—black pupils, black irises. She feared him more than she did before, possibly because she knew him better. "Can you bring back the dead?"

He stepped into stride with her, and they walked side by side. "I wouldn't if I could. I always go forward. I don't take away what you lost or give it back. I only help you incorporate the loss into who you are now."

She thought about that for a while. "The pain of the loss makes it hard to do that."

"The pain makes it possible. And after death comes a new version of life."

She stared at the sand, her feet making marks in its smooth surface that would sooner or later be wiped away. "I wish." There was no answer, and when she turned to him, he was gone.

The carnival seemed interminable, and yet it did end, gradually yielding to hotels, condos, and vacation cottages of all shapes, sizes, and colors.

"How did you like your prize?" The voice at her shoulder was exactly where Death had been, but it belonged to a woman.

Startled, Echo turned and found Estelle, whom she had also met at Jeph's scavenger hunt, walking beside her. She still wore the linen dress with threads of silver, and her face held an expression of friendly curiosity.

"The prize," Estelle said. She seemed to think Echo wasn't tracking her question. "Is it what you thought it would be?"

What could Echo say? This woman had connections to Jeph. Would she tell him?

"Hey, I just paid him to let me into this world," she answered before Echo could speak. "I bought a mirror for myself from his friend Cain."

"Partner." Echo spat out the word.

"They told me they were associates. Oh, well, you hardly ever know what someone means by a term. Are you still on a mission?"

"I need to go. I promised to meet someone."

"Jeph?"

"God, I hope not." The words escaped before Echo could stop them.

"So that's how it is."

"What would you have won?"

Estelle smiled. "A place in Jeph's organization. I still might."

Fear thundered in Echo's ears. Was she a plant? A spy? Were they all going to report her to Jeph? "What was the consolation prize?"

Estelle's smile took on a knowing quality that chilled Echo to her bones. Was it the music? Or had Estelle been a sinister presence all along?

Echo had to ask. "Do you know someone named Galynn?"

"Black-haired girl, smart like a raven?"

"That's the one."

"Jeph told me about her. He said you sent him your replacement when you quit. She brought the key. He said you would know what he meant. He was grateful."

Echo's fingers twitched. "I need to be going now."

Estelle smiled. "Yes, I think you do. God's Thumb is straight ahead at the end of the beach. You can't miss it."

"Is Jeph going to be there?"

"He said he'd see you in Portland." Estelle veered away from the ocean with only a brief glance back Echo. A chill climbed Echo's back as she watched the other woman go.

It seemed like a four-day walk, but the Carnival ended, and then the City, leaving only a few mannequins flying kites on the beach or throwing tennis balls to mannequin dogs in the surf. Echo found a driftwood log and sat facing the ocean. She went through her esuoh, through her basement, then walked up the vast expanse of dry sand leading to the old woman's house. It was closer than she remembered, and less gloomy than it had been before, although there was a new grave there with flowers in cerulean, bronze, and mauve. She stopped at the freshly turned earth and whispered an apology she knew Lazar would never hear, then went into the house with river stones shoring up its walls.

The old woman seemed to be sleeping in her chair. Echo sat in the other chair, waiting until she woke to ask her questions. The hours stretched long, punctuated by nothing but a damp wind that sighed through the trees. The old woman slept, and Echo sat with her pain rising around her until she feared she would drown. And then the pain receded until she felt she could bear it. The woman woke, wiping away tears.

"You'll see them both at God's Thumb." She closed her eyes again.

Echo went back through her esuoh and turned off the radio. Then she returned to the beach and kept walking.

CHAPTER 12

# Crime in Depoe Bay

Traffic slowed to a crawl as Travis's SUV crept across the Highway 101 bridge over Depoe Bay. Gray, looking down to the harbor parking area, saw a dozen vehicles with flashing lights, crime scene tape, and people in pale-blue coveralls inspecting, measuring, and photographing. "What's going on?"

Travis glanced toward him and back. "You tell me. I need to watch the road."

"Something happened down there. Lots of cop cars, ambulance, people in suits and uniforms standing around talking."

Travis glanced again. "I can't see. The angle is wrong."

At the turnoff to the port, the street was blocked, and a sheriff's deputy stood there answering questions and sending people away.

Travis put on his turn signal and turned left at the next block, then took another right, maneuvering back to their destination. But it was no good. A sheriff's deputy was waiting at the corner, pointing back out to 101.

Travis stopped and rolled down his window. "We've got an appointment down by the docks."

"It's been postponed." The deputy spoke with a practiced deadpan.

"What's going on?" Gray leaned across the car to ask the obvious.

"Crime scene," the deputy said.

"Any idea when the dock will be open?"

"Probably later today," the deputy said, then stepped away from the window and waved them toward 101.

Back on the highway, the traffic picked up speed, and Gray couldn't see anything useful.

At the north end of town was a small building with cars and pickups parked out front, and Travis turned in and parked. A faded sign over the building read "The Busted Scupper."

"This looks like a bar. What are we doing here?"

"We're going to ask the grapevine."

Gray followed him into the poorly lit building. Several tables had four to five men sitting around, each with a pitcher of beer in the center. Their conversation was quiet, and their faces somber. Two men in their twenties played at the pool table, and even the clack and thump of the balls on the table seemed subdued and melancholy. Over the bar was a big sign in a pirate script: "Welcome to Depoe Bay—A sleepy drinking village with a fishing problem."

Travis went to the bar. "A beer and water for me." He turned to Gray. "What do you want?"

"Water."

Travis handed the man a ten-dollar bill. "Keep it." Then, "Do you know what's going on in town?"

The bartender filled the glasses. "A murder. Down on the dock."

"Damn." Travis leaned on the bar. "My brother lives in town. Do you know who it was?"

"New guy in the area." He pointed with his chin toward a big man sitting alone at a booth in the corner with a vodka bottle and a glass in front of him. "His son, Lazar Kyrillovich."

Gray felt his stomach drop to his knees. Travis had already thanked the bartender and gone to sit in the booth next to the grieving man's.

They sat a while, Travis's beer like a centerpiece on the table, untouched, and the two of them sipping their water. Gray wanted to get up and *do* something, but the stillness on Travis's face meant he was waiting for the right moment, planning the right words. If there were any right words.

Finally, Travis turned and spoke to the other man over the back of the booth. "I heard about your son. I'm sorry for your loss."

The man—a larger, older version of the man who had helped Gray put on his armor in his dream, without the scar on his face—looked up and grunted, then poured another glass of vodka.

Travis got up and slid into the booth across from the man. "We're sorry to bother you at this time, but we're looking for a girl who was looking for Lazar."

Lazar's father gave him a long stare, skeptical beyond questions. He drank the glass before him, then poured another and drank it like water. He sighed, and a belch came out with the exhalation. "What you want with her?" He had an accent, like the one in Gray's dream, but thicker.

Gray came out of the booth to join the conversation. He pulled up a chair and sat at the end of the table. "She's my friend. Her eyes are closed, like your son's. She was trying to save him." He didn't know that, but he *knew* it.

The man's hand closed into a fist on the table.

"Lazar came to me in a dream last night." Gray couldn't believe he was telling this stranger, but the words poured out. For most of his life he had been afraid to open up this way, but if it would help him find Echo . . . . "I've never met him, but he had a scar below his right eye. He was kind to me, and he told me to go to God's Thumb."

Travis was staring at him, open-mouthed.

The man looked at Gray, lips trembling, a brightness in his eyes that *was not*, refused to be, tears. "She saw—" He caught his voice wavering. Stopped and steadied it. "She saw Jeph kill my son. *Merzavetz.* I saw nothing. The girl saw everything."

Gray exhaled. He hadn't realized he had been holding his breath. "Did they catch her? Will she have to testify?"

"Testify." He said it like a curse and slammed his glass on the table. "The police took twenty years of my son's life and never believed him. I sent her away."

"Where?" Travis asked.

He shrugged and nodded to Gray. "She said Lazar told her to go to God's Thumb."

"Was anybody with her? Anybody driving?"

"No. She fell in the water. She swam away. Nobody waiting with a car."

Gray and Travis looked at each other. "How long ago was that?"

The man looked at the bottle as if it were a timepiece. "Couple of hours."

"Where's God's Thumb?"

He pointed vaguely north. "Past Lincoln City."

Travis patted his shoulder. "Thanks."

Lazar's father watched them in fury and sadness as they left.

# Chapter 13
# The End of the Road

Travis drove north from Depoe Bay. Gray, who had gotten acquainted with the map app on his phone during the long, winding drive from Ashland to Depoe Bay, now watched it obsessively. The cliffs fell away along the coast and then the beach emerged about the time they arrived at the edge of Lincoln City.

Gray held onto his dream of traveling north with Travis as a drowning sailor holds onto a piece of ship wreckage. In the dream, Travis had driven along the beach until it was almost too late. The highway veered away from the beach at the Siletz River, and Gray thought they had missed the place where he had seen Lazar, but the highway veered back, and the beach continued. He couldn't see the beach from the highway; it was blocked out by shops and houses, but every so often he caught a glimpse of the distant horizon, slate-blue water sparkling under a clear sky.

When 101 turned inland to go north, Gray felt the panic he had felt in his dream. They had gone too far. He told Travis to turn, and they followed a street north, paralleling the coast.

A sign said they had arrived at Road's End State Recreation Site—basically a parking lot and restroom on the edge of the beach. Gray said, "Park here. I'm going to look for her."

Travis parked the car in a spot overlooking the beach. "Do you want me to come along?"

Gray hardly thought about it. "Not this time."

"Fine by me." He pulled a copy of *Moby Dick* from the side pocket in his door and leaned back in his seat to wait for a while.

Gray took the blacktopped path to the beach and walked in the sand toward pointed rocks that stood like the teeth of a long-dead dragon. He looked for signs that this was the place in his dream, but what came back to him was the smile of the man who helped him and the humiliation and hope of getting his armor on correctly.

He tried to hold onto his memories of the eternal ocean, but he was very conscious that this was not it. This was the ocean of time and change, tides and storms, transportation and commerce. He walked north along the coast, looking for Echo, but he didn't see her. He realized with pain that he might not know her in this world, even if he saw her. But he told his pounding heart that he would know her in any disguise.

A sign close to the edge of the sand said, "GOD'S THUMB TRAIL." He weighed his options. It was hours until sunset, when the man said Gray was to meet her at Road's End. He couldn't just wait, so he followed the trail through woods and meadow up to a peak of land with views over the coast, north and south. It was inspiring, but there was no Echo.

Gray had gone a couple of hours from the beach and hadn't found her, and the shadows were lengthening, so he hurried back.

At Road's End, Travis's car still sat in the parking lot, with Travis barely visible in the driver's seat, possibly reading, possibly sleeping. Beach-goers walked, ran, shot photos, played Frisbee, tossed tennis balls into the surf for joyful Labrador retrievers. The sun bathed the coast in glorious splendor, but there was no Echo.

The sun sank into the ocean in an explosion of fire, and darkness followed it, eating the light. And still there was no Echo.

Gray sat on the sand, put his head on his knees, and despaired.

## CHAPTER 14

# Rendezvous at God's Thumb

The path took Echo up away from the beach, through mountains reaching the sky, to a statue of a giant so tall that its face was lost in the clouds.

She trod a narrow path up the statue, sometimes having to leap chasms, sometimes climbing the rock face of a fold of clothing. There were people here, translucent like ghosts in brightly colored clothing, wearing backpacks and floppy sunhats, but she ignored them.

She came to the giant's arm—a narrow footpath over a ridge that curved down into emptiness on both sides. She didn't look back at the face, intuiting a danger in seeing the face of God, but kept walking forward, looking for Lazar. If he wasn't—she didn't know what she would do, except eventually climb down again.

But then the thumb emerged from the clouds, pointing to the sky, and Echo hoped that was a good sign. A light hovered above the thumb, like a blue sun breaking through dark clouds, and silhouetted in the light was a man whose face she couldn't see, but she knew he was Lazar.

As she came closer, he walked out to her. "May I come into your house?"

"Of course."

He stepped in as if through a wall and stood for a moment looking out her window. "That was quite a journey. Would you like to see it from my perspective?"

"Yes." She felt strange. "Is it OK?"

He smiled. "For a short time, it is permitted."

She went into his house. "But you're—"

"Dead. Yes. But the bus driver is waiting for me, because you and I have some things to discuss."

They were standing in his lighthouse, with its windows still showing what he saw: the eternal ocean and what the physical world looked like to more or less everybody. Echo gravitated to the physical reality; she found that she missed it sometimes. God's Thumb was not a mystical statue, but a rock formation with magnificent views of the coast. Hikers dressed like the ghosts she had seen stepped by them, muttering something polite but not really making contact. Something about that nagged at her, but she didn't have the attention to spare.

Lazar pointed to the Eternal Ocean. "Let's go sit on the beach."

She followed him out the door of his esuoh onto the endless beach. It was warm in his presence, and the sun was setting in a sky streaked with crimson, coral, and red-orange. In the midst of the glowing sky, the portal glowed blue-white, shaped like the pupil of a cat's eye. Lazar sat cross-legged on the beach, and Echo sat beside him.

"I want you to know I'm sorry," she said. "It's all my fault. Gray tried to tell me, but I didn't listen. Your mother tried to tell me, but I wanted to change history. I wrecked everything and got you killed, and now your poor father—"

He pulled a tangle of string from his sleeve and handed it to her.

She turned it over and over in her hands. It was a mass of everything, from heavy jute to the finest fishing line. There were colored threads and threads wound into ropes. "What—?"

"Untangle it."

It was a perfect image of the hash she had made of everything. She looked at it in despair and felt tears welling up in her eyes.

He pointed at it. "Find one loose end and work it free." He spoke as if teaching a great work to a young child.

The waves lapped the beach and slipped away, and their rhythm calmed her mind. She found a loose end and began working it. As she touched different strands, she felt as if she were touching something alive, something trying to talk to her.

He waited, watching her calmly. "Do you understand what happened?"

Tears begin to flow again. "I helped him murder you."

"Look again. How many strings do you see?"

"Are you kidding? It looks like what collected in my hairbrush when I had long hair."

"Look closer. Sizes, shapes, colors. How many?"

There were red, green, blue, fuchsia, clear. Cotton and jute and nylon. Thick strands and thin ones. "OK. A lot, but I don't know how many."

"What about the one you're pulling?"

"It's thin and red and not the longest."

He looked over at the mess. "When you finish pulling that one out, will it be untangled?"

"No."

"Keep working."

As she touched the strands, she began to get flashes of images. A man in a room full of goods for sale doing a friendly two-finger salute on his way out the door. A high school gym decorated for prom with people dancing in old-fashioned clothes. An old man pushing a shopping cart across the street against a don't-walk light. A car wrapped around a tree, steam rising from what was left of its radiator. People captured in cages like dog kennels, not knowing they were in prison.

She gasped and dropped the mess, and the wind caught it and blew it across the sand. She looked up at Lazar, and he nodded toward it.

She ran to pick it up.

"What is this?" she asked, coming back.

"It's a tiny piece of the map of everything." He held out his hand, and she placed the mess in it. He stroked it, covered it with his palm, lifted it to the sky, and opened his hands slowly, like a magician. "This." He held it up by a corner, and it was a bit of cloth, the size of a handkerchief.

Echo took it from him and looked it over carefully. The colors of the threads she had been untangling ran through it in intriguing patterns, but there was no picture. She turned it over. The patterns were different on this side, suggesting something recognizable, but she couldn't make sense out of it. "I don't see anything."

He laughed at that. "It's one of a billion-piece jigsaw puzzle."

She held it flat between her hands, and the images came rushing in. The ones she saw before and more, too many to count. "Do you know what the whole thing looks like?"

He nodded toward the portal, shimmering faintly in the sunset. "I will, I hope."

"I want to come with you."

"That's why I'm here. To tell you it's not your time. You have important work. Do you see that thin red thread?"

"Yes."

"If it's not there, the picture will change."

"You said yourself, it's just one of a billion-piece puzzle."

"I didn't say 'just one.'" He reached across. "Touch there." He pointed to a dark place. "With the cloth between your thumb and forefinger."

She did. She saw the cages again. Metal bars, mesh floors, stacked three, four, more high. Hundreds of people, sitting, standing, some working, some sleeping, caught in recurring motions in one small space, as if they didn't know they were caged.

In one cage a black-haired girl drove a yellow Mustang convertible down a four-lane highway whose backgrounds repeated like in Hanna-Barbera cartoons. She looked familiar. Echo gasped. "Galynn."

The cloth evaporated to fog in her hands.

"I have to go." Lazar stood. "There's more to you than you think there is."

"But what can I do?"

"The next true thing." He walked toward the portal but turned back, smiling. "Accept help where you find it." He walked into the light like stepping across a threshold into bright sunshine. The portal closed, and she was sitting alone on the sand.

GRAY SAT ALONE ON THE COLD SAND as the voices of the beach-goers died away. Fir-scented smoke trickled by from a nearby driftwood fire. Darkness fell like a blanket, and the tide came and went with its constant susurration. He feared that aloneness was not only his present but his future as well.

After a time that felt as long as a walk along the Eternal Ocean, he heard the soft squeak of footsteps in the sand. Assuming it was a passing beach-walker, he didn't look up.

Then he felt a warmth beside his shoulder and a tingle of electricity. He looked over in fear and wonder and found a slim girl with hair cut short, her face bearing scars like a broken mirror. She looked at him with a crooked, shy smile and closed eyes.

"Echo!" How could he think he wouldn't know her?

She stared at him, eyes wide behind closed eyelids. "You're in the—I was going to say 'real'—I guess I mean physical—"

"I came looking for you. Crossed into Oge right after you left, then lost my rorrim in a bus accident. I hired the detective who worked on my mother's murder to help me look for you. He's waiting in the parking lot to take us home." He wanted to hold her, to make sure she was real. But his attraction to her was so strong that when she touched his hand in the Ugly Mug, only a few days ago, it was like grasping a live electric wire. "Are you OK?"

She was silent for a second. "Yes. But I'm not finished yet."

Gray held his breath. He had found her, hadn't he? "Not finished?" He had reached the end of his journey. He had found Echo. Wasn't that finished enough?

"They killed Lazar," she almost shouted; now her voice dropped to a whisper, losing none of the intensity. "They're stealing souls."

There it was again, leaping like a flame in a childhood memory, the fire-lit story, the expressions of the listeners ranging from the adults' comfortable boredom to the children's shock and horror. The grandmother who told the story had crinkles at the corners of her eyes, as if she didn't quite believe it herself, but she spoke with the authority of one who had seen it happen. Douglas, the man who adopted him, at the time the leader of the Srelevart, didn't believe in soul theft, and neither did his son Quig, who had taken his role in the pilgrimage. The stealing of souls was a quaint idea, backward and unsophisticated, unless reinterpreted in light of the last hundred years of Srelevart research into the intersection between Ytilaer and depth psychology. *Stealing souls isn't real*, he told himself, more wish than assurance. "We'll talk about it later," is what he said to Echo.

"But—" she said.

"It's late," he said. "There's nothing more to do tonight."

She was silent a few seconds, seeming to take that in, then she nodded, got up, and came around and kneeled in front of him. "Are you looking at me?"

He laughed at the wonder of it. "Yes."

"I mean, can you see me?"

He sat cross-legged and leaned forward to look directly into her closed eyes. He was so full of love and gratitude he could hardly contain it.

"You're not horrified?"

"At chasing you to the end of the world?" He thought about it. "No, not even that."

"I mean about my face."

He stared at her face, yearning to see her eyes again. Her scars like the cracks in the primal rorrim. Even in Oge, she seemed to radiate light. "I love your face."

She stared at him for another second, then turned and sat beside him again, her shoulder and upper arm close to his, but not touching. He felt her warmth and the inner delight of knowing she was real and *here*. She sat quietly beside him for a time, then leaned away to face him, her face silhouetted against the starry night. "I guess it's time to get back to Portland. Aunt Doris will be frantic."

"Travis is waiting to drive us." He stood and held out his hand to her.

She took his hand, then fell back on the sand as if she'd had an electric shock. "I had that coming. Now I know what it felt like." She got up and followed him to Travis's car.

CHAPTER 15

# Sanctuary

IN THE DARK EARLY HOURS OF THE MORNING, Travis pulled up to the front walk of Quig's house. "Need help?"

"I've got it." Gray slid out of the car and turned to wake Echo. "Thanks," he said to Travis. "When you get it figured out, tell me how much more I owe you."

With a combination of nudges and whispers, Gray roused Echo enough to walk to the Sanctuary in the basement of Quig's house. He heard the SUV's engine as he opened the creaking gate into the backyard. He led Echo through the outer door and stopped at the silver-framed rorrim that hung outside the inner door, where Gray entered Ytilaer for the first time in what seemed like weeks.

From the first day Douglas had brought him—an eight-year-old boy stubbornly refusing to leave Ytilaer—here to meet the Srelevart, Gray had seen this place as an expanse of white walls with sparkling windows bringing abundant light to a room of quiet and order. Honey-brown wooden benches, arranged in groups, each group with its own gate, provided a sense of safety. The homecoming feeling comforted him now, with the brilliant light shining despite the physical darkness outside.

Above the podium at the front of the room, a giant, wide-hilted broadsword hung point-down on the wall. During meetings of the Srelevart, the leader of the pilgrimage—formerly Douglas, now Quig—would address the members from a white wooden lectern.

Echo walked through the chapel. "Thank you for coming to get me. I don't know how I would have gotten home without you." Then her eyes opened wider. "Home! I need to call Aunt Doris."

"I texted her while we were driving. I didn't want to wake her up if she was sleeping. She texted back right away. I told her you were safe and would see her tomorrow—today, actually."

She turned to take in the room. "What is this place?"

"We call it the Sanctuary. It's in the basement of Quig's house. House, not esuoh. There are a few people around Portland who travel in Ytilaer, and we meet and tour together. We call ourselves the Srelevart."

"You and your backwards words. Tomorrow I'll have to write that out and see what it means in everybody-else language."

"You'll meet them this morning. I also called Quig while we were driving, and he decided to call an emergency meeting. Not everyone will be here, but they want to hear your story."

"Oh, good," she said. "Maybe they'll be able to help us stop Jeph and Cain."

"Stop them? We're not dragon slayers. We've got people who can help with defensive measures like improving our locks or identifying trouble early in an encounter. We leave Ytilaer to take care of Jeph and Cain."

"Defensive?" Echo's tone was at once challenging and disappointed.

Her tone demolished his comfort; all he had done, all he had risked, wasn't enough for her. The sky outside turned dark, and rain dripped down the windows. A blues dirge played somewhere, as if in a different room.

Echo shook her head. "No." Then quieter, as if to herself. "No." She opened a door into her esuoh and went in, leaving the door open behind her.

"May I come in?" Gray asked.

She waved him in, only glancing back to say, "That's why I left the door open."

It wasn't exactly a textbook invitation, but he walked in anyway. Passing her windows, he glanced out at the Sanctuary as she saw it—a strip-mall storefront meeting hall with cracked display cases along the wall, broken linoleum flooring, drop ceilings with fluorescent lights in ugly yellowish green, about a third of them flashing at random intervals. At the front was a wooden dais made of shipping pallets. A simple steel lectern stood on it with a battered guitar and an old-fashioned microphone beside it. And outside the storefront's big plate-glass window a storm was raging: heavy winds, torrential rain, and a greenish sky that presaged tornadoes.

The music coming from somewhere in Echo's esuoh was an old woman with a creaky voice, playing and beating time on a twangy guitar. If the song were a recipe, it would be three fourths sorrow, one fourth anger, and seasoned with a heavy dollop of fear.

Echo reached across knickknacks on a shelf and turned the radio off. Silence fell.

She opened a door next to her windows and stepped outside. A look back at Gray around the door frame was her only signal to follow. She led him out to two Adirondack chairs side by side on a narrow porch overlooking a vast chasm and sat in the farther one. Gray took the one beside her.

They sat in silence for a long time. Just as he was thinking it was time to leave, she said without looking at him, "There are usually eagles here."

That was out of the blue, and he didn't know how to respond. "Oh?"

She pointed to a rocky bluff that might have been miles away. "They seem to have a nest over there."

"Eagles," he said noncommittally. He had been away from Ytilaer for only a few days, but he felt he had lost his sense of meaning. It wasn't that he didn't understand the *concept* of eagles—freedom, power, fierceness—but concepts are inadequate bridges between Oge and Ytilaer, and he couldn't fit the concepts in with what he knew about Echo.

"I see them flying together over the abyss sometimes." She spoke longingly, continuing to stare out over the canyon. Then, "But they're not there now," very matter-of-factly, and she didn't say anything else.

The silence filled him like a continuous noise that rattles the bones, and then the *presence* of it died away, and he heard only the sounds of Echo's slow breathing.

He waited a while longer, and then he rose quietly to go into his own esuoh for the first time since his journey began.

WHEN QUIG'S WIFE, JULIA, CALLED THEM up to breakfast, Gray went to fetch Echo. He knocked at the door of her esuoh, calling, "May I come into your house?"

"Just come in." She spoke with some annoyance. "Can I give you an open invitation, or do we always have to knock?"

A few steps down the center aisle of her esuoh brought him close enough to see that she was at her table, partly obscured by velvet curtains, sorting and shelving her sketchbooks.

"The Srelevart will be here soon."

She looked up at him. "Can we persuade them to help? Or are they just going to teach us to run away?"

Gray shrugged, a little embarrassed. "They're not some warrior caste or anything. Just people who explore Ytilaer together, without going into its dark underside."

"But Lazar told me to ask for help. Who else is there?" Her eyes were brown with flecks of emerald, and her gaze pierced him like knives of ice.

"Echo—" He took in breath for a sigh, but let it out slowly and quietly. "Ytilaer has her own way of handling things like this."

"You keep saying that, but I don't know what you mean. Is Ytilaer like God or something?"

"No," he said—too fast. "Not that." He tried to think how to say what he meant. "More like a pattern."

"Lazar mentioned a tapestry. But too large to take in."

"More like a dance. Or if it's a tapestry, it's an ever-repeating pattern from macrocosm to microcosm, like a Mandelbrot set."

She shook her head. "Tell me this, then. How do dancing fractals stop a monster?"

She was watching him, expecting a reply. There was none of the mischievous banter he was accustomed to seeing in her expression, only an earnest question that he couldn't answer because he was lost among the green stars in her copper-colored eyes.

The eyes turned away from him, looking at the books again, and he felt their loss like the extinction of the sun. "Come on up to breakfast," he said. "We'll work something out."

She turned back to the table and started tossing the sketchbooks into three piles. "You go. I need to prepare."

"Prepare?" This was mildly disturbing. Echo had never been one to prepare for anything.

"I need to show them." She flipped through the books, glancing inside each one and tossing it onto one of the piles on the table. "I have an idea how to explain things quickly. Tell them I'm still sleeping or something."

"But you're not sleeping."

She sighed. "Then whatever it takes to get them to leave me alone for a while."

He shrugged. "I'll tell them you'd like to be alone for a while."

She laughed. "What a concept. Do that, then."

When he came back an hour later, before the others began arriving for the meeting, she was outside her esuoh. In front of her was a dark-wood conference table that hadn't been there before, and on it was a model lighthouse on a windy beach.

Gray felt the ground shift under his feet. She was imposing this experience on him, just as Jeph and Cain had made him small and ridiculous in Jeph's office. *It's not the same*, he told himself, but he was shaken at the power and audacity of it.

Echo walked toward the lighthouse, becoming the right size for it as she strode across the sand. She didn't seem to shrink but just to move quickly into the distance. She stood on the sand outside its door, the wind whipping her tunic around her shapely legs, and gestured for him to follow her. Waves licked the foundation of the lighthouse. At the door, a tiny something on a string swayed from the lintel.

When he caught up with her, she held out the thing by its string for his attention; it was a tiny silver cross. "I got the idea from Jeph's scavenger hunt."

Gray stared at her. "We don't practice illusions" were all the words he could muster. They didn't capture his fear and wonder.

"Even true ones?" She searched his eyes, and he felt more than saw disappointment in hers.

*How long does it take someone in Ytilaer to gain this power? More than a few days.* Theo sometimes talked about what she had learned in her training as egam krad. By her telling, she wasn't much older than Gray and Echo when she left the segam krad and accepted the way of the Srelevart. Even so, Theo said her practice had lasted years, not days. Had Echo been coming and going in Ytilaer all along? But he stopped himself. This was Echo, who never saw a secret, much less kept one. Still.

She stood there, holding the cross by its string. "Just touch the key to go in. It's a copy of Lazar's key and a copy of Lazar's esuoh."

He hesitated. "You made a *key?*"

"It's easy. Just make a thing and load it up with meaning." When he didn't answer right away, she gave him another once-over that told him he wasn't measuring up to expectations. But she didn't *make* him small, as Jeph did, even though he felt that way. "It's the only way I can think of to make them understand," she said.

"We don't—" He stopped. There were too many ways to end that sentence. *We don't make keys. We don't manipulate perceptions. We don't take on other people's Ytilaer problems.* The last one stung. Certainly Douglas, his foster father, had helped Gray with his Ytilaer problem. But Douglas was dead, and the Srelevart explored from the safety of the Sanctuary but didn't rescue. "Changing others' perception is how Jeph and Cain manipulate people" was Gray's lame attempt at explanation.

She took a step back and looked at him with her eyes wide and her mouth tightly closed. After a beat, she nodded. "OK. But *I'm* not lying, and I'm not trying to manipulate anybody." She touched the key and the door opened. "Come and see before you decide. I want to show you what I found in Lazar's esuoh. He wouldn't mind, and besides, it's all from *my* memories, so it really doesn't belong to him anyway."

For Gray, her display brought nagging questions, literally laying them out on the table. Deception, manipulation, control. Whether it might be necessary to walk dangerous paths for the greater good. Might there be a right or responsibility to shape others' view of reality? What is the cost of inching toward evil in this way?

On top of that, the size and scope of this illusion was on a par with the illusions Cain had forced on him—maybe beyond it. Gray had never tried anything like it, but he was sure that if he did, the results would be like making a sand castle from dry sand.

But she was looking at him like a child sharing her first batch of cookies, holding out the key to him. He touched it and felt its subtle electric buzz. The door disappeared, leaving an opening into a small lighthouse with a table and a woodstove and windows looking out in all directions. "How did you do this?"

"The same way you make a chair."

Gray stepped inside and was immediately drawn to the windows, looking out to both the harbor at Depoe Bay and the Eternal Ocean. "Both worlds?"

She stood beside him. "This is what Lazar could see out his windows—and he could cross over with a blink." She paused as if waiting for that to sink in. Gray stood looking out the windows, a rift forming in his reality. When he didn't answer, Echo said, "Let's go upstairs."

She led the way up the spiral staircase, chattering as she went. "His esuoh is different from most people's. His long-term memories are stored downstairs, for one thing."

In the upper room with a three-sixty view, two men stood in frozen conversation near a small table, stiff as historical figures in a museum diorama. The windows showed featureless ocean as far as Gray could see, but a slight movement of his head brought into view the touristy harbor, with its sailboats and cabin cruisers gently rocking at the dock. Viewing the two worlds made him dizzy, so he turned his attention back to the men. One was middle-aged and the other old but hardy, both with identical horizontal scars on their cheeks below their right eyes. They were like twins born decades apart.

"Wait. I know him."

"You do?" She eyed him with curiosity.

"He came to me in a dream," Gray said, and the man's connection with that dream made Gray more comfortable with what he was seeing. If she had learned from the man who prepared his armor instead of from Jeph . . . . "But keep going. I want to know the rest of it."

She pointed to the ancient man next to Lazar. "This is his soul." She turned to Gray. "He eliminated the distance between his esuoh and his inner chamber. Is that unusual? All the souls I visited were far away."

*All the souls I visited . . . .* Gray shivered as if a spider climbed down his back. He wished he could ask his mother that question—or the old woman with the gold tooth, the wisp of memory from the time in his childhood when memories and dreams felt the same.

"I can't make them move," Echo said. "I hope that doesn't destroy the illusion too much."

"If anything it's too real," Gray said. "The Srelevart—"

"There's more." She created a door in the middle of the room, then walked through it into the downstairs, to a small doorway on the ground floor that opened at her touch. "Lazar said he kept his memories in here, but he didn't use them much. I never went there in his esuoh, but I've put relevant parts of his past here—what I know of it—so that the Srelevart can see what Jeph did to him."

The rooms were arranged in sequence along a hallway. The first one was a prom. In the still life, a figure that looked like young Jeph poured something into the drink of a figure that looked like young Lazar, while Lazar and a figure that looked like young Cali Zielinski stared into each other's eyes and didn't notice.

"They look fake because I didn't actually see these things myself. Do you think it will be OK?"

Gray had a growing sense that it would not be OK. Yes, what she did was "wrong"—but he no longer understood why. He was awed at the power and effort she had taken to tell her story. Surely there would be no harm if it enabled her to capture the attention of Quig and the others long enough to get them to stop and listen before judging.

In the next scene, like a prison yard from a movie, a figure that looked like Cain talked to a figure that looked like Lazar in his early twenties.

"They met in prison?" Gray asked.

"They weren't there together very long, just long enough for Cain to get hungry for Lazar's soul."

"Do you have proof that Cain is a soul-eater?"

"I saw them try to take Lazar's—and another guy's also. The other guy—Chandler—died before Jeph—" A shiver ran through her. "I'm pretty sure it was Jeph, and I'm pretty sure he died before Jeph could take his soul." She looked down at the table. "I hope so," she said so softly he could hardly hear her.

She looked at her display again. "I wasn't sure what was happening at the time. Looking back, it's obvious that's what he was doing. But come and see. Tell me what you think."

She took Gray to the next room, this one containing three overlapping scenes that almost seemed to move, like a flipbook cartoon. In one, Cain moved in with a net of light to capture Lazar and his soul. In a second one, Lazar stood alone, the ego and soul combined into one—taller, stronger, more present than before—and threw a crown onto the ground. In the third one, a portal like the pupil of a cat's eye opened, and blinding blue light spilled out. Cain, alone now, kneeled, hiding his face. The scenes in this display were much more real than in the other two.

"This is your memory?" Gray asked.

"Don't answer." The voice came from behind Gray, and Quig walked into the room, followed by Edward Paladin and Theo Greenwood, the Srelevart leadership committee.

"Did you see the rest of it? Did you get the story?" Echo asked.

"I don't know if Gray told you what we do here," Quig said.

"You should know he didn't. It was against your rules to tell me anything."

Quig spoke over her words, not waiting for her response. "We do not manipulate other people into believing our private imaginings are external truth."

"I got the impression that you opposed evil." Echo waved a hand, and her display collapsed into a pile of sketchbooks. "Sorry if I was mistaken." She slid them all together and took them into her esuoh.

CHAPTER 16

# The Srelevart
# behind the Bulwark

ECHO PUT EACH SKETCHBOOK INTO ITS SLOT on the shelf very slowly, willing her anger and humiliation to melt away—at least to a controllable level—before she went out to meet the group. It was tempting to just leave them all, find a park bench somewhere, and go looking for Galynn alone, but that was beyond her ability, and Lazar had told her to get help. She sighed and left her esuoh.

All evidence of the table and display she had created was gone, leaving the abandoned strip-mall store she had seen when she first arrived. Seven people sat in battered folding chairs arranged in a ragged circle with Quig facing them from the chair furthest from the front door. A timeworn lectern stood beside him with a battered acoustic guitar leaning against it, head and neck upright. Gray's chair was opposite Quig's, and an empty chair awaited Echo beside him.

She knew some of the others in the circle. The dragon woman Echo had met at the train station nodded severely at her. And Edward, who had been at Jeph's game, gave her a subtle wink inconsistent with his ornate robes and beehive hat. And of course Quig, Gray's perpetually preoccupied guardian. Echo had never seen him wield his authority with any show of power, but here he stood in kingly robes with a sword in one hand and a scepter in the other, looking as if he knew how to use both of them.

That left three Srelevart she had never seen before: Two women—one middle-aged with goat horns extruding from her bobbed and frosted hair and one slightly younger, holding two pitchers of water which she poured from one to the other. The third was an aged man holding a lantern attached to a staff.

And then there was Gray, wearing an off-white peasant's shirt belted with leather, over pants that bloused out over knee-high boots.

It had taken a few seconds to scan the room, and during that time, Echo was acutely conscious that they were all watching her as well. With an attitude of defiance, she replaced the metal folding chair with a three-legged wooden stool and sat down with one foot perched on a rung.

Quig stood. "I call to order this pilgrimage of the Srelevart. We welcome Gray's friend Echo into our company."

Echo wasn't sure she believed the "welcome," but it was better than being singled out for condemnation.

"Now the invitation," Quig said. "May I come into your house?"

They all repeated the question, including Echo.

All replied, "I invite you into my house," except Echo, who said, "Please come in." She felt awkward and out of step.

And then she was alone. All she could see was a scuffed wooden floor beneath her feet. Blinding lights shut out her vision of what was beyond. She realized with sickening horror that she was on a stage, and outside those lights were people, *looking* at her—seeing her scars, her torn clothes, her ugliness—and expecting her to *do* something. Explain herself? Entertain them? *Inspire.* Using her hand to shield her eyes, she peered past the lights to the silhouettes in the audience. There seemed to be a multitude, waiting for her performance. *Where is Death when I need him?*

She looked to her left, and Quig was there, standing among curtains, holding his scepter but not his sword and making a "go on" circle gesture with his hand. On the other side, Gray watched with concern and excitement, like a dad at a toddler's ballet recital. He gave Echo a two-thumbs-up. She took a deep breath, stepped toward the bright abyss and stopped on a red circular rug in the middle of the floor. "I began this journey Monday afternoon . . . ."

As she told the story, she felt the pages of her sketchbooks flipping in her esuoh. The audience laughed and cheered for Aunt Doris, and when Echo's story came to Jeph's game, a flash in the corner of her eye made her look up. Behind her, huge screens projected the pages for everyone to see. Her memories had changed without her awareness: insertions, strikeouts, circles and arrows, and marginal notes filling every space of the page like a madman's manifesto. The words flowed out of her in such detail—she had to tell it *all*—what she knew then and what she knew now—sometimes correcting herself, sometimes backing up to catch a detail she had forgotten—so that they could *understand*—that she felt a huff of impatience from the audience, a squeaking of chairs, the rustle of restless feet. A heckler shouted, "This isn't making any sense!"

*Stick to the highlights*, she told herself.

At that moment, a two-walled platform rolled onto the stage, pushed by black-clad stage hands.

The platform held a mockup of Edward's esuoh—the cozy library, with Edward reading in a comfortable chair. It was all fake, of course, from the books painted on the shelves to the green and red spotlights combining to make yellow light coming down on his shoulder.

A wave of applause crested and retreated as Edward stood from his chair like a father-in-law inviting her to dance. Echo hovered at the doorway, glancing into the wings. Both Quig and Gray were gone.

A band was playing from somewhere, with a trumpet screeching the high notes, and Edward stood beside his desk, which now looked like something from a late-night talk show, with a second chair beside it. The back wall had morphed into brick with windows revealing an Impressionistic painting of nighttime Portland from east of the Willamette.

Edward stood, waiting politely as the music repeated, until Echo understood that her role was to sit in the chair and entertain the audience with light banter.

Despite her lack of banter, Echo pushed herself to walk across the stage. *It's my time to shine,* she told herself, but she didn't feel shiny. She felt awkward and ridiculous, and she painfully remembered how Edward had both defended and betrayed her at the trial.

He took her hand and drew her in for an air kiss, but she pulled back, looking at him and wondering who this man was and why he seemed so familiar after so little history.

"Good to see you, Echo," he said, sitting in his chair behind the desk. "The last time I saw you was—"

"At my trial," she finished for him. Applause from the audience, as if it were a movie they remembered.

"Good times, good times," he said, playing with a small wooden box on his desk.

Echo did a double-take: it looked exactly like the wooden box Jeph had kept his rorrim in. "Is that—?"

"Ha ha." He didn't laugh; he actually said, *Ha ha.* He opened the box and showed it to her. It was empty. "I'm trying to quit."

The audience roared with laughter. Edward winked at them as if they were in on the joke. Echo wasn't.

"So, I understand you won the game that night," Edward said. "Quite an accomplishment on your first try. How did you do it?"

She stared at him. "You were there."

He shrugged and laughed. "It's a good story, and these fine people haven't heard it.

The audience erupted into whistles and applause.

*The game.* Echo hadn't had time to think about it for a while. "I'm pretty sure it was rigged," she said.

Edward looked at her with concern on his face but merriment in his eyes. "Why do you think so? What made Jeph choose *you*?"

"I was the mark. Naive and stupid." Scattered laughs from the audience; scattered boos. Echo shrugged. "All the players wanted something with different levels of desperation. I was the only one who wanted it badly enough to march into the unknown believing everything Jeph told me."

Edward looked at her sympathetically, and the audience said, "Awwww," in a way that infuriated her.

"You played the game," she said. The audience gasped. "What did *you* want?"

He tapped a couple of pencils on the desk in a nervous tattoo. He looked into the wings and out at the audience, as if they were about to hear a secret he didn't want to tell. "I was trying to get you to see what you were getting into."

It was disturbing that he was lying to her. "You didn't try very hard."

His eyes narrowed in accusation. "You got your wish." The audience contributed an "oooooh" to the moment.

"But no one told me what it would cost," Echo said.

Hoots and jeers from the audience; a heckler shouted, "Where's my tiny violin?"

Edward gave a sad smile. "No one ever does." Exultant applause, cheers; the band started up with an energetic exit song, and Edward's stage began rolling back into the wings.

Echo stood, surprised by the movement, and as the set rolled offstage, she stepped back and watched it leave her like the last lifeboat leaving a deserted island.

But no. Another stage was rolling in from the other direction, this one containing an oval conference table with three people looking across it at a single empty chair. Each chair had a small screen and a big microphone in front of it. Each of the people—Echo recognized them as the Srelevart she hadn't met yet—wore massive over-ear headphones.

"Echo," the first one said with the friendliness of a gambler for a new mark. She was the one with the blonde bob and goat horns.

The second, pouring her two pitchers of water—now reduced to the size of travel mugs—back and forth, looked up from her task with an expression of sympathy.

The third, the old guy with the lantern, raised an eyebrow at her and then dropped his head as if he were sleeping.

Music was pulsing, the anxiety-ridden cacophony she had heard among the mannequins, and a voice-over boomed: "It's time for the CRM podcast. Exploring worlds from our perch in the basement. We're Caryn, Rachelle, and Mitch—Can't Remember Meaning."

The woman in the middle, Rachelle if the order of their names matched the layout, gave Echo a little wave of invitation to the empty chair.

The voice-over continued: "Today we're talking to Echo, who wants something from us—as they always do. Join us as we find out where she's coming from—and maybe where she's going."

*Well, this is*— Echo was thinking *weird*, but that didn't begin to capture it. She strode toward the empty chair and pulled the headphones over her ears. A cavelike silence dropped over her. On the tablet computer propped in front of her, comments scrolled upward on the screen.

"Greetings from Ashland! It's a jungle down here! —*Ashlandify.*"

"First! Damn. Guess not. —*Salem Omega.*"

"Anybody know what happened to Lazar? We miss him. —*Depoe Mode.*"

Echo adjusted the mic to be in front of her mouth, and her breath flowed through the cave like a stray wind from a distant storm. "Uh, hi," she said. Her words reverberated like the voice of a god—a young and stupid god with great power and no sense. She tried to still herself, but the reverberations continued like a deranged heartbeat, developing a rhythm: Ta-TAH ta-TAH ta-tah-ta-TAH—increasing in pitch, volume, and intensity until her feet and fingers were tapping, and she couldn't sit still in her chair. The others were looking at her—Caryn with irritation; Rachelle with pity; Mitch with an inscrutable expression. She gathered herself. "I was born in Pennsylvania—"

Caryn broke in, popping the silence like a bubble. "Not that far back."

Quiet remained inside the headphones, but the mystical silence had gone, leaving only a mechanical one. *You're nothing but a pack of cards* ran through Echo's mind, but she simply said, "How far back, then?"

Caryn stuck out her tongue in a mischievous grin. "We want to know how many people you killed."

Echo counted them on the fingers of her hand hidden in her lap: *Three, four, five. Is that all?* She shivered. The week wasn't over yet.

The chats scrolled by on the screen. Someone had paid twenty dollars to ask, "Why did you kill your sister? —*Cain Hermana.*"

Excuses ran through her mind like floodwaters taking out a bridge: *It was an accident. I didn't mean to. My father was driving, not me.* But she thought of Lazar spending twenty years in prison for a crime he *really* didn't do, and the truth came out of her mouth: "Envy."

Caryn opened her mouth to speak again, and Echo answered the question before it was asked: "Chandler because of wrath. And Lazar because of pride." Boos and scattered shrieks from the audience washed over her like a wave of regret.

"Thanks, Caryn," Rachelle said. She adjusted her microphone and poured water from one pitcher to the other as if it aided her in thinking. Caryn eyed Rachelle maliciously, but stayed silent as if recognizing that in this game—whatever it was—it was Rachelle's turn."We both know that for human beings, motivations are mixed, at best *and* at worst."

Someone in the chat paid fifty dollars to ask, "When do we get our two minutes' hate? —*Orwell Awakens.*"

Rachelle poured the water back into the first pitcher, muttering under her breath, "What is, what was, what is to come," like a tuneless song. Echo recognized the rhythm from her first moments in the headphones. Rachelle turned her attention on Echo again. "What did you learn?" she asked, pouring the water again.

Echo inhaled to speak. She knew the "right" answer—*Don't envy; don't be greedy; let go your pride*—but as Rachelle poured the water from pitcher to pitcher, the sound was like a mountain stream running over rocks, clear and clean and honest, hiding deeper truths like gold in the sand. Envy, greed, and pride were flags above huge battalions, but the actions that made up those battalions were small, often interchangeable. "Slow down," she said. "Be aware. Tell the truth. Ask for help."

Rachelle nodded, sat back in her chair, and looked to Mitch.

Chats rolled up the screen:

"Miiiiiitch! It's been ages. —*Mitchmatch.*"

"How's your soul, Mitch? —*Mindfuck Mission.*"

"Come back! We need you! —*Jeff the Joker.*"

Mitch sat with his arms folded on the table staring through or past Echo for an uncomfortable length of time.

After a while, Caryn snapped her fingers at him. "Mitch! It's called a livestream for a reason."

He shifted in his chair and brought his attention back to the circle. "What did you lose, Echo?" His voice reverberated painfully, as if he'd gotten too close to the microphone.

The question hit her like a kick in the gut. The illusion of ever having an apartment in Sellwood. Then her bag, with all its stuff of different kinds of value. Her illusions about the world and about herself. Lazar, Galynn, Chandler, maybe even Gray. She didn't want to name it all, so she said, "Everything."

He gave a little nod that said, *Just as I thought.* He continued to examine her face. "And where are you going?"

"I'm going to find and stop Jeph. Alone if I need to."

He nodded thoughtfully then spoke to the air behind her. "Where is Jeph?"

"You mean in the dream world or the real world?"

He looked at her as if she were a math student solving a problem in a way that was both understandable and disappointing. "There is no unreal world. Every step you take is in both worlds, whether you know it or not. You've been given the gift of knowing it." He asked again. "Where are you going?"

It felt like an important question, and Echo berated herself for not knowing the answer.

The chat pestered her:

"If you don't know where you're going, how can you get there? Huh? —*Jungle Justice.*"

"Your problem is that you drift like a bottle on the ocean. —*Nikolai was here.*"

"Yeah, but you forgot to load the message. —*Lost Eco.*" Three emoji at a forty-five-degree angle, laughing with tears.

Echo half stood to leave, but then she felt twelve-year-old Echo looking out her window, meeting Mitch's scrutiny with fierce intensity. Echo had been afraid of her younger self until now, but feeling nothing about Diana in the energy, she embraced it. "Wherever it takes," she said. She sat in the chair again with her arms crossed in defiance. "I don't even know the next step."

He nodded. "When you're walking in the unknown, every step is a crisis." He let the responsibility and terror of that sink in. "You say you've lost everything, but I say to you, not yet." He took off his headphones, leaned back in his chair, and dropped his chin to his chest as if he were napping.

Echo looked to Caryn and Rachelle. Rachelle, her pitchers standing on the table, was typing on a keyboard, and Caryn was taking off her headphones and hanging them on a stand next to her spot at the table.

"Wait," Echo said. "Is that all? What about my mission? I need help."

"Seems to me," Caryn said, "you've got a cleanup on aisle four, and now you want us to fix it." She closed her tablet with more force than necessary and stood up.

Rachelle poured water from pitcher to pitcher three times, then gave Echo a sympathetic lift of the eyebrows and a slight shrug, then took her pitchers and left.

At Rachelle's departure, the lights turned off, leaving Echo in semi-darkness as in the mouth of a cave. She stood and rose to leave, wondering what to do next.

The wooden floorboards had been replaced by a white stone slab, and she stepped out of shadow into blazing sunlight.

The myriad audience was arrayed in a semicircle stretching up the sides of a bowl-shaped valley. The people talked among themselves, pointing at Echo as if she had committed some scandal. She turned her back to them, looking to where the stage ended in a two-story facade with doors and windows but no interior. In her hand, she held a mask, an exaggeration of her own face, with spiky orange hair on top, like the plush creatures Chandler and Warren had, and scars like a broken mirror radiating out from between two huge, round eyes. She put the mask on and tied the leather laces behind her head.

A person in a black floor-length robe with a huge raven mask came out of one of the doors on the first floor of the facade, and the Raven and Echo turned together toward the audience.

Echo gave a small bow to the Raven and then spoke to the thousands watching from the stone seats: "Have you come back to bring Lazar's key? It's too late now."

The Raven cocked its head to one side, then replied in the voice of a woman who was not Galynn. "In a prison dark and deep, I hang like a shiny bauble in the shadows. Annihilation without end."

A chorus line of six—three male and three female—mannequins danced into the open area in front of the stage, their arms extended and hands on the others' shoulders. They sang a series of nonsense syllables in a harsh and sorrowful harmony until they had spread themselves across the stage, and then their words became very clear:

> Echo the Fool,
> rash and reckless,
> claims another victim.
> Who will be next?

As the sound died from their words, they all turned to her, and Echo saw that they, too, were wearing masks, but theirs were the blank face-shaped expanse of the mannequins she had seen at the beginning of her journey. Each mask had a mouth forming an O of surprise or horror.

When Echo turned to the Raven again, she was gone, replaced by a man in a mid-calf-length tunic wearing the mask of an arrogant and powerful king, with long, curling hair and a huge spiky crown. The man wore a sheathed sword and carried a scepter. Even though he didn't look like the Quig she knew, she recognized him as if she had checked his entrance on the playbill.

Quig strode to the center of the stage and addressed the audience:

> We are the Srelevart,
> Travelers in Ytilaer.

He spoke in a booming, bombastic voice unlike that of Gray's mild-mannered brother. At his words, the members of the audience stood, holding their right arms across their chests with their hands flat, palms downward. They recited the words with him as if they were a sacred pledge.

We map the Underground.
We follow the ancient paths
To discover the familiar
And know it for the first time.
Shunning deception and incivility,
We value reason even in dream.
We preserve the mysteries of the Srorrim.
We uphold the sanity of the world.

When he finished, they cheered and sat down again.

The mannequin chorus, still holding their arms across their chests, bowed to Quig, then lowered their arms and stood at attention as he spoke.

"Srelevart," Quig said, "I have come to praise Echo, not rebuke her. She is a bright girl, of quick wit and hasty temper, spinning through the Great Ballet aware of neither the plot nor the music. Who can blame Gray for being fascinated with the glittering mirror-ball at the center of the dance? But Gray is young and easily drawn aside from established paths onto the wild and dangerous ways encroaching from the borderlands."

"We are the Srelevart. We discover the familiar," the mannequins replied, in such perfect synchrony that it sounded like one voice in many different pitches.

"But," King Quig said, "neither Gray nor Echo understands that the monsters are within, and fighting the inner demons as if they're outside makes the demons stronger and more dangerous."

"We are the Srelevart," the mannequins sang. "We value reason even in dream."

Quig's voice rose to a roar of exhortation. "By shunning deception and incivility, we preserve the sanity of the world!"

A shriek came from behind, like the cry of a red-tailed hawk with an undertone of a lion's growl. A dragon with shining red scales soared down from the second floor of the facade at the back of the stage. Making a soft landing and folding her wings behind her, she revealed herself to be the dragon woman.

She stood at the center of the stage, in front of Quig and Echo, speaking to the audience:

> Hear and prepare, O Srelevart!
> Believe my prophecy if you dare.
> The Fool is your hero,
> And folly is her champion.
> Fear and outrage grip the Areopagus
> While sanity trembles in sanctuary.
> Your grip on stability is slipping;
> Unreason is the snake squirming in your fist.
> The tapestry unravels at the edges,
> And monsters overrun the center.
> Will you rise in courage or cower in despair?
> Cursed Cassandra has spoken.

The audience stood in their seats, jeering and throwing fruit at the stage. Echo and Quig stepped back, and the mannequins turned toward them, joining the audience's hubbub with unintelligible grunts and howls. The sounds of their voices were like a zoo when the apex predator begins to plunder it for food. Quig and Echo exchanged a look, and the terror she felt matched what she saw in his eyes. The dragon looked around the audience, disgust meeting resignation on her reptilian face, and flew back to the top of the facade at the back of the stage.

Echo gave a nod to Quig, then walked off the stage, into the empty storefront, and out the door onto a street of broken windows, burnt cars, and graffitied words she didn't understand.

She stopped on the broken and spray-painted sidewalk, listening to invisible cars whoosh slowly by. She held in remembrance the quiet streets, the summer sunshine, the carefree existence she had given up when she set out on this journey. She allowed herself a moment of nostalgia for the comfortable illusions of that other world, then focused on her memory of how to get from Gray's house to Aunt Doris's house.

*Annnd she's gone again.*

Gray watched open-mouthed as Echo walked out the door, leaving in her wake a whirlwind that wiped out the Greek theatre and everything else she had imposed on them. Her illusions flew away like scraps of cloth held together by soap bubbles. The scene called to mind the day Echo walked out of the bank, leaving Gray attached to Cain. Again he was rooted in place, but this time it was to persuade the Srelevart to support Echo's mission.

The meeting of the Srelevart returned to its usual format—the participants seated in the pew boxes that bore their names. They blinked like dreamers waking from a deep nap.

Caryn spoke first. "What. The. Hell."

Rachelle poured water from pitcher to pitcher. "Did we all see the same thing?"

Gray stood. "I saw Echo try again and again to communicate the importance of what she's doing. I saw one of our leaders"—he looked to Theo—"affirm what she's trying to say. I saw the rest of you demean and dismiss her."

Quig was—*Still? Again?*—wearing the king mask from Echo's drama, and he spoke from the lectern at the front of the chapel. "Think of what you're saying. This danger didn't come to *us*; it came to Echo, who refused every chance to say no. You're both young, and you're too emotionally invested to see the peril."

"No," Gray said, but a voice within him asked, *What if they're right?* The Srelevart had been with him ever since Douglas rescued him from the foster system after his mother died, and they continued to support him even after Douglas's death. No one ever told him the monster he feared wasn't real. But the foundational understanding of the Srelevart is that the battle against evil is always fought with reason and personal ethics. But, Gray wondered, is there any difference between a monster that isn't real and a monster that succumbs to reason and personal ethics? "What if reason isn't rational and rationality isn't enough?" he said finally.

"Did you get that from Echo?" Quig asked. "She's a bright girl, but do you really trust her view of the world against thousands of years of lore about Ytilaer?"

They looked at him now, concern wrinkling their foreheads, not so much judging as diagnosing with sympathetic detachment. So confident that they couldn't imagine a challenge to their reality.

In the face of their confidence, Gray's wavered. He felt like a bug in a collection—pinned and labeled, categorized, diagnosed.

"You've had enough trauma for a lifetime," Quig said. "We're trying to protect you."

But the past few days had brought huge changes for Gray. He had left the safety of a job and raided his college fund to hire Travis to help find Echo. He had lost his rorrim and learned to navigate Oge. He had found Echo and brought her home. These were all realities the Srelevart didn't have time to know. "What if it's time for me to be the protector?"

Quig smiled. "A worthy goal for a young man. But our dragons are not soul thieves. They are the everyday struggles of life, revealed through Ytilaer in their mythic form." He shrugged. "What do you know about Echo's— adventures? Only what she told you."

*Only what she told me.* Gray wavered between two views of the matter at hand: a girl had entered a magic world unprepared and had gone at least a little mad from misinterpreting what she saw there, or a girl had been called into Ytilaer for reasons even she didn't know and had accidentally discovered a horror that was unimaginable to people who explored Ytilaer regularly and knew all the lore about it.

Quig's version versus Echo's. Who was right? What did he know? *Lazar came to me in a dream, helped me put on my armor, and told me to meet Echo at the End of the Road.* The man's face was as clear to Gray as if he stood there right now. Gray asked that man, Ytilaer, and the universe for truth.

"The cycle continues—" An old woman answered, speaking beside him. Gray turned to her in surprise and found an almost-forgotten familiar face, gold tooth sparkling in the firelight. She glared at him and pointed to a chair across from her at a small table covered with a fringed cloth, with a clear but unspoken command to sit.

She laid three cards upon the table: middle, left, right. The card on the left held a wheel with monsters ascending and descending on it. The one on the right was a prince in a chariot drawn by black and white lions. The one in the center was a man between two women with Cupid hovering above, arrow nocked.

She tapped the center card with a gnarled finger and looked up at him. "Ah, love," she said. Her voice had an indulgent tone, but her gaze was sharp. "Love is decision—small and large, every moment of every day."

She pointed to the card on the left. "Wheel of fortune. Hard times create greatness; greatness creates easy times; easy times create weakness; weakness creates hard times." She looked up at him again, a grim smile around her mouth. "The wheel is always turning."

She pointed to the card on the right. "What will you choose to be? A champion in victory? Or—" she lifted the card, revealing an empty space beneath it. She raised one eyebrow in a questioning expression and faded into transparency.

Gray turned to Quig. "Did you see that?"

Quig's face was uncharacteristically angry—and something else, too. "Did Echo do that?"

"Echo is gone," Gray said. "And besides, she couldn't produce my great-grandmother." He squared off to face Quig directly. He was tall enough to look his foster brother in the eye, which wasn't true in Oge and had never before been true in Ytilaer. He felt something knock lightly against his leg and saw that it was the sword Lazar had given him at Road's End. "It's time to stop worrying about the means of communication and *listen* to what's being said."

"You don't know what you're asking," Quig said. "Death is waiting."

Gray nodded. "There are worse things than death."

CHAPTER 17

# Echo Fights Alone

As soon as Echo opened the door to Aunt Doris's house, she knew she was too late. The door pushed a broken chair leg out of the way, and the house *smelled* empty; she had no other way to describe it.

The rooms were derelict: wallpaper peeling, plaster falling, furniture disintegrating as if beaten down by the dust of ages.

"Aunt Doris!" she called, knowing it was of no use.

She heard a scritching from the kitchen and the tinkle of broken glass. The sound gave her an existential foreboding. In an abandoned house in Oge, it might be rats or raccoons, but in Ytilaer, there was no end of what it could be. She raced up the stairs instead.

She found Aunt Doris on her bed, silently sleeping on her back, sheet and light blanket pulled up to her chin and her arms outside the covers beside her. Echo ran to her, kissed her wrinkled cheek, and called on her to wake up. But the old woman was cold and unresponsive, like an aged Sleeping Beauty to the wrong prince.

Echo hesitated only a moment before rushing into Aunt Doris's esuoh, which was as dilapidated as her physical house. Her esuoh was very much like her kitchen—same wallpaper, same silly cat clock, same layout of doors and windows. But now the furniture and appliances were gone, and the linoleum flaking off the floor. Echo went to where the basement door should be, but she found only three steps leading downward to a blank wall.

*No basement?* Even Chandler had a basement when he was closing in on death. *But he lost his upstairs first.* Echo searched for an upstairs. The door opened into half darkness that became nothingness a few stairs upward.

The only thing in Aunt Doris's esuoh that seemed whole was the cat clock that had been hanging on her kitchen wall as long as Echo had known her. Amid all the dead and silent things, its huge eyes still moved back and forth as its dangling tail marked the passage of seconds.

It subtly vibrated like a key. She put her hand toward it, as if she were testing the heat of a stove, and the cat began to speak.

"Hello, Echo!" Its voice high and squeaky like in a 1930s cartoon. "Lost your beau?"

*Wait. Gray? He hadn't had time to get involved in this, had he?* "Where's Aunt Doris?"

"Oh? Her?" The cat said. "Jeph is keeping her safe. Grab my tail, and I'll take you to her."

Echo jerked her hand back. Jeph was a liar, but she believed two truths about what the cat said. Jeph had taken Aunt Doris, and if Echo touched the cat's tail, it would take her to Jeph. But between those two truths lay a realm of lies and darkness.

*Keeping her safe.* She remembered Chandler asking to be taken to a beach where he could live in contented illusion forever. Aunt Doris wouldn't ask for that, but maybe she didn't have a choice. Echo was sure Aunt Doris wasn't dead, because if she were, there would be no esuoh to enter.

*An esuoh to enter.* She left Aunt Doris's esuoh for her own to create a message for Gray, hoping he would still follow her to the end of the world.

AT THE TOUCH OF THE CLOCK CAT'S TAIL, the scene changed from Aunt Doris's ruined kitchen to a balcony high above a city, with a ribbon of river glinting in the summer sunset far below. The sliding glass door from the balcony to the condo was open a few inches, and through it drifted sounds of laughter and female voices, the clink of ice in glasses, and music—a heart-felt song about deep longing and lasting love, sung with no feeling, with sarcastic comments between the verses, trumpets shrieking and trombones blatting. And then Jeph was at the door, wearing a maroon brocade smoking jacket. He smiled at Echo, but fear and hunger lingered around his eyes.

"Echo! I knew you would come." He stood aside to make room for her to enter through the door. "Have a drink. I owe you some money." He looked her up and down as if appreciating the lines on a new sportscar. "You're my best student."

A crash of musical notes, like someone sitting on the piano keys. A knot of people clustered around the instrument, helpless in laughter. Jeph took it in with only a glance, then turned his attention back to Echo.

"You're just in time for the celebration. I've got some clothes you can wear." Like a magician, out of thin air, he produced a small, sparkly knot of strings and patches of cloth. He leaned in, the smell of whisky on his breath. "You could be almost pretty if you fixed yourself up."

His words rankled, and she pushed the costume away. He eyed her, a smile playing around his mouth. She told herself to remain calm—remaining calm was something her soul had tried to teach her. But now—with Jeph's crimes strutting through her mind like a parade—she wasn't sure she had gotten the lesson. Listing those crimes wouldn't solve anything; her goal was to get Aunt Doris out of prison. After that? She had promised to stop Jeph and Cain, and she already felt overmatched and unprepared.

"Everybody!" Jeph shouted as he sauntered toward the piano in the enormous room. Jeph's esuoh bore a vague similarity to what she had seen in the game the first night she met him, but it was vastly larger and—nastier—she had no other word. Shag carpet on the floor, with evidence of spills and splatters. Stained white furniture. The pictures on the walls were erotic poster-sized ads for cars, except for one old masterpiece of a bowl of fruit that had been used as a dartboard. A small silver cross hung in a glass-fronted wooden display case on the wall. Lazar's key—like a trophy of a noble beast shot from a helicopter. On the coffee table, among the empty drink glasses, used napkins, discarded garments, and drug paraphernalia, sat an anomalous bowl of walnuts.

Jeph took one of the walnuts and tossed it into the air. His head changed to a condor's, which snagged the walnut in flight and swallowed it, then changed back to Jeph's head. He looked a little fresher, a little more like the image she had seen when he first spoke to her at the coffee shop. The whole action took only a second or two, and then he strode casually to stand among the "everybody" he had shouted to.

One was a piano-player who looked like a robot creepily close to human. Otherwise, most of the party-goers were women in thongs and pasties who jutted out their breasts and bottoms and gave open-mouthed smiles and licked their lips whenever Jeph looked at them. There were a dozen of them of all shapes, sizes, and colors, including the blue and green of Star Trek aliens, but they were enough alike that they appeared to be lifelike dolls. And the faces—

When she focused on the faces, she saw Marlo, Galynn—and Aunt Doris. *Are they real? They can't be real.* Why Marlo? Why now? Why Galynn, who had brought him the key? *And Aunt Doris.* A shiver wracked Echo's body and made her want to scream at Jeph. Having lost all capacity for calm, she fought for self-control.

"Everybody!" Jeph said again. The piano player stopped, and so did the singer, somewhere, and the horns faded as the air died out of them. Everybody stood there, hungering for Jeph, hungering for Echo. "This is our hero!"

The women squealed, even Galynn, even Aunt Doris.

"She made it possible for all of us to be here this evening."

The women shouted and bounced, clapping their hands, their long, brightly painted fingernails glinting in the light.

Marlo, Galynn, and Aunt Doris—*Fake, fake, fake,* she told herself. This can't be them, can it?—came toward her like mean girls running to meet their queen.

"I thought you might betray me," Jeph said to Echo in a stage whisper, "but fortunately you chose one of my own as your confidant."

He reached out and draped an arm around Galynn's shoulder. She was not the raven as Echo knew her, nor the stripper of just a moment ago. Now, looking childish in a schoolgirl's uniform whose short, plaid, pleated skirt exposed her long legs, she leaned into Jeph as she spoke to Echo. "I told you I wasn't 'normal people,' but you didn't believe me."

"You—" Echo said to Galynn, but words failed her. "You—" she said to Jeph. Looking back now, Galynn's betrayal seemed inevitable—Echo had to admit the temptation would be strong for her as well if she, like Galynn, had gotten a glimpse of this world and then Echo's promise of more, subsequently revoked. The shock of seeing what was there all along was worse than if it had been a complete surprise.

Jeph drew Galynn tighter to himself and gave a little shrug. "I wish I were brilliant enough to put you two together." He shook his head. "Some people say the dream world has a will and plans. It seems like complete bullshit to me, until a lucky break like this comes along to make me won-der." He let go Galynn's shoulder and smacked her on the rear. To Echo: "Let me introduce you to a couple of others you'll recognize."

Marlo stepped forward, dressed like a Las Vegas showgirl with a foun-tain of scarlet feathers on her head. She looked Echo up and down with a dismissive smile that didn't quite reach her eyes, then turned to Jeph and shook her head. "I told you she wouldn't do."

Jeph and Marlo locked eyes for a few seconds, their expressions inscru-table. Then he recovered himself. "But look! I got everything I wanted—and her, too."

Marlo glanced at Echo as if the younger woman was an inadequate rival. "I see you've attached yourself to Jeph's visionary inspirations. You won't need a resume now."

*Jeph's visionary inspirations*—where had Echo heard that? It came back to her: that distant Tuesday morning when Marlo, stern and sophisticated, had introduced Echo to Jeph-as-employer. Marlo had hinted at a division between herself and Jeph, but now she eyed him with the adoration of a politician's wife at a campaign event. Jeph also seemed to embrace Marlo with his eyes, even when he wasn't looking directly at her. They were like two magnets at once attracted and repellent to each other.

Echo felt a nudge and found Aunt Doris standing beside her, not the porn star with an old lady's head, but Aunt Doris in stripper garb, poking Echo in the ribs with an elbow. "He's quite a looker, isn't he?" She jiggled her saggy breasts and well-padded hips. "You said you wanted to step off a cliff and see where you fly. Now here you are with your 'special skills.'" A rapturous smile lit her face. Was it really Aunt Doris? Echo now understood why the answer to that question is another question—*What is real?*—because the experience was present and visceral, and Echo felt a scream rising at her own part in making all this.

Jeph stepped between them, filling Echo's vision with his form that had once seemed so attractive. He was too close. She stepped back, but found her way blocked by something behind her. She couldn't even turn to see what it was, because Jeph held her attention the way a snake fascinates its prey.

Jeph made a complicated series of steps, his arms outstretched like one of those bird mating dances, never releasing Echo from his gaze. Something deep inside her was screaming that she needed to get away. What had Lazar done to escape? She couldn't remember, but the thought of Lazar brought a fresh breeze that woke her up a little. She expected the net of sparks, but it didn't come.

"In fact," Jeph said, his tone soft and intimate as a lover's in a perfume ad, "I have a trophy for you."

*Lazar's cross!* Echo could hardly believe her good fortune. She didn't expect it to be useful in any way, but it was an offense for it to be here. "It means nothing to you," she told him. "You don't deserve to keep it."

Jeph glanced in the direction of the shadow box hanging on the wall and shivered subtly. "No." He spoke with a quiet firmness that was far from the inane persona he had been portraying up to now. "That's a trophy from a different fight."

"You didn't even try to take Lazar's soul," Echo said. It was an accusation. "You knew that if you left Cain to take it alone, it would destroy him. Is that why he isn't here?"

"You saved me," he said in an intimate whisper. "When you stepped in between him and the knife, he pushed you out of the way. You gave me the opening I needed."

Echo saw Lazar's body fall lifeless on the deck—as Jeph would have seen it—a memory he had just dropped into her as they stood there in conversation. She felt Jeph's triumph and her own guilt and anger for Lazar's death.

Jeph stood so close that she could see the feather pattern woven into the cloth of his jacket. From somewhere, nowhere, he pulled out a bloody knife, exactly like the one he had used to kill Lazar. He offered it to Echo, handle toward her. "You deserve this."

Rage enveloped her like a forest fire. The people around her became like shapes in an incandescent cloud. She took the knife's handle, felt it solid and icy in her hand, and thrust it forward into Jeph's deserving abdomen, pulled it back and drove it where his heart would be if he had one, pulled it back and—

She heard the crowd laughing from far away, as if watching a clown's hilarious pratfall.

Echo wiped a spot of dampness from her hand onto the apron she wore over her pink gingham uniform. A streak of red spread down the starched white surface. She sighed and went to the hand-washing sink. Where had the ketchup come from? That family with the kids must have spread it everywhere. As she washed, she was surprised at how much ketchup swirled down the drain.

Then the bell dinged, alerting her that her next table's meal was ready, and she wiped her hands on the towel and went to pick up the orders. Number 6 and number 4 for the two men next to the window. She set the plates in front of them: pancakes, sausage, three eggs, and biscuits for the thin older man with the guarded watchfulness of an off-duty cop. Just two eggs and toast with melon for the younger man with the dark eyes and soulful expression. He was so fascinating that he made her heart beat faster. She wanted him to look at her, to meet her eyes like they do in the movies. But a voice inside her asked, *What would he see? A freak. A horror.* Didn't matter. Their eyes would meet, and he would say, *I feel like I've known you forever, and she would say, I feel the same.*

But neither man looked up at her.

"Coffee?" she asked, adding a cheery waitress tone to the question.

The older man nodded, working ravenously at his pancakes. The younger man, looking out the window at the bleak rural town, green and gray on a cold November day, just shook his head and didn't look at her.

She sighed inwardly and tried to keep her voice bright. "I'll bring the coffee in a minute."

She went to the table where the ketchup family had left and started clearing. She made sure the lid of the ketchup bottle was screwed on tightly. She put the tip into her pocket and felt something hard and damp there. She looked down. Tucked behind her order book was a bloody knife.

Terror shook her. Where had it come from? She looked at the old cop, talking to the fascinating young man, who answered in single syllables, if at all, never looking away from the window. There would be awkward questions. She couldn't tell anybody about the knife until she remembered how it got there.

She carried the load of dishes over and put them into the tub for the dishwashers.

Echo wiped a spot of dampness from her hand onto her apron. A streak of red spread down the starched, white surface. She sighed and went to the hand-washing sink. Where had the ketchup come from? That family with the kids must have spread it everywhere. As she washed, she was surprised at how much ketchup swirled down the drain.

Then the bell dinged, alerting her that her next table's meal was ready, and she wiped her hands on the towel and went to pick up the orders.

CHAPTER 18

# The Sleeping Princess

GRAY HOPED HE WAS RIGHT THAT ECHO would check in with Aunt Doris before setting out on her next "mission." The last thing he wanted was to face that formidable woman with the news that he had lost Echo *again*.

But when he came to the Craftsman bungalow with its tree-shaded yard, he found the front door ajar. He knocked and called, but got no response, so he pushed the door open and went inside.

Everything was calm and quiet, with an atmosphere of abandonment that made him step carefully and quietly, not sure what he was looking for or what he had found. There was no one on the main floor, and the basement door opened into darkness. He closed it and went upstairs.

The first closed door was Echo's room—jumbled and messy like her esuoh. He smiled a bit in spite of his worry and went on to the room at the front of the house. What he saw there made him catch his breath.

Aunt Doris was arranged on the bed like a queen in state, and Echo draped across her like a mourner. Both were cool and still as death, and he couldn't find a pulse in either. With a feeling like sinking in quicksand, he sat on the floor and surveyed the prospect of a world without Echo—a world without light or laughter or beauty. Pain pierced his heart, fear gripped his guts, and the washed-out image of emptiness clouded his vision.

Time passed, the pain eased, and a pinpoint of hope appeared. Gray considered his options. If he had his rorrim, he would try to go into Echo's esuoh to get more information. But he didn't have it and cursed himself again for its loss.

He could go back to the Sanctuary and ask to borrow one or cross over and come back, but that would cost valuable time.

Or he could call someone.

He didn't reach Theo on the first try and was debating calling Travis when she called back.

"Are you in Ytilaer?" he asked her.

"I'm driving home," she said.

"I need your help."

"Give me a minute to park."

It might have been more than a minute, but it seemed like hours as Gray paced the room, checked the medicine bottles on the nightstand—finding no information he could understand, but at least it was something to do—and then he heard Theo's voice again. "May I come into your house?"

"I invite you into my house," he replied, his voice cracking with grief and fear.

And then another person's presence—Theo's—tickled his consciousness.

"They're dead, Theo—Echo and her Aunt Doris. How could this happen—to both of them?" He walked around the room holding the phone to his ear, and looking everywhere except the deadly tableau of a double murder he had found on Aunt Doris's bed.

Theo's voice came to him like a voice from a daydream. *You need to look at them.*

Gray steeled himself as he turned toward the women. "How could this happen? I was only a few minutes behind her. Poison?"

*Closer,* Theo said with annoying calmness.

He moved in closer. "You can't do anything. I should have called an ambulance."

*Lift the older woman's eyelid.*

He did. Her eye was blue and the pupil wide open.

*Is that what color her eyes were?*

"I'm not sure. I only saw her once in Oge and I wasn't paying attention."

*What about Echo's?*

"I need to move her. What if it's a crime scene?"

*If you can move her, it will tell us something.*

He turned Echo and arranged her on the bed beside Aunt Doris, then bent and pushed her eyelid open. Her iris was ice blue, and the pupil very wide.

*What about her? Have you seen her eyes?*

"Yes." He struggled against tears. "They're brown with green flecks."

*Stay there and wait for me.*

"But the police—"

"Don't *do* anything." Her voice was coming from the phone again. "*Don't* call an ambulance."

"What is it?" he asked more insistently, almost shouting.

"Listen to me." Her voice took on the dragon quality from the Srelevart meeting earlier. "Where's your rorrim?"

Shame overwhelmed him. "I lost it."

Long pause and then back to business. "I'll scold you later. They're not dead. They've been stolen."

His legs gave way, and he sat abruptly on the floor. Of course that was a possibility—he knew it even when Quig didn't believe. But when you walk through Oge on a sunny June afternoon, such things don't seem possible. His breath caught as if lost in the labyrinth of his throat. "Jeph and Cain. Probably Jeph."

"The men who killed Lazar?"

He nodded, unable to speak.

She didn't need his reply. "Stay there and wait for me," she said again. "Traffic is bad, and it may be half an hour. I'll bring a rorrim for you. But *stay there* and don't do anything."

He sat on the floor beside the bed, his hand on Echo's hand. It was too cold, and he felt nothing of the electricity that at any other time would have such a stormy effect on him. As he stared at the wall because he couldn't bear to look at her face, a story came back to him, like a song he'd heard so long ago that he'd almost forgotten it. Was it from his mom or her grandmother? Didn't matter. A beautiful princess enraged the court magician because she wouldn't help him supplant her father. He stole her soul and the soul of everyone in the kingdom, then went away and left them all asleep where they'd fallen. After a hundred years, a prince came, having heard there was a treasure inside the palace worth more than a kingdom. The prince had to fight his way in through terrible trials—quicksand, a guardian monster with poisonous teeth and claws, and roses with thorns like daggers. Eventually, tired, dirty, and wounded, he found the princess asleep in her chamber, and she was so beautiful—here he turned to Echo and thought *yes*—that he was overcome with love and kissed her lips. She awoke and said, "I knew you would come," and he discovered she was the treasure worth more than a kingdom.

He stood and looked at her again. It was stupid, of course, in the way magical things are stupid in Oge, but he bent down and brushed his lips across hers.

Then he heard a noise behind him and found the door open and Theo standing in it with a grim half-smile on her face. From behind her, Quig looked over her shoulder with the expression of a man who is walking to the firing squad.

"Did it work?" Theo asked, coming to stand beside him as Quig, Edward, and Rachelle followed her in. All three were in their work clothes—Quig's gray suit; Edward's old-fashioned, double-breasted suit, also gray; Rachelle's simple dress with a scarf around her shoulders.

"A story," Gray said, feeling his face flaming red, "from my mother's—"

Theo nodded. "There's a version of it in Oge, too." She shrugged. "Worth a try." She reached into her bag and pulled out a small box like a gift from a jewelry store. She opened it and held out the rorrim to him. "Go see what you can see."

"Me?"

She pushed it toward him again. "You're more likely to have permission than any of the rest of us. You can check Doris's esuoh, too, if you can get in."

He took the rorrim and crossed over. Aunt Doris's comfortable, if dated, bedroom, had become a stone bed chamber with rich rugs and tap-estries on the walls, well-made furniture, and a canopied four-poster bed with a beautiful princess lying on it next to her old nanny. Obviously, the reason the kiss had had no effect was that he hadn't gone through the necessary trials to earn it.

He looked over his shoulder. Theo was there, in her red woolen robe and dragon's face; Quig still wearing the mask of the ancient king from Echo's Greek tragedy; Edward in his beehive hat, looking pale and nauseated; and Rachelle with her two pitchers of water. There was a frantic quality to her pouring, but she didn't spill a drop. Mitch and Caryn were absent, but Mitch had been unpredictable since he found his soul, and Caryn was often more difficult than helpful.

Theo gestured toward Echo with her dragon's chin, and Gray went into Echo's esuoh.

It felt empty in its deepening darkness, despite all the things on her shelves. He made a lamp and set it on a counter, where it shed a small pool of light that emphasized the abandonment. He called to her, but his voice died in the stillness. The door to the outside was not just locked but gone, and he couldn't find a door to her basement. Her window were shuttered from the outside.

He tried to open a door into Aunt Doris's esuoh, but it was impossible—for him, at least.

As he was turning back to leave, he heard the subtle buzzing of a key and traced the vibration to a toy on an upper shelf among various science fiction figurines. It looked like a trash can on wheels. He reached for it, and when his hand neared it, a voice that might have been Echo's—the sound quality was too tinny to be sure—said, "Help me, Eleven. You're my only hope."

The name smacked him. Some of the kids in high school had started calling him that a couple of years ago, so Gray assumed it was an insult. But—

Jeph *would* leave a trap key, but only Echo would know the name had any significance to Gray. She must have meant him to find it. She had to.

Did the logic hold? If it didn't, he could find himself in whatever trouble Echo was in, unable to help her.

"Help me, Eleven. You're my only hope," the voice from the toy robot said again.

He held his hand out again, hesitating, then shook his head and reached for the key.

When he touched it, a holographic projection of Echo in a cheap science fiction costume stepped forward and spoke to him.

"I knew you would come," she said. She looked over her shoulder. "That bastard took Aunt Doris. It must have been in the middle of the night, after you texted her." She looked around again. "I hope he didn't stop to look at your text." She looked thoughtful for a second. "If you're seeing this, I guess I'm gone, too. He left a key in Aunt Doris's esuoh." She looked at the ceiling. "I need to follow her. I owe her so much, and this could be a way to get to Jeph." She paused again. "I don't really have a plan. Big surprise, right? But I'm going to use Jeph's key to fix this."

Gray's stomach flipped, and his knees felt weak.

"I understand why your Srelevart won't help. I can't blame them, and I won't blame you if you go home and get on with your life." A softer look crossed her face, a look of fondness—even love, if he dared believe it. "I don't believe you'll do that, so you need to prepare before you ride off into battle."

Gray's heart was pounding. He wanted Echo to *be* there, to talk about this. But all he had was a secret message, left specifically for him, so he tried to focus on what she was saying.

". . . But Lazar did his best to prepare me for this. He helped me meet my soul. He said it was important—I'm not sure why—so let me tell you how to meet yours."

*Meet my soul?* The one thing his mother's grandmother and the Srelevart agreed on was that the journey to meet your soul was a terrifying adventure to the unknown, and nobody ever came back from it unchanged—and many never came back at all. The difference would probably be that the Grandmother would say that's why you do it anyway, and the Srelevart say you make little forays into the Underground so that you're prepared to meet your soul on the road to death.

That journey had ended Mitch's life as most people knew it. He'd lost his family, his job, his friends—aside from the Srelevart—and now he spent his days searching for something, he said, that he hadn't known he was missing. And look at Echo. Even she had come back almost unrecognizable.

*Unrecognizable*— Did he and Echo have a future, even if she overcame whatever danger she was in? The distance between them was even wider now than when he'd kept his secret of Ytilaer from her. But if they were ever to be together—or even if he were to go on alone with Echo somewhere in the world—he had to do this.

". . . The thing is," she was saying, "you have to go through the doors."

*Wait.* What had he missed?

"It seems like the most terrifying thing in the world," Echo was saying, "but you *have* to do it. If you don't, you might as well just go home."

The robot was blue and orange, with a domed top and various vents and lenses. No "pause" or "reverse" buttons. He waved his hand at it, but Echo kept speaking.

"At the bottom of the stairs after the last door—three seems to be the pattern—you'll come out on the sand at the Eternal Ocean. You'll know where to go. If you don't let the barriers stop you, you'll find it. I don't know what it will look like, but you'll know it when you see it. When you meet your soul, do what he tells you to do.

"I probably didn't need to tell you any of this. If you set out with firm intention—or maybe not even that—if you set out with intention to intend, you'll arrive—I think.

"Last thing. I—" She stopped, her eyes wide. "I can't do that to him," she said in an undertone. "Last thing," she started again, "you're free. I don't know how all this will work out, but I hope we get a chance to talk again."

The toy robot made a whirring, clicking sound and disappeared in a puff of white smoke.

He reached to snatch it from its destruction and run the recording again, but his hand closed over empty space.

He slumped to the floor in terror and despair, his arms clutched over his abdomen. The image of Echo lying in an unending sleep that he hadn't been worthy to break haunted him. The knowledge of how Quig and the others would react when he told them his plan—tenuous and half-formed—made it even harder to carry out. He *could* pull an Echo—make a door into his own esuoh, open his basement door, and start this journey without telling the others.

But he owed it to them, even though he was afraid they would stop him. Maybe small acts of courage prepare you for bigger ones.

He went out to tell the Srelevart he was going to meet his soul.

IN THE STONE CHAMBER, GRAY FACED THE SRELEVART who had come for him. "Theo's right," he said. "Jeph took her." He looked down at the two sleeping women. "Aunt Doris, too, as bait."

None of them spoke for a while. The dragon's lip curled, revealing dagger-sharp teeth. Edward leaned against a wall, looking sick. Rachelle slowly and thoughtfully poured the water from pitcher to pitcher, and the mouth of Quig's king mask dropped from the grimace of decision to the downward turn of tragedy.

Quig spoke first. "Then of course we'll have to take action. We'll start in Jeph's office." He turned away from Gray. "Edward? Theo? What do you recommend?"

"I'm going—" Gray started to say.

Quig turned back to him. "You're too young. I promised Dad—"

"And I promised Echo."

Quig turned to the other Srelevart. "What's the plan?" he asked, as if Gray hadn't spoken.

Theo gave Gray a quick glance but answered Quig's question. "We need someone to stay with Echo and Doris. They will probably be fine, physically, for a while, but if some helpful person finds them this way, Oge medicine could kill them before we release their souls."

Quig nodded. "Good point." To Gray, "Stay here and watch over them. We'll let you know if we need you."

Gray felt a fire growing in his lower rib cage. There was anger in it, wounded pride, and something else—determination. "I won't be able to do that. I'm going to my soul."

All four of them stared at him. Quig's mask showed narrowed eyes and an angry sneer. Theo squinted at Gray as if she were seeing him for the first time. Edward leaned against the wall with his arms folded. Rachelle had stopped mid-pour, her eyes wide and the water paused in streaming from pitcher to pitcher, as still as in a photograph.

Gray felt the need to explain. "Echo left me a message—"

But Quig interrupted him. "So if you can't go with us, you won't do anything to help?"

The fire in Gray's belly burned colder and hotter at the same time. "I'm going to my soul," he said again, his voice steady and strong this time.

"And how will that help?" Theo spoke kindly, for a dragon, but with a roar undertone.

"I don't know what good it will do. Even Echo said she didn't know"—Gray shook his head, as frustrated with Echo as with the Srelevart—"but she said it's important, and I'm going."

Quig shook his head. "If you're not going to help, could you at least not make things more complicated? You understand that if it comes to a choice between rescuing you and rescuing Echo, we'll choose you."

"I don't need rescuing. This is how Lazar prepared her, and she told me how to go about it." He hoped his voice displayed more confidence than he felt.

"You realize you could come out, at best, as crazy as Mitch and as out-of-control as Echo," Quig said.

Gray opened his mouth to speak, then closed it. Quig was still utterly calm and rational, and Gray felt more anger toward him than at any time since he'd known him. He nodded and went into his esuoh.

GRAY STOOD IN THE QUIET DARKNESS OF HIS NEW ESUOH, his heart pounding. He already regretted how the conversation with Quig had gone.

After more than ten years in the Burroughs family, Gray had never chosen his own will over either Douglas or Quig. Quig blamed Echo for the rift between himself and Gray, but Gray could think of several candidates for blame—Jeph, Cain, Quig for not listening, and, yes, even Gray himself—but he kept coming back to what Jeph did, who Cain was, and Echo. Gray knew he might be wrong, but it was a wrong with no remedy.

He felt more than heard a presence beside him and, turning, found Theo at an open door.

"May I come into your house?" she asked.

He sighed, realizing he had had a brief hope it would be Quig. "Of course. Always."

She stood for a moment, taking in his new esuoh—the high ceiling, dark wood, thick rug in browns and blues, the suit of armor standing beside the door. She didn't say anything about the room; she just looked Gray up and down and nodded to him. "I brought you something," and she walked over and sat in one of Gray's chairs near his memory cabinet. She pulled a small item out of a pocket he hadn't known she had, unwrapped it carefully, and held it up to him.

He reached for it, and she jerked it away from him. "Damn it, Gray. You know better than to reach like that. It's a key. Sit down and let me tell you what it's for."

He dropped onto a chair. "I never imagined you'd—"

She shook her head. "Don't depend on the limits of your imagination to ensure your safety in this world. You have to be aware of what's possible."

He held up his hands, palms out. "Sorry. I'm listening." The world around him, as well as within, had changed over just a few days.

She glared at him for a few more seconds. "It's a key," she said again. Gray wanted to ask about it, but decided he should just let her tell it. She waited, gauging his attention, before beginning again. "If you touch it, it locks you out of Ytilaer forever."

Gray's fingers tingled as if he had come too close to a buzz saw. "How? Did *you* make it?"

She wrapped the key again and held the package in her lap. "I made it for myself to escape my former teacher." She looked at Gray significantly. "The egam krad."

Gray sat with his hands closed around his fingers, wondering how this woman who had been like an aunt to him since his childhood could have made such a terrible thing.

"I was desperate," she said. "Meeting Edward brought me into the Srelevart and saved me. I left all that behind, but I kept this key in case I might need it someday." She held it out to him. "*You* may need it."

He sat back in his chair, eyeing the thing as if it were a snake rising to strike.

She held it out to him. "It doesn't kill. And it doesn't work through the cloth."

He didn't reach for it. "It cuts you off from Ytilaer? And you say it doesn't kill?"

"It doesn't kill," she said again, with more emphasis. "It cuts the communication between Ytilaer and the whole person."

"How is that not death?"

"Slow death, maybe. But that's not what I'm talking about."

He got up and walked away from her. "It's terrible. How could you even make such a key?"

"Desperation."

"Who do you expect me to use it on? Jeph? Cain? Echo?"

"Will you sit down and discuss this? I don't *expect* you to use it on anybody. Maybe on yourself."

"Myself?" He shook at the horror if it, like moving from a home of lush greenery and bright flowers to an alien desert where the only neighbors were Nothing and Nobody.

Steam came from the dragon's nostrils, but she didn't say anything for a while. Finally, "I'm not forcing anything on you. But please sit down and listen."

He looked around the room, half-expecting Quig to come in and hold him down so that she could touch the key to him. But that wasn't something Quig would do, nor Theo. He took a few deep breaths and sat again.

"I don't *want* you to use it," Theo said. "I only thought that if the worst happened, it might be better than the alternative."

"The worst? You mean going to my soul?"

She batted away his question like an annoying fly. "That? No. I don't know why you insist on going to your soul, but that's not what I'm worried about. I know you plan to go and rescue Echo by yourself the first chance you get."

Well, she was right about that. "OK."

"You could get into a situation where this key is your best option."

"My *best* option?"

"Where's Echo right now? Where's her aunt?" She locked him in her gaze. "Quig may be having trouble believing what's happened to them, but I'm not, and I'm surprised if you are."

"You think I'd force Echo—"

She shook her head. "If you *can't get* Echo out. If you get trapped yourself. If there's no way out—" She sighed. "Well, it's a way out."

"Suicide?"

She glanced upward and sighed again. "Yes and no. Maybe. I don't know. I've never used it. I don't want you to use it. But I can imagine a situation where you would find it your best, only option. Better than whatever Jeph or Cain has in store for you." She held it out toward him. It was a squat, fist-sized, square-jawed man carved from black onyx. Looking at it, Gray felt an urge to slide a finger over its sharp edges and smooth planes. Theo wrapped it in the heavy cloth and tied it with a leather cord.

This time, when she held it out to him, he took it from her hand.

She walked toward the door, stopping at the suit of armor that Lazar had given him. She looked back at him with a slow, thoughtful nod. "You should probably wear this." She went out the door.

Gray sat for what seemed like a long while, holding the horrible thing in his hand, his heart pounding at what he had taken on. Then he got up and looked out his window at Echo and Aunt Doris, sleeping the sleep of death. He hid the key in his cabinet of memories and went to find his soul.

CHAPTER 19

# Trials of the Prince

GRAY OPENED HIS BASEMENT DOOR and stepped into a half-darkness that felt like walking into his own grave. He ran his hand along the wall—cold, sterile tile, lacking features or decoration. He closed the door behind him and started his descent in a dim and flickering fluorescent light that came from everywhere and nowhere.

As soon as the door closed, he heard voices—too distant to understand, but distinctly voices—laughing, shouting, squealing, cursing. It was as if high school had returned to reclaim him, but there were adult voices among them, deeper and louder, and fear gripped him as he wondered what he was walking into.

Endlessly down and down the unchanging stairway Gray descended, with the voices gradually coming nearer, but their source never appearing. Sometimes it seemed they were talking about him—as when he stumbled on a stair and nearly fell and the voices erupted in unanimous laughter. He felt pursued then and looked back to see where the door to his esuoh was, but it was lost in the distance, where Echo slept the sleep of death, so he turned forward and kept walking.

At last he came to the bottom of the stairs. Across a short space of polished concrete was a cave mouth with a cloud of bats pouring out of it like smoke. Their flapping wings and twittering voices seemed to be the source of the conversation he had heard along the way. As he entered the cave, the half-light halved again and again with each step, until he peered into utter darkness going forward, seeing nothing.

And then there was a wooden door with a peeling brass knob that looked both strange and familiar. It was perfectly visible, but gave off no light to illumine the darkness. Gray touched the doorknob and felt fear, anger, and endless pain behind it. A monster was waiting for him there. He snatched his hand back and started walking again.

He had gone only a few steps further when he remembered Echo's warning that he had to go through the doors. Was this one of them? He looked back. It was still visible in the wall of the cave, but it seemed to be fading. He dashed back and ran through without further thought.

He entered a woman's bedroom, with yesterday's clothes hung over the back of a chair and tomorrow's neatly folded on the seat. The dresser was strewn with things—makeup, keys, hairbrush, a Lightning McQueen car—and a pocket-sized mirror lay on the floor reflecting the ceiling light. His mother's room. As the recognition struck him, he was a boy again, standing beside her bed, watching her open her eyes. She was not much older than Echo was now, and she was beautiful, with olive skin and luxuriant dark hair. She looked at him, and her smoky brown eyes poured such love upon him that he felt like crying. "Did your dream scare you?" She reached out to hug him.

"Somebody came in the back door." Gray turned to look at the door that he, the child, had come through. "I heard glass break in the kitchen."

She threw back the covers and stood, vulnerable in her pink nightgown, her gaze darting around the room. "Get under the bed." Her tone brooked no argument, and Gray slid under. There were toys under the bed—Matchbox cars, Ninja Turtle figurines, building blocks—like Gray's former esuoh. The pink coverlet dropped over the gap where Gray had slid in, and beyond the edge of it, the woman's bare feet turned this way and that. Looking for a weapon? A place to hide? But it was too late. Red cowboy boots entered the room with heavy footsteps, and Gray's mother turned to face the door.

Gray shimmied to the foot of the bed and reached out to take the mirror lying on the floor. He felt a twinge of guilt that he had pulled it out of its case to look at it without his mother's permission and had forgotten it on the floor. But more than that, he feared the intruder and hoped the mirror would give him a superpower to make all this right again.

He looked into the mirror and touched its wavery surface, and he felt the shock of crossing over—the sense of drowning and then recovery. It was dark here, and the monster now walking in his mother's room had legs with coarse black fur ending at  huge hooves that thundered when he walked.

"Get out!" His mother's bare feet squared off as she faced the monster, and her voice did not falter. "There's a restraining order."

The monster laughed like a wolf growling and moved a step closer. "Calm down. I just want my mirror back." It spoke in Cain's voice, and a shiver ran down Gray's spine.

"It's not yours. It came from my grandmother." His mother's voice was pitched a note higher now.

He sighed. "OK. I'll give you money for it." Coins clinked on the bed above.

"Get out. I don't have it."

The monster screamed like an angry tiger. "What did you do with it?" The beast stomped around the room, breaking toys and kicking shoes out of the way. Sounds of drawers opening and things falling. Then a pause. "Where's the boy?"

His mother's feet came closer to the bed and turned toward the room, as if she could shield her son from the monster.

The black hooves came nearer.

"OK, OK. The rorrim is in the closet."

He moved across the room and bent down. A scaly black-clawed hand came from above to pick up the mirror's leather covering that lay on the floor near where the mirror had been. Gray's mom stepped away and struggled with an electric cord.

"Here's the—" The monster turned. "A lamp? So that's the way we play it." A struggle, and something—the lamp—crashed against the wall. Gray's mother ran past the monster, but he pivoted toward her. Confused noises. Then her feet were lifted off the ground, and a great weight like a tree fell on the bed. A storm struck with lightning and clashes of thunder. The bed shook. Muffled screams, heavy exhalations, and pounding on the bed. Gray shrank away toward the wall, lying in a fetal position, his hands on his ears, tears running down his face. The lightning and thunder continued, and the pounding of the blood through his veins was like the roar of a tornado. Then, after a while, quiet fell like a sigh for a time that could have been minutes or days.

There was a movement above, and the hooves thumped to the floor. A claw lifted the cover, and a face appeared, black on black, with red eyes and a mouth that grinned with obsidian teeth. The monster held out an ash-black hand with long claws, and Gray put the mirror on it.

It beckoned the boy with a claw, but Gray lay prone on the floor, peering over the redoubt of his folded arms. The monster growled. "I'll come back for you, kid." It walked away, heavy-footed on the cheap apartment floor.

Silence fell eventually—outside first—and then the beating of his heart quieted as well. The boy cried out in rage and fear and frustration. He went to his mother, who was naked and not breathing, her pink nightgown tossed aside on the floor. He pulled the blanket over his mother and lay next to her, waiting for what would happen next.

Then he was standing outside the door in the cave. Tears still flowed, but the darkness and silence engulfed him, leaving him empty of feeling and imagination.

He kept walking until he came to the second door.

This one was massive, double wide, and opened to a colosseum, where a black-robed emperor presided over thousands of people, all looking down in stern judgment. Caged beasts stood poised to lunge at him, watching with their eyes wide and their tails twitching. He stepped back at the sight of them and bumped into something that turned out to be a knight in blue-silver armor, who looked down at him, visor raised, and the crinkles around his eyes made Gray feel a little safer.

But he brought Gray to the center of the colosseum and left him facing a man dressed in black leather with an executioner's hood, with holes in the black cloth barely revealing his eyes and mouth. He told Gray to raise his right hand, which Gray did, but the man said, "No, your right hand." Gray looked at his hand; it seemed to be the right one, but he raised the other instead. The executioner nodded and asked if Gray would promise to tell the truth. Gray nodded, but the executioner said, "You have to say the words, 'I do.'" So Gray said, "I do," and the executioner pointed to a high platform with a chair on it, and Gray climbed the steps to the top.

A huge chocolate Lab came out to him. Gray had met this dog before, and knew him to be friendly, but here he seemed different—more stern, if a Labrador retriever can be stern—and so large that he could look directly at Gray's eyes even at the top of the platform where he sat.

The Labrador retriever led Gray through the story of his mother's death, leaving out the part about the mirror—"It's not important," the Lab had said. Gray answered, "Yes," "No," "Yes."

The dog asked, "Do you see the man in this room?"

Gray pointed at the absorbing darkness who had killed his mother. "That man." The monster smiled at Gray, black on black, his mouth a fissure in the darkness revealing deeper darkness and pointy black teeth.

The Lab smiled at him and went away.

Then a hyena came, smelling of death and smiling at Gray in a way that said it was hungry. "So you were hiding under the bed during the attack. Is that correct?" the hyena said.

Gray nodded, noticing the animal's sloping back and sharp teeth.

"You need to answer out loud, please."

"Yes," Gray said.

"Then you saw his face when he looked under the bed at you."

"He bent down to look at me under the bed."

"You said you saw the attacker very clearly."

Gray nodded, then remembered he had to speak. "Yes."

"But the psychological reports say that you've had your eyes closed since you were found after the attack."

"I see everything," Gray said.

"That's good," the hyena said. He stepped between Gray and the monster who killed Gray's mother. "Would you tell the jury in your own words what the man looks like?"

"He's a black monster. So black that he sucks light away from everything else."

The hyena yipped triumphantly and walked away from Gray. The audience in the colosseum shouted, cheered, booed, stamped their feet, and the hyena walked on its hind legs around the arena waving its forepaws at them all. The emperor rose in fury and shouted at everyone, causing them to return to silence. The man Gray knew as the Blue Knight came to lead Gray from the colosseum, and the black, black man—not black of skin but black of soul—showed Gray his terrifying teeth.

It had taken a long time—until years later, when Douglas explained it—for Gray to understand what had happened that day. But on the way out of the colosseum, as strangers gathered around him and asked questions he couldn't understand and didn't know how to answer, a man came close to him, pushing through the crowd. He whispered in Gray's ear, "You're not crazy." Something the size and shape of a coin pressed into Gray's hand. "Use that to get out when you're ready."

Gray slid it into his pocket. Later, when he was alone, he looked at it. It was a small rorrim, the size of a nickel, wrapped in a leather covering. As he gazed at it, the surface shimmered, and his finger hovered over it.

He slid it back into its case and put it into his pocket.

Only when Douglas Burroughs had invited Gray to come live with him and be his son did Gray realize from whom he had received the rorrim. And at his death, Douglas's natural son, Quig, had continued to support Gray.

But Gray had never used the rorrim until a few days ago, when he also lost it.

And then he was back in the corridor only a few steps from the third door, double doors again, metal, dirty, with their paint chipped and scratched, and he knew by the smell and by the raised hair on the back of his neck that it was middle school.

He entered a long, institutional hallway, dimly lit because most of the light fixtures were broken, and the remaining lights were a sickening yellowish-bluish color that strobed in a way calculated to make a person sick—or mad. On each side were cells large enough for a couple dozen people. The prisoners—fellow students at Sellwood Middle School—leaned against the bars, staring out at Gray with hostility and derision.

He stopped to put things on a shelf, and a light out the corner of his eye caught his attention. It was a bubble of sky and sunlight enclosing a girl—a teen-aged warrior princess. She carried the light with her all the way down the hall and stopped at the shelf next to his.

Gray turned away from her, unable to bear the prospect that she would react to him way the rest of the class did.

Echo—for that's who it was—fiddled with her shelf for a while, then sighed. "Do you know how to work this thing?" She was looking at him, with closed eyes, of course, as everybody did. Then, when he turned to face her, she said, "I'm sorry. I didn't notice—"

"No problem." His heart pounded with something stronger than fear. "What are the numbers?"

She told him, and he felt the locker dial, focused on the feeling in his fingers, and opened it on the first try.

"That's amazing. I've never seen a blind safe-cracker."

He laughed. "Not blind, not cracked, not a safe." He felt something different, just being close to her, hearing her laughter—not at him, but to him, as if he were not a misfit, but someone worth knowing. He wanted to know her—and more surprising, to be known by her—almost enough to pull out the rorrim he always carried and cross back into the world everybody else saw. He stood at the branching of two paths. One took him back to the world as other people knew it. He could be normal, with friends, hobbies, activities. And with this girl who had brightened his life in only a moment, he might have a relationship. But the complications were enormous. Explaining why his eyes were open, learning to function as other people did, without the workarounds he had made for himself in this reality. And the biggest complication was the litany of what-ifs that had hounded him from the time he was seven: What if the monster comes back? What if I have no warning? What if I don't know him? Gray chose the familiar path, and the door closed.

Gray was back in the cave, which now had enough light to walk by. It quickly became a corridor and suddenly opened onto the sand. He looked around at the beach, with the steel-gray sky overhead and the distance scent and sound of the Eternal Ocean.

Where to now? he asked the absent Echo and heard her reply, You'll know where to go.

He sat on the sand until his heart stopped pounding, then stood up again and turned a full circle. He felt a tug in his chest upstream of a creek that poured itself into the ocean, and he followed it into the thick dark forest just inland from the beach.

His course took him sometimes through the forest, sometimes over the stones of the creek, sometimes wading through the cold water itself. It was a long walk, but much better than the cave. And then the creek turned a bend and widened out to a wetland of marsh grasses and dead trees.

GRAY STOOD AT THE EDGE OF THE WETLAND, water soaking through his boots. The stream widened out here to a marsh of grass, straggly bushes, and the snags of dead trees. At the center of the bog, a rocky mound protruded from the water. With imagination, he could see the remains of a stone castle. With less imagination, it was just a pile of rocks. Nevertheless, something pulled him toward that place like a winch attached to his rib cage.

He shrugged off the pull and tried to follow the creek upstream, but the draw was too strong, and he understood what Echo meant when she said he would know where to go. That pile of rocks was his destination. The only problem was that it was on the other side of brown water and black mud, and the pile of rocks on the island seemed like a good place for vermin to hide. He didn't want to go there, but Ytilaer made it clear that she didn't care what he wanted.

So he walked up and down the stream bank, looking for a route that went over or around the water. But the island was the only land that bulged above the surface, and everything around it seemed to be thick black muck that would be trouble to cross. Sometimes the only way is straight through. He took a deep breath, as if he were diving into a rorrim and took his first step into the ankle-deep shallows. Then he paused to look around for a rock or something to give a foundation to his next step.

But in that brief moment, his foot sank calf-deep in mud and kept sinking. He lunged forward, tugging his back foot out while the forward foot sank to above the knee. He flopped on his belly, pulling himself free from the mud, and when he stood to walk again, he sank chest-deep and got a mouthful of disgusting water. With great effort, he extracted himself by gently kicking his feet and clambering with his arms until he could make progress horizontally, shimmying like a salamander through mud and weeds too shallow to swim through. His heavy clothing was a drag on his progress, but he kept moving, pulling himself along by weed stems and rotting underwater snags, sometimes clawing through the mud.

Eventually, he flung himself on the bank of the island—panting, trembling, and covered with muck.

He pushed himself to his feet and wiped his hands on his pants, but they came away wetter and dirtier than they had been. His white shirt was now as brown as the water, he was covered head to foot with mud, and he trailed rotting vegetation like a swamp creature. He shook his hair from his face and started climbing, not the pile of rocks he had seen from the opposite bank but a stone plateau jutting out of the earth with almost vertical cliffs all around. When he came to a level spot about halfway up, he sat on a knee-high boulder to catch his breath. A giant stood up from behind a rock and shouted: "Who goes there?"

Gray leaped up to gape at the creature—man-shaped, greenish brown, with shaggy hair dripping swamp water. The monster's body was so caked with mud that it was impossible to say if he were naked or clothed. He held an alligator's jawbone poised to strike.

Gray stopped and held his hands out to both sides. "Who are you?"

"I asked first," the swamp creature said. "What are you doing on my island?"

"Your island?" Gray said. "I'm pretty sure it's my island."

The monster growled and raised the alligator jaw above his head but didn't come any closer.

"If you were going to attack me with that"—Gray tried to project a bravado he didn't feel—"you would have done it by now."

The ogre squinted at him but didn't lower the jawbone.

"Who are you?" Gray asked.

"Nobody."

"I'm pretty sure you're somebody," Gray said.

The ogre shrugged, then peered at Gray with his eyebrows drawn together. He lowered the alligator jawbone as if he'd forgotten it, but then lifted it again. "Did you come for the treasure?"

"Treasure?" Gray asked.

Now the ogre did lower the jawbone. "You don't know about the treasure? Why would you cross that water, then?"

"What treasure?" Gray asked again. "I came here because I have reason to believe my soul is up there."

The ogre scratched his head and looked over his shoulder up the cliff toward the top, which was invisible at this angle. "Somebody lives up there?"

"You've never been up to meet him?"

He shook his head solemnly. "I've never been invited. I'm just the threshold guardian."

Gray paced back and forth across the flat space a couple of times. "Who are you guarding it from?"

The ogre raised the jawbone again, as if posing for a movie poster. "Pretenders." He let the jawbone drop.

"You stop them with that?" Gray asked.

The ogre looked at the jawbone as if it were suddenly growling at him. "I use it to scare them away."

"What do you do if it doesn't work?"

The ogre gave a fearful glance up the cliff behind him. "The roses finish them off."

"Roses?" Gray asked. Quicksand. Monster. Roses. I know that list.

"They have thorns like daggers," the ogre said.

Naturally. "What happens to the pretenders?"

The ogre shrugged. "They run away."

"So someone could have gotten in?"

The ogre shook his head. "Not past the roses."

Gray walked to the cliff and examined it closely for a way up.

"You'll never make it," the ogre said.

Gray looked over at him, his hands already gripping rocks jutting from the cliff. "I think I will. There are handholds and toeholds here, and it's my island." He scrambled up the rock face like the mountain climber he had never been.

At the top, the roses covered the island as far as he could see. Taller than a tall man, they entirely hid the rocks, structured or unstructured, he had seen from the shore. Their blossoms were huge, with colors ranging through the red spectrum from palest pink to bold crimson. Their thorns were shining steel blades, from a half inch to six inches in length, and they seemed to be in constant movement, as if searching for prey. About two feet of bare rock separated the roses from the cliff edge, leaving room to walk around the island without engaging with the roses themselves.

Behind Gray, the ogre was pulling himself to the top of the cliff. "I'll come with you." He rolled over on his back, panting.

As Gray took a step toward the roses, a sudden wind hissed through their branches, and their knives rattled. The ogre shrank back, watching, cringing in fear.

"You say pretenders tried to get through the roses?" Gray asked.

The ogre looked uncomfortable. "Cut through, climb over, dig under."

Gray nodded. "How many pretenders have there been?"

The ogre shook his head. "Just one. He had red cowboy boots, and when he didn't defeat the roses, he gave up."

So Cain was here looking for me. I can see why he left. Gray circled the island looking for ingress. Gray was relieved that the thorns protected the princess until he took into account that they were still protecting her even from him. The rose blossoms turned toward him as he walked, and at every step, wind hissed through their stems and the knives rattled.

He kept remembering the fairy tale. He was the pretender, unworthy to wake Echo with the lover's kiss. When footprints in the dust showed he had returned to his starting place, he accepted that there was no path through. He had swum over the quicksand, and the monster—here he gave a quick glance back at the ogre sitting on the edge of the cliff, staring vacantly out at the panorama—had turned out to be less dangerous than he looked, so maybe the roses . . . ? Anyway, if Echo was waiting in the center of the island, he would find her. He plunged into the brambles.

Behind him, the ogre shouted, "Hey!" And then sounds of tumbling and crashing in his wake told him the monster was following.

But Gray was receiving vicious cuts and scratches all over his body. Some sliced his skin; some stabbed into his muscles. His clothes were quickly shredded, and even his boots were destroyed so that he left bloody prints from both hands and feet. And yet for all that, keeping the image of Echo always before him, he made progress through the thicket.

At last he looked up and saw an end to the branches and a clearing with a well-built stone house in the middle of it. In the excitement of victory, he stood and pushed the last branch out of his way. It slipped from his hand, and one of the thorns pierced his heart.

He cried out in pain and frustration, and darkness overtook him.

CHAPTER 20

# The Princess Awakes

ECHO WIPED HER HANDS ON THE TOWEL and went to pick up the orders. Number 6 and number 4 for the two men next to the window. She started to set the plates in front of them: pancakes, sausage, three eggs, and biscuits for the thin older man who looked like an off-duty cop. Just two eggs and toast with melon for the younger man with dark eyes and a thoughtful expression. He was . . . .

*What was that?* A sound, or maybe not. A presence, an absence, that shook the world like a distant explosion. "Did you hear that?"

The two men turned to her with blank expressions, as if the sidewalk had suddenly spoken to them in a strange dialect and they needed time to understand what it said.

She was standing with their plates sliding to the edge of the tray. Listening. The reverberation seemed to shake the world, but it was dying away, and she still had the tray of plates in her hands.

*Who am I? And why am I working this job?* It started as the kind of existential question anybody might ask after a long day at any work, but the plates seemed too familiar. It wasn't just that she had been doing this very thing forever; she had been doing *this very thing* forever.

She had to break the pattern. Embracing her existential frustration, she threw the plates against the counter, and they fell with a crash. Everyone in the diner looked at her open-mouthed, but now she saw that "everyone in the diner" consisted of exactly three people, herself and the two men, plus the cook's arm, raised above the bell to call her to pick up plates.

How long had she been serving breakfast to those two men, cleaning the dirty table—discovering the knife? She pulled it out of her pocket and looked at it again. It was a long switchblade with a black and silver handle, and it was covered with blood. She had seen it before. She set it on the table between the two men. "Do you know who this belongs to?" It was a real question.

The older man looked at it thoughtfully, but the younger man rose from his seat. "Let's go." He took her hand in his. It was as warm and familiar as her own spit.

She pulled her hand back, disgust fighting attraction and winning. "Who are you?"

"I feel like I've known you forever," he said. Quoting her daydream felt fake and manipulative.

Her heart *was* beating faster, but it wasn't blossoming romance. It was something darker.

"Do you feel the same?" the young man said, coming closer, putting a hand on her waist.

It reminded her of someone whose touch had a magnetic pull. But this being—whatever it was—had a reversed polarity. She pushed him away.

"We can get away," he said, moving closer again, almost touching her face with his lips but not quite. "I've got a car out front."

She pushed him away so hard he sat in the booth again. "No! No! No! You don't drive!"

She ran to the door, pulling off her apron as she ran and tossing it behind her. She burst through it—

And instead of the gray-green landscape of the rural November town, she was in a cage like ones for dogs in research laboratories, just tall enough for her to stand and wide enough for two steps lengthwise and one step across. Outside the cage, the darkness breathed like a dragon sleeping on a stolen hoard, every exhalation releasing the smell of fear and death. Everything from the diner was gone except the knife, which lay like a bloody accusation on the wire floor.

She felt bewildered, disoriented, as if she had just awakened from a powerful dream. The knife. She had tried to kill someone.

Images came back to her, ones from the diner mixed with—something else. A party, women in bikinis, a man who enraged her. Was he the one in the booth? No. Relief flooded over her. The one in the booth was based on someone real, the way a wax museum display is based on a historical person.

And the noise that woke her up? She focused on the sounds. Air. Inhalation and exhalation, rattling the walls of her cage, and outside all that, the heave and fall of the ocean.

Remembering the ocean made some memories fall into place like the key to a puzzle. She still didn't know where she was, but she knew who she was. *I am Echo.* And her name was the word she had heard. *Where is Gray?* She felt the pain of emptiness where her heart should be. Did she leave him, or did he leave her? Her eternity in the restaurant faded like the last shreds of a dream. The young man who had offered to take her away. She didn't remember him, but she remembered thinking he was handsome. She tried to recapture his eyes, but it was no good.

She studied the knife. She had tried to kill someone. She had failed—or had she?—but she felt more ashamed of failing than of trying.

There was a place, her place, always with her. The diner was better than what she was seeing, but that wasn't it.

Her esuoh. How did she get into it? She remembered a voice, someone she thought was attractive, saying, "Turn around. Stay there and turn inward." It hurt to remember that. She felt like a fool. But she let the accusation go. She had to get out of here, and it wasn't helping to remember she was a fool.

*Turn around. Turn inward.*

And she was in the familiar place with the busy, colorful decorations—faded now—and the table with dusty curtains sheltering it and the window to the outside, covered with boards as if in preparation for a disaster. The condition of her esuoh frightened her. Lightning had struck, leaving a burned streak down one wall. Termites ran along the walls and floor, and her sketchbooks were scattered about. Some lay in a pile in the corner, partially burned. There should be an upstairs, accessible out the door. But outside the door was only the cage. The porch she expected was not there, nor was the ladder to the top.

Under the rug should be a basement door, but it wasn't there. Just floor, scuffed and scratched. Did she remember correctly?

She picked up the sketchbooks from the floor and set them carefully on the table. They were only partially destroyed, and she chose one that seemed to be in the best shape to open. The ink had faded in places, but the story engaged her interest. Gray appeared there as someone kind and helpful, someone the writer of these books had loved. She felt like a stranger in this house.

There was also someone named Lazar. She had no memory of him except that he was dead. She stared at the knife. Did she kill him?

Gray was the only name she trusted, without even knowing why. She opened the door and leaned out into the dark and breathing stillness and shouted the name. The sound was muffled, as if the cage were swaddled in cotton. No one could hear her, but at least shouting broke her own silence.

CHAPTER 21

# The Lost Boy

GRAY'S EYES OPENED. What was that noise? In his dream he had thought he heard Echo shout for him. But he was lying in his own bed—

No. It wasn't his bed. It was comfortable, if a little hard and creaky, but the room was different, and two men looked down at him, one old with very white hair and the other just an overgrown—very much overgrown—child. It took Gray a minute to recognize the younger as the ogre who had followed him up the island, all cleaned up now and dressed in clothes like Gray's. When he did recognize him, the experience came rushing back, and he sat up all at once. A piercing pain in his mid-chest region knocked him back again.

He sat up more slowly this time, with the help of the old man and the ogre child, and he noticed that there were no cuts on his arms or anywhere else.

"Take it easy there," the old man said. "The last cut is the deepest." He tossed clothing on the bed—white shirt, blue pants, leather belt and boots indistinguishable from what Gray had worn—and ruined—on the way here. "You probably have questions. We'll wait for you in the other room." They went out.

Gray slipped into the pants and laced the boots. Bending was a challenge, and he moved slowly and carefully. Then he slipped into the shirt and fastened the leather belt around his waist. When he stood up, he felt more like himself. The room was stone, like the one Echo was in, but the furniture was darker and heavier—as if he and Echo were guests in different rooms of the same house.

He went out the door and found the old man and the ogre sitting in sturdy wooden chairs at a rough but well-polished table, drinking mugs of something that smelled of smoke and spices. There was a mug at a third chair, and the old man got up to pour steaming brown liquid from an iron kettle, then set the kettle on the hearth again before Gray sat down.

When the old man came back, Gray asked the question that had been tormenting him. "Where's Echo?"

The old man's eyebrows went up in surprise. "Did you lose her again?"

Gray's only answer was to hang his head.

"If she were here, you would know. No one comes here without your permission," the old man said.

Gray nodded to the ogre. "What about him?"

The ogre looked scared and sad. "You gave me permission."

The old man said to Gray, "He allowed *you* to pass. That should tell you something."

Gray pondered that riddle for a while, looking between the two men, companionably drinking from their wooden mugs. He took a sip of his own; it tasted like campfire smoke on the beach, like a winter evening when moonlight shines on snow, like a comfortable chair upholstered in leather, like fog caught in the branches of a coastal pine. The warmth eased the pain in his chest, and the ogre and the old man, sitting across the table watching him, seemed to merge into each other and then slide into separateness again.

Gray shook his head and rubbed his eyes. "What did I just see?"

In perfect synchrony, the old man and the child-ogre looked at each other and back at Gray. It was a clearer answer than they could have given in words. "Are you his soul?" he asked the old man.

"Yours, too," he answered.

Gray wondered about that, watching the steam rise from his mug. Then he looked up at them again. "Are we brothers?" Gray asked them both.

The old man smiled. "Something like that," he said, "only closer."

*Closer?* Gray thought of Echo's display, Lazar merging into his soul to protect himself from Cain. "You're my soul," he said to the old man. "You must be." Then he turned to the ogre, big but small for a giant, with a child's vulnerable face and wide-open eyes. "And you—"

"A lost boy," the old man said. "Someone left behind. He's been waiting for you."

The ogre smiled at him—a shy and hopeful smile.

"Is that all you're going to tell me?" Gray asked him.

"It's enough for now," the old man said.

"All the cuts are gone except the one in my heart," Gray said.

"The cause and cure are love."

Gray nodded. "I need to find Echo now."

The old man didn't answer, but watched with a beatific smile.

Gray rose to leave. The ogre followed him like a shy puppy hoping to adopt a new human. The old man followed both of them with a smile that said he was glad for the company, also glad for the company's departure. The roses still had knives for thorns, but a trellis formed a tunnel through their stems. "Say goodbye, Ogre," Gray said, and the ogre hugged the old man as gently as if he were his grandfather, and they walked together under the rose vines to the edge of the island.

FROM THE END OF THE ROSE ARBOR, a bridge led across the creek directly to a door on the streambank. Gray opened it and the ogre followed him into his esuoh.

Nothing had changed there. Outside the windows, Rachelle sat on a chair by the four-poster bed, pouring water back and forth, slowly and thoughtfully, as if were a task of mercy, like reading to a comatose patient.

The ogre gazed around Gray's esuoh with a smile of childish pleasure. He walked through the room, touching things as if his fingertips told him more than his eyes did. He turned back to Gray with a huge smile. "Let's play."

Gray shook his head. "We can't play now. I've got work to do."

"I want to help."

"The first thing you can do is be quiet. I need to think."

The ogre looked peevish and sat in a chair while Gray went out into the world.

At the first subtle movements of Gray's return, Rachelle stopped pouring and looked at him. "Quig, Theo, and Edward left a little while ago."

"How long have I been gone?"

Rachelle shrugged. "Ten, fifteen minutes, maybe." She poured the water twice more. "Did you find your soul?"

Gray nodded, overwhelmed at the experience. "And brought back someone." He called into his esuoh. "Ogre, come out."

The ogre came into the room, and his presence made it feel smaller.

"Nice to meet you," Rachelle said. She stood from the chair to look closer into his eyes. Her attention seemed to comfort him, and he leaned down to look closer at her. "What's your name?" she asked.

"My mama calls me Guaril."

Startled, Gray searched the ogre for something he hadn't seen before. The name had shaken loose a memory kept locked away for a reason.

"That's a nice name," Rachelle said. She glanced at Gray but kept talking to the ogre. "I bet your mama loved you very much."

Tears welled up in the creature's eyes, so incongruous as to be terrifying. "She told me to be a big boy and wait on the island."

She set down one of the pitchers to reach up and pat the ogre's shoulder. "I'm sure she would have come back if she could."

The ogre's mouth curved downward, and the tears poured like rain from an overflowing gutter. "I know. Something bad happened to her, and I couldn't help."

Gray found this conversation extremely uncomfortable. Having returned with an ogre was itself shameful, but a crying ogre was just cringeworthy. To top it all off, Gray felt like crying, too, and he didn't have time to fall apart about the times he had failed the most important women in his life.

But Rachelle was unusually oblivious. "How old are you?" she asked the ogre.

"Seven."

She glanced at Gray but continued talking to the ogre. "Were you seven when your mother left you, or are you seven now?"

The ogre looked confused. He shook his head. "It seems like she left a long time ago, but it also feels like just a few minutes."

Gray couldn't stand anymore. The pain had returned to his chest, and the two of them stood there talking as if he had no stake in the conversation.

He went into his esuoh and out onto its front porch. The scene surprised him in its quiet beauty. He had hardly ever used the porch of his old esuoh—it was just a braided rug looking out over a messy bedroom floor. Now it was a perfectly manicured lawn stretching as far as he could see, punctuated by black-barked trees with umbrella-shaped crowns, where light breezes made music in the leaves. A sense of calm washed over him, as if the wind had blown away his wounded pride and anger. His attitude toward the ogre was now more curious than resentful, and he went back inside to his cabinet of memories to fetch the box with the monster drawn on it.

He returned to his porch and created an Adirondack chair, where he sat with the box on his lap. Waves of emotion poured out of the box before he even opened it, surging like high tide in a storm. He didn't have names for all the feelings—but they gripped his guts, seized his neck, sent waves of pain up and down his back, and renewed the ache in the hole in his heart.

*Mama told me to be a big boy and wait on the island*, the ogre had said. The pain in his heart was so sharp that he folded over with his head on his knees until it faded.

When the pain was bearable, he started taking photos out of the box. There was the one of Cain tossing the black-haired toddler into the air that Cain had shown him from his own identical box in the Ugly Mug Cafe. Revulsion twisted Gray's stomach. There was a photo of Cain with Gray's mother, side by side at a carnival, with a merry-go-round behind them. *Sylviana, her name was Sylviana.* Anger burned his chest and shoulders, and his hands gripped the photo as if they would tear it. But Gray set it down and picked up the next.

It was a photo of Gray on the first day of school in second grade, the last first day of school before his mother died; he didn't know what came before that. Seven-year-old Gray stood outside the school door, with his hair all crazy and a goofy smile, wearing dark pants and white shirt. Gray knew it was himself, but the face was also the ogre's face. He flipped over the photo and saw written there, "Guaril—my small champion."

Memories flooded him like scenes from forgotten dreams. Riding a big dog bus in darkness, his mother's arms around him. Her whispered admonition that his new name was Gray; he must remember never to answer to the old one. The two-bedroom apartment with the dark green carpet, and the loneliness of being away from the grandmother and all the relatives.

And then Cain arriving in the new place in the middle of the night . . . .

A deluge of rain was falling on the park outside his esuoh, settling into deep puddles with blades of grass barely breaking the surface of the water. Wind ripped through the leaves so that the sound that had been peaceful before was now wild with anger and fear and loss.

He closed the box, hiding the monster's picture with the palm of his hand because he couldn't bear to see it now. He went inside, put the box on its shelf, and came back to the window to watch Rachelle's conversation with Guaril. She had handed him one of the pitchers, and he sat beside her chair like a happy child, taking turns with her to pour the water back and forth between the pitchers. Gray took several breaths to calm himself and went out into the room.

They both turned to him as he re-entered their circle—Rachelle with a thoughtful expression, Guaril with a hopeful half-smile.

"I remember," Gray said. It was all he needed to say.

Now Rachelle was holding both pitchers again without ever exactly taking the one back from Guaril. "Guaril has been telling me," she said. "It must be painful to have to leave part of yourself behind like that."

"It's OK," Gray said; it was almost OK. "But I think he's come back at the right time." He extended his arm to help Guaril stand. They grasped each other's wrists in a rescue grip, and Guaril disappeared from his view, but Gray felt his presence even more strongly. The scale of the room had changed: The floor was farther away, and the furniture was smaller. He went into his esuoh, and found it substantially the same, except one wall was now the hard, bright red of the most vivid roses on the island, and a red scarf had been tied around the arm of the suit of armor near the door. He didn't see Guaril anywhere, but he could feel him everywhere.

He looked out the window again at the sleeping Echo and Doris, with Rachelle meditatively pouring her pitchers beside them.

"Yes," he said to Guaril. "I think you can help." He went out into the world, crossed over into Oge, and called Travis.

## Chapter 22

# Return of the Blue Knight

Gray watched out the window of Aunt Doris's living room for Travis to arrive. Even in Oge, Gray felt Guaril's presence. He felt taller—although he certainly was not; stronger—he had carried Echo down the stairs in a fireman's carry. And another feeling—lightness, even playfulness, had short-circuited the gloom and dread he felt only a little while—*a few minutes!*—before.

When Travis arrived, Gray carried Echo out to his SUV and placed her gently in the backseat. Travis hopped out to help. "What happened to her? Hospital?"

"Your little research project." Gray watched Travis's expression change as he made the connection to the forensic bulletin board in his living room. "Two more victims, and now we know for sure that Jeph and Cain are the culprits."

Travis's eyes narrowed, and his jaw clenched. "How can I help?"

"We need to start at Jeph's office. I don't know if he'll be there, but maybe we can get a trail." Gray clicked a seatbelt into place over Echo and headed for the passenger seat.

Travis got into the car and closed the door. "So no hospital for her?"

Gray shook his head, assailed by panic. "The hospital will kill her, not knowing she's not already dead."

Travis nodded and climbed into the driver's seat. Driving over the Sellwood Bridge, he turned to Gray. "How long do we have?" He slipped into a faster-moving space in the right lane and accelerated.

"You mean how long do *I* have?" Gray tried to remember the stories his mother had told him. They came in snatches and snippets, dark dungeons ruled by terrifying monsters. Nothing coherent. "I have to go into the dungeon and let her out." He looked at Echo in the back seat, her body processes slowed to the point that it looked like death. He was angry at her for leaving him again. He was terrified at having to follow her. But he would follow.

"You there?"

He looked over at Travis. "Sorry. I guess I was drifting. What did you ask?"

"I asked how long until she really dies, but maybe a better question is the address of Jeph's office."

"Twenty-seventh floor of the US Bank Tower. Maybe Marlo can tell me where to find him." He thought about the other question. "I don't know. A day, maybe? If I knew a doctor who understands Ytilaer—"

Travis was looking at his phone.

"Uh—are you supposed to do that while you're driving?"

He handed the phone to Gray. "Call that wheelchair rental agency and have them deliver it to the US Bank Tower parking garage. I don't think you want to take her up twenty-seven floors in a fireman's carry."

TRAVIS HELD THE DOOR OPEN AS GRAY PUSHED ECHO in the wheelchair into the office of Jeph Blackthorne, Reputation Management, et cetera. No one was at the reception desk, and when the door swung shut behind them, a disturbing quiet descended on the place.

"Where is everybody?" Travis asked.

Gray shook his head. He pushed Echo down the corridor toward the entrances to Jeph's and Marlo's offices.

In the cubicle labyrinth, two people appeared to be asleep at their desks. Gray pointed, unable to speak because of the horror gripping his throat.

Travis went to the first man, who seemed to be in his thirties and had a spreadsheet open on his computer in front of him. He picked up the man's flaccid wrist, checking for a pulse.

Gray set the brake on Echo's wheelchair and followed Travis. The man's face lay on his keyboard, mouth open, gibberish in the file cell where his cheekbone had typed for him.

Travis checked his pulse. "Dead."

Gray moved in to close the man's mouth and check his eyes. They were pale blue with wide pupils like Echo's and Aunt Doris's. "No," he said with more confidence than he felt.

Travis gave him a doubting look and went to the next cubicle, where a Spock figurine stood at attention on the shelf. An overweight thirtysomething bearded man lolled back in his chair, feet sprawled, neck drooping backward, glasses askew on his face.

"Let's get him on the floor to straighten his neck." Gray took the man's shoulders and Travis took his feet, and they laid him on the floor near his desk. Gray put the man's glasses on the desk.

A shriek came from the corridor, and then a young blonde woman—with her hair wild, her makeup smeared, and her eyes wide and terrified and red from crying—shouted at them, "What are you doing here? You have to get out before Jeph gets back!"

Gray stared at her. Her fear flowed outward like ripples in a pond, with the ripples having been caused by a dynamite explosion. He had seen this woman before, but not in Oge. He remembered her as a sea turtle, long and lithe, sunning herself on a warm yellow beach—Jeph's receptionist, Meghan. "I was here a couple of days ago." He focused on the sea turtle, trying to speak to that aspect of who she was, instead of the panic that roiled her now. "Do you know what happened?"

She looked unsteady on her feet, and Travis helped her to sit in the heavier man's chair.

"They were fighting. I heard shouting but didn't see." She took deep breaths, trying to recover her calmness, while her smeared makeup gave her the face of a tragic clown. "Both saying the other one didn't keep his end of the bargain. And then it went quiet."

"Jeph and Cain?" Travis asked.

She nodded. "I came down the corridor to see what was happening. Jeph's face was red; Cain was lying on the floor. Jeph looked straight at me. His eyes were closed, but he was looking at me, and he scared me. I ran to the women's bathroom and waited a while."

"About how long ago was that?"

"I don't know. I left my phone here and was afraid to get it back." She looked at the two men unconscious at their desks. "What happened to Jack and Chris?"

Gray and Travis exchanged a glance.

"That's what we're trying to find out," Gray said. "Is Jeph still around? Do you know?"

"I haven't seen him for a while—I just came back to get my purse so I can leave." As if thinking of it for the first time, her face took on the look of a hunted animal, and she started to rise.

"Please tell us the story before you go," Travis said. "We want to help."

Her eyes shifted back and forth, Travis to Gray, as if calculating the odds. She sat leaning forward on the seat, ready to spring away, her arms against her abdomen as if holding a life preserver.

"When was the last time you saw him?" Travis asked.

"Five minutes ago, an hour. I don't know." She covered her face with her hands and leaned over her lap for a moment, then sat upright. "He came into the bathroom. I was scrunched up on the seat in one of the stalls and trying not to breathe. And then a couple of women from another office came in. One asked what he was doing there, and the other called him a pervert. He made a noise like an angry dog and left."

"OK," Travis said, "then what?"

"I sneaked out after him and followed from a distance. I saw a man getting on an elevator. I thought it was Jeph, so I went to get my purse so I could leave. But then I saw him walking down the corridor toward his office. He was talking to himself and twitching like a zombie. I ran through to the back door and up the stairs a few floors and out to the restroom on that floor."

Travis nodded, finished with Meghan for now. He asked Gray, "And you really think they're alive?"

"Alive?" Meghan almost shrieked. "When they look like—that? Why aren't you doing something?"

Gray felt her panic like an electric shock. He turned to Travis in desperation. *Come up with something*, he begged silently.

Travis made a quick, almost imperceptible nod and said, "It's a new kind of poison, absorbed through the skin. Most hospitals don't have the antidote, and the wrong treatment can kill them—" and here he gave Gray a lifted-eyebrow look that said, *You'd better be right about this.* He gave a half-shrug. "We'll get them to a specialist we know."

"What about Marlo?" Meghan asked. "She was here this morning."

The thought of Marlo suffering this fate hit Gray harder than he might have expected. He had met her only once, but she had been kind to him and had given him the path to find Echo. It had been clear that she loved Jeph with a deep and painful loyalty. Gray led the way to her office, where they found Marlo on the sofa in her office, looking as elegant as if she had drifted off to sleep. She had no perceptible pulse.

Leaving Travis and Meghan with Marlo, Gray pushed Echo into Jeph's office through Marlo's door. It was the first time he had seen it in Oge, huge and bright with reflected light. Jeph wasn't there, but Cain, dressed in black, lay sprawled on the floor like a disconnected shadow.

Also there, conferring among themselves, with quietly raised voices and many gestures, were Quig, Theo, and Edward. They looked up as Gray entered, and Theo asked, "Who was screaming?"

"Meghan, the receptionist," Gray said. Meghan entered the room as if on cue, with Travis following. "And this is Travis, who's been helping me."

Travis stepped into the room and stopped, taking everything in. He blinked in the blinding light, his eyes stopping at the supine Cain, then at the three people standing to the side, staring at him and Gray, their mouths agape.

"These are the friends I've told you about," Gray told Travis, "Quig Burroughs, Theo Greenwood, Edward Paladin." Meghan stared at them. "They're the specialists who might be able to solve this," he told her, surprised at his growing ability to lie. Meghan looked skeptical, and Gray had to admit that in this world they didn't look like the awesome characters he knew them to be: Quig the slightly frumpy attorney; Theo, black-haired and middle-aged, with hairstyle and makeup of the "artistic" type; and Edward, in a tailored but frayed gray suit, with a frailty that Gray had never noticed in Ytilaer.

Travis went forward to shake hands with the three Srelevart, speaking a meaningless greeting and observing each one with a penetrating glance.

Gray bent down to Cain and found his eyes moving back and forth like someone in REM sleep. "Cain is here!" he said.

The Srelevart gave him a look that said that was what they were discussing. Meghan looked at him as if Gray had declared Cain a snake. But Travis crouched beside Gray. "Alive?"

"Listen," Gray said quietly to him, hoping Meghan wouldn't hear. "He might be dying. I've got to talk with him before he's gone."

"And?" Travis said.

"Can you get Meghan out of here? Send her home? Put her to work?" Gray said. "She shouldn't see this."

Travis walked over and in a low murmur told the Srelevart of Gray's concerns.

Quig took a short, silent survey of the others and immediately took charge. "Meghan, it's nice to meet you. You can leave now. We've got this under control."

Suddenly the crying maiden became a warrior princess. "I don't know who you are or where you're from, but the people who work here are my friends, and I'm not going to just go away and leave them with a bunch of strangers. How do I know you're not working with Jeph?"

Theo said to Meghan in a calm and soothing voice, "Let's go together and look for other victims, then."

Meghan gave her a dubious look, "But what—" Whatever she was going to say died on her lips as Theo touched her shoulder with an expression of concentration.

"We'll just walk around the floor," Theo said, "and see what we can find."

"Just a quick walk around the floor," Meghan said, following Theo out.

Gray didn't have time to think about whatever manipulation might have happened there. He was already searching Cain for a rorrim, and in his front shirt pocket, Gray's fingers wrapped around a familiar object, smaller than he remembered. It was a leather-wrapped rorrim about two inches square. "My mother's." He stood up. "I need to talk to him now, because he can help me, if he will, and he's dying."

"If he's not like the others," Travis asked, "should I call 911 for *him*?"

Gray hesitated. As far as he was concerned, Cain deserved to die. He would likely die anyway, help or no help, but Gray didn't want to be the one to make it happen. On the other hand, if the EMTs came, they wouldn't stop with Cain. Marlo and the others, *Echo*—getting intubated, their stomachs pumped, *declared dead*. "No. I've got to do this. No outsiders."

Quig came to stand beside him. "What are you planning?"

"I've got Cain's key," Gray said. "He gave it to me. I want to ask him what happened to Echo."

"You say he's dying, but do you know what will happen if he dies while you're with him?" Quig's voice was not harsh or dismissive, but seemed genuinely concerned.

"No," Gray said. "But what other lead do we have?"

Quig looked worried but didn't answer.

"How will we find you if you get lost?" Edward asked, his worried frown belying his calm tone.

"I don't know that either, but I'll send you a message somehow." Gray looked around the room at all the sparkling mirrors. "How many of these are srorrim?"

"At least some," Edward said. "We hadn't been here long enough to discuss them when you arrived."

"I think you should collect them and put them in Travis's car. It may not be possible to keep the police away from this scene, and we don't want the srorrim to end up in evidence."

Travis looked around the room with his shoulders stiff. "This is a crime scene."

Gray looked Travis in the eye. "If we're successful, all these people will be alive and conscious, except possibly Cain, who won't have any obvious cause of death. If we're not successful, Oge police will have a mystery they can't imagine the solution to, and the srorrim will just endanger the whole crime scene team. You can store the srorrim in your car for a while, and if worse comes to worst, you can drop them off at Quig's house."

Travis pinched the bridge of his nose between his thumb and forefinger, then nodded. "How do I know which ones are which?"

"Quig and Edward can tell you. Don't forget to check Marlo's office and the conference room."

Gray sat cross-legged on the floor beside Cain, loathe to enter. He looked back at Quig. "I have to do this. He gave me his key."

Quig nodded. He opened his mouth to speak and shut it again. He waited a beat, then said, "Do you want me to come with you?"

Gray shook his head. "I don't think he'll talk with you there. I'll be back." He took a last glance at the room. Travis was already opening drawers and removing srorrim, and Edward checked a hanging display of mirrors on the wall behind Jeph's desk. Gray focused on the rorrim Cain had stolen from Gray's mother on the night he killed her and crossed over.

## CHAPTER 23

# Reunion

GRAY ENTERED YTILAER ON THE STREET of a Western ghost town. He stopped for a second, absorbing the scene. Tumbleweed lay piled at the doors of abandoned buildings, and cobwebs filled their windows. The horse troughs were dry, and the sun blazed like a consuming fire.

Cain, wearing his monster's head and cowboy outfit, lay sprawled on the street like an outlaw shot down in a gunfight.

As Gray came close to him, he rolled to his side and coughed. "Water."

Gray squatted beside him. He leaned down and loosened the cowboy-monster's dirty red bandana, disgusted but no longer afraid of him. "May I come into your house?" He felt the irony of asking this of someone who marched in uninvited wherever he wanted to go.

There was no answer, only a groan.

Taking that as a yes, Gray went into his father's esuoh. The last time he was here, the cabin had seemed sturdy if old-fashioned. Now it appeared to have barely survived a fire. Holes let in dusty light through blackened walls, and the floor crackled when he walked across it, shifting in places, threatening to break. Most of the furniture was burned, and the rest was broken beyond recognition. Animal droppings littered the floor. The boxes of memories on the shelf had crumbled to ashes, except the box Cain had shown him, which still sat on a high shelf, seemingly untouched.

"Are you back, you bastard?" Cain, now wearing his human head, sat on the floor leaning against a wall like a discarded rag doll. "You already stole everything."

Gray stepped carefully across the broken, blackened floor and hunkered down beside the decaying ego of the man who had fathered him.

The petulance broke, and a smile that captured something of the old cunning came back to his face. "Son of a bitch! It's you. I never expected you to rescue your old man."

"I'm—"

"We don't have much time. Lift me up. We've got to get Underground before this house falls apart."

Gray hardly hesitated to think. The house *was* about to fall apart, and he needed information. He leaned down and lifted the old man to his feet. He felt strength flow out of him and into Cain until Cain could stand on his own. Instinct told Gray to run away, but the sacrifice was a small price to pay to find Echo and end all this. When he did let go, Cain shook out his limbs and walked a few steps. The house looked sturdier as well. Gray felt as drained as he would after a long day of intense stress.

Cain opened his basement door and held it open for Gray to lead the way. "Are we going to your soul?"

"Ha! I got rid of that parasite decades ago. I am the king of my castle." He waited for Gray to step into the darkness and descend a few stairs. Then he closed the door behind them, shutting out all the remaining light. "Such as it is." Cain's voice, slightly crackly like his floor, came out of the thick darkness like a ghost's. "Next time it'll be something more modern."

"Next time?"

He clapped Gray on the shoulder, almost knocking him down the stairs and leaving him feeling even more tired. "Wait'll you hear my plan."

Gray found his way by touching each riser with his heel and setting his foot solidly on the step before beginning the next. "It's slow going. Aren't there any lights down here?"

"I don't need lights. You can make some."

Gray decided against that expense of energy. "You should go first, so I can hear your footsteps."

Cain laughed. "I want to keep an eye on you."

The stairs ended abruptly when Gray ran into a stone wall.

Cain gave a loud guffaw behind Gray and pushed past him. He pressed his hand against the stone, and a starlit beach appeared through a door-shaped opening, with the Milky Way like a river of diamonds in the sky. A track through the sand led away from the ocean.

"Follow that." Cain gave him a little push, and at his touch Gray's energy flowed away. Gray grew weaker with each of these nudges, and fear beat at the door of his esuoh as he wondered where Cain was taking him.

He could, he hoped, turn off the path and run somewhere to escape. He hoped but wasn't sure, and for now this was his only route to Jeph, to Echo, and possibly home. He was pretty sure Cain was operating on borrowed time, and since it was Gray's time he seemed to be borrowing, that was a matter of concern.

A gravel road began, with fist-sized chunks of rock that rolled under Gray's feet as he walked, threatening at every step to throw him off balance and pitch him to the ground.

A black shape emerged from the treeline, like an eldritch god crouching to sniff for prey.

As they came closer, the shape resolved into a building of black stone, its design a cross between Art Deco and the Palace of Cthulhu.

"Beautiful, isn't it?" Cain's voice came disembodied out of the darkness.

"Not the word I'd choose."

Cain pushed Gray toward a vertical rift in the monstrosity, high enough for Godzilla to pass with its head held high. "Here's the door." Gray shuffled wearily in that direction, torn between hoping he would find Echo and hoping she hadn't been exposed to that monstrosity.

They entered the portico, carved in characters that repeated at different intervals like letters in an unknown language. Out of the corner of his eye, the figures depicted savage appetites, a thirst for madness, a hatred for everything illumined by goodness. But when he looked directly at them, they were simply letters in an unknown language, like sociopathic schoolboys pretending to be good when the teacher's watching.

The building was dark and empty of people but held a warren of intersecting passages with half-height windowed doors into rooms too small to stand or move inside. The doors stood open, and the cells were empty. The place stank of fear and death.

"You should have seen this place before Jeph got me. Somebody in every room. I know you think I'm a monster, but I was good to them. I gave them a nice reality to live in. They were content. They were just a calm and constant source of power, saved from what's beyond the blue light. This is what he did to me."

Gray looked at Cain with panic. "Jeph did this?"

"Emptied it from bottom to top." Cain sounded half outraged, half admiring.

Gray surveyed the building again. "He released them? How?"

"Released them? You're dumber than I thought." He wandered through the cells, occasionally looking inside one and closing its door. "He took them to the prison *I* helped him build." He turned to Gray, indignation distorting his face. "He wasn't stronger than I am—was—until he betrayed me." He walked closer to Gray, fists balled at his sides.

Gray waited calmly, the knowledge of what Cain wanted from him slowly dawning.

"You're making plans already," Cain said. "I can see it in you. Look, I tried to tell you, between Jeph and me, I'm not the bad guy."

Gray held himself very still, looking directly forward, willing himself not to roll his eyes. "Why should I believe *he* betrayed *you*?"

"Lazar was the key to it. If everybody is a Christmas light, that guy was a fucking power plant—and he knew nothing about himself or the dream world. I tried to take him a few times while I was in prison, but he was too quick for me. I accidentally taught him some things, and that made him stronger. I managed to add a few souls to my collection there, but it wasn't enough, and Lazar told the rest of the inmates to stay away from me."

"Why are you telling me all this?" Gray asked.

"Because it's important, goddammit." He shouted and waved his arms like an old man yelling at the TV. "Lazar was *mine*. I set up the plan. *I* warned Jeph that Lazar was planning to get back at him—although he didn't figure out my part in it until later. *I taught him how to take a soul.*" The place seemed to shiver in sympathetic passion, and Gray took a step back from him.

Cain reached forward and grabbed Gray's shoulder with a clawlike grip. He spoke more quietly but with the same intensity. "He was supposed to help me. I wasn't strong enough alone, but the two of us would have been. There was only one Lazar—we couldn't split him or anything—I get that—but Jeph would have been well compensated"—and here he gave a quick sharp look at Gray that spoke some nameless horror about the compensation—"but he sacrificed it all because he couldn't stand for Lazar to continue to exist, even when Lazar could never be any danger to him."

"What could Lazar do to Jeph?"

Cain grimaced. "That's where my hook paid off too well. I got Jeph interested by telling him Lazar had new evidence of Jeph's role in the crash. There's no statute of limitations for murder."

"But Lazar was just living his life, wasn't he?" Gray asked.

"Oh, but that life. Laid out before me like a condemned man's last meal." He paused in remembered rapture. "If you had seen it, you would understand."

"Like Echo," Gray surprised himself by speaking aloud—she was blindingly bright and lit every corner with her exuberance.

Cain nodded with a lustful smile. "Gotta give it to you, boy. You know how to pick them."

Gray had loved Echo from the first day he saw her and never quite knew if others in Ytilaer saw her as he did. But now Cain stood in stark contrast to the Srelevart, who wanted her to mature before entering Ytilaer, whereas Cain and Jeph wanted to bring her in to eat her light for their own power. Gray's knees buckled, and he recovered himself to find Cain's hand clutching his forearm. "Look, if you wipe me out, I can't do anything for you," Gray said.

"We haven't established that you're going to do anything for me anyway," Cain said, but released his arm. "If you bring them back to me, I'll release the girl."

"What about my mom?"

"You're not in a position to negotiate. I'm your last hope."

"And I'm yours."

Cain gave him a sharp look. "You know her body's dead and buried." He raised an eyebrow at Gray, who felt the guilt that his childish call to 911 had caused his mother's death in the county morgue. "If she comes back to me, I'll keep her alive. If you let her go, she'll be burned in the blue fire."

Gray remembered Echo's display for the Srelevart. "You mean the portal that opened when you killed Lazar?"

"What do you know about it?" Cain leaned into Gray's space, his eyes wide and nostrils flaring. "You weren't there."

Gray resisted the urge to retreat. "I saw Echo's memories."

"I didn't kill Lazar. That son of a bitch Jeph did, to keep me from taking his soul. And the light—oh, God—the light burns like fire. You saw what happened to my house." Cain stared at the ground, looking older and more decrepit than ever.

Gray waited for Cain to go on. After a while, he asked his own burning question—that didn't come out as a question at all. "Echo didn't say anything about the fire burning."

Cain looked at him now, and he could swear the pupils of Cain's eyes glowed red. "She wouldn't know anything about it, would she? There's something out there—bigger than the world—and it hates people who threaten its power."

The ground shook, and a crack opened across several nearby cages. Cain sagged against a wall. "You saw my esuoh. Jeph killed Lazar and me at the same time and let Lazar get away from me." His attention drifted to a spot over Gray's shoulder and then came back to Gray— "And that girl of yours helped him. I don't let that kind of thing go lightly, but if you'll help me—"

Cain was fading fast. Gray could almost see the toothless old monster under the face of the man, ravaged like a cancer patient. A new emotion crept through, one he would never have expected to feel for this man: pity. His only fear now was that Cain would die before telling him how to rescue Echo. He grabbed Cain's arm and held him up until he could stand alone. "How do I release them?"

"Release?" Cain struggled to stand on his own legs. "Not release, you bastard. Bring them back." His anger and bitterness gave him a boost. "If I tell you, you have to bring them back." He sagged against the wall again, mumbling. "They're all that can protect me from the blue fire." An earthquake shook the place again, but Cain stood himself up to his full height and looked Gray in the eye. "A promise. In Ytilaer. My prisoners for the girl. You can keep her, you can let her go, but that's the deal." He smiled his cunning smile.

Gray felt weak. The effect of Cain's withdrawals from Gray's energy bank were accumulating. His knees and hands were shaking, and there was emptiness in the pit of his stomach as if he hadn't eaten in days. He well understood what Cain was demanding—more than the captives—and promising—more than Echo. If he fulfilled this bargain, taking the captives into himself even temporarily, he would become what Cain was—or, worse, what Jeph was. And Echo would *belong* to him. He could keep her in prison or let her live in the outside world, but she would be *his*, not her own. As tempting as that could be at certain moments, it was not tempting now, when the decision was on the table. But would it be better to have her in those circumstances than leave her to Jeph?

In his weakness, Gray felt despair like the weight of the ocean, and despite all he knew, he began to waver in his resolve to reject Cain and all his darkness. In that moment, Gray opened his mouth to speak but stopped when he heard a voice in his esuoh whispering to him. Cain watched Gray, pleased and cunning, aware that he had Gray cornered. But the voice inside insisted, "Hey!"

Gray left Cain where he stood and went into his own esuoh.

An ancient man was there, sitting in Gray's leather chair, an older version of Cain. *Cain's soul?*

"Cain said you were dead," Gray said.

"Not dead yet," old Cain said with a grin. "You woke me up."

Outside his esuoh, Gray heard Cain shouting, "Where are you, you bastard? Listen to me! I deserve an answer!"

"Lock the door," the old man said.

"I've never been able to keep Cain out," Gray told him. "He just marches in." Outside the window, Cain was red-faced, shrieking. "And here you are."

"Just lock the door," the old man said. "I'm all the strength he's got left, and we need your help."

Gray created the best lock he knew and braced himself for the pitch.

"Don't say another word to Cain, but listen to me. When the portal opens, Cain will go in screaming, and I'll go after him. You have to let us go, no matter how pitifully we beg. After we're gone, the last earthquake will destroy his esuoh and crack his prison. There'll be a fissure in the wall. Go straight through, turning neither left nor right. It will take you to the road to Jeph's prison. From there, you're on your own."

"Why are you doing this?" Gray asked.

"I have a question you can't answer: What is the value of a single act of love?" Old Cain looked intently into Gray's eyes. "That's why you must do exactly as I say: Don't answer Cain in any way, and allow us to enter the portal. If you accept this gift I give you now, we *might* live. If you try to save us, we die."

"But death comes to everyone," Gray said.

"Death comes many times, causing all manner of fear and upset. But the one death is more monstrous than all our fears. And facing those fears is the price of surviving it."

Gray studied his father's soul, who, in return, eyed Gray intently, as if appraising his capacity for—he had no idea what. As he reached the door, the old man said, "Hey." He was pointing at the armor Lazar had given him. "You might need that."

Gray allowed the old man to help him put it on. Then he went out to await death with his father.

ALTHOUGH GRAY HAD LEFT HIS ESUOH WEARING THE ARMOR, when he returned to the horrific chamber which had held Cain's prisoners, he could neither see nor feel it on himself. He didn't have time to worry about it, because Cain looked up at him with a petulant expression, pushed himself away from the wall, and walked toward Gray with his hand held out.

Gray stepped away from him. It was too late for Cain, and Gray didn't have much more energy to give.

"What the hell?" Cain said. "After everything I've done for you?"

Gray opened his mouth to respond, but he remembered Cain's soul's words. *Don't say a word.* As hard as it was not to protest or explain, Gray held himself in a rigid silence.

"Where did you go, anyway?" Cain asked. "We were negotiating."

Gray held his head as still as his tongue. He didn't want to give any answer to Cain's request, neither yes nor no, because he didn't want to become entangled in any sort of promise in Ytilaer.

"What happened to you in there?" Cain asked. "You chickened out, didn't you? I knew you were worthless."

Gray breathed very slowly, wondering when the end would come. Whatever Cain's faults—and there were many—he was observant. What would happen if he knew that Gray had conspired against him—with Cain's own soul? Would it make Gray's mission more difficult? Impossible? When the portal opened, how hard it would be to do the thing Cain's soul had asked. Why would he listen to Cain's soul anyway? Cain himself was a liar; was it reasonable to think his soul was different?

Cain's focus had zoomed in on Gray, watching the march of his thoughts across his face.

"You've got a plan," Cain said, "and I'm out of it." He pushed himself closer to Gray, close enough to grab Gray's arm, but his hand closed on nothing, like an invisible force field enveloping him. Lazar's armor. Gray was relieved.

Cain was outraged. "You lying son of a bitch!" he shrieked. "You're worse than me. Worse than Jeph!"

The insults reached Gray more successfully than Cain's touch. Gray's own outrage grew in response, but he held himself under strict control, until the earthquakes started again.

Cain was jumping up and down like Rumpelstiltskin on being named, and at each landing, the building shook, causing cracks to split the walls and pieces of the ceiling to fall. Gray sheltered his head with his arms, but none of the falling debris touched him.

And then there was a crack so loud that it seemed the earth was opening to give birth to a moon. An almond-shaped hole in reality opened; it had white margins that shaded into blue-black darkness at the center. Cain screamed, piteous and terrified, and Cain's soul appeared beside him. He gave Gray a significant look, then took Cain's elbow and guided him toward the light. Cain fought him and pulled back, and his soul shepherded him as if he were a small child reluctant to see the doctor. But as they drew closer to the light, they were both screaming, the flesh searing off their bones, and their skeletons walking against a great wind, their skulls' mouths open in a soundless scream.

Gray turned away. *We might live*, Cain's soul had said. *If you try to save us, we die.* As if Gray had any way to save them from that. And yet for the first time, Gray felt something for his father—not hate, indifference, or even grudging acknowledgment of one supremely adept at evil. A sense of loss, sadness for what might have been, and a small flicker of something that might, under other circumstances, have been love. It was there and then gone, like a diaphanous flame leaping out of an ember and dying away again, but leaving the ember awaiting the next breath to awaken it.

When Gray turned away from the cave wall, the entire prison was gone, leaving him alone in a huge cavern with a crack in one wall wide enough for a man to slip through.

CHAPTER 24

# The Labyrinth

EYOND THE CRACK WAS VELVET DARKNESS, heavy with hopelessness and fear. Holding one hand against the wall of the cave—*Go straight ahead*, Cain's soul had said—Gray took a step forward in the darkness, then another and another, and he was walking again. With his right hand trailing along the damp wall and his left hand stretched out for obstacles, he shuffled through the gloom.

The ground sloped downward, and water rose to his ankles, knees, chest, chin, mouth. And then, still tasting the sharp salt flavor, he walked upward as the water level went down. Drenched and cold, he kept walking.

The cave ended at a glass wall with a wooden door in it. He recognized it as the office of Jordan Ross, CEO of Talking Autism PNW, as it would appear in Oge, even though he had seen it only in Ytilaer. Could there be a connection between Jeph and the job Gray had held for about four hours Tuesday? But Cain's soul had said, *Go straight ahead*, and Gray opened the door and walked in.

Inside, there were details about the office he hadn't noticed through the glass. For one thing, the rug in warm browns and blue seemed to have come directly from Gray's esuoh. And the dark wooden desk had a brass nameplate saying "Gray Birdsong."

That sent a shiver down his spine, because in his secret wishes for the future, he held a dream of being responsible, competent, respected. He looked around the office again. It felt like that dream.

On the credenza behind the desk was a picture of a woman. She looked like Echo, but different. No scars on her face, which shouldn't bother him because he had never seen them until recently. Something else. The eyes were cast down. The smile seemed shy and uncertain, lacking Echo's bold directness. He turned from the photo and was about to leave when there came a soft knock on the door Gray had come in through. He waited for it to open, but the knock came again, just a trifle louder.

"Come in," Gray said.

A tousle-haired blond man in his mid-twenties peeked around the door. He wore an off-the-rack suit and a shirt too wide at the neck. "A minute?" The face looked vaguely familiar, but the voice was unmistakable. It was Buzz, Gray's supervisor from his half day of internship.

Gray measured him with his eyes. "Sure."

Buzz entered, and the world beyond the door was sensible carpet and beige walls, not the cave Gray had arrived through. "I'm sorry," Buzz said, looking like he meant it. "It's about the new intern."

Gray was intrigued. "What about him?"

"I don't think he's going to work out. He seems smart, but . . . ." He made a face with his mouth downturned.

Gray waited a beat for him to finish, then prompted him. "But what?"

Buzz looked up into a corner of the room, as if a random spider might provide an answer for him. "It's like—" He stopped, tried again. "He thinks he knows the hard things, but he doesn't know the easy things."

"Can't you teach him?"

"Teach him to read?" The guy shook his head. "I asked him to bring me coffee, and he came back with Caroline's mug."

With a sinking stomach, Gray recognized that intern as himself. He picked up a random page off his desk and looked it over. The words flowed into him in all their jargon-laced glory; he saw a typo. He easily checked the total of the column of five-digit numbers. These were mystical powers of Oge he had never learned. Until crossing over, he not seen the meaningless squiggles on paper in Oge, and they certainly had never spoken to him, unless through some chance of Ytilaer, he found the deeper meaning within.

His hand trembled slightly as he set the paper back on his desk. Was this a warning, premonition? A temptation to leave his mission? He felt it. To be competent. Respected. To have problems that could be solved by sending two employees to lunch to get to know each other better. He took a last glance at the young man, waiting for his answer, and at the woman in the photo, Echo and yet not Echo. The beige walls spoke to him louder than the words on the paper. He turned and walked through the wall opposite the door and into the cave again.

The cave was dark and wet, with ocean on its breath. He kept walking.

He came to the front door of the house Quig had inherited from his father. Inside, the living room and dining room were the same, but the furniture was different. Two children sat at the dining room table, the older girl—brown-skinned with thick black hair—doing homework, the younger boy—with spiky red-gold hair—coloring. They weren't Quig's kids. He looked around the rooms—everything was tidy and in order. Julia, Quig's wife, was highly organized and disciplined, but she couldn't keep things this neat.

A woman stepped out of the kitchen—the Echo/not Echo from the photograph—and asked how Gray's day had gone. She was as put together as the house was. Not 1950s formal, but her long hair was in a neat pony-tail, and her clothes were well-kept and attractive. "Dinner will be ready in a few minutes," she said to the kids. "Better get cleaned up." They calmly and quietly began putting away their projects. Then to Gray, "Can I get you a drink or anything?"

Gray's heart was pounding. Was this life a possibility? If he continued in the illusion, would it become his reality? If he did, what would happen to the Echo he knew and loved? He practically ran through the house and out into the cave.

The third door opened to the Srelevart's sanctuary, but there was no Snow White rorrim beside the inner door. Gray walked in Ytilaer; he hadn't left since he joined Cain on his journey to death, and yet in this dream within a dream, he was in Oge, in the carpeted basement of Quig's house with stacking chairs arranged in a circle and a simple wooden lectern at the front. The people in the chairs turned to watch him walk in, and he realized with a shock that none of them had their eyes closed. It was a meeting of the Srelevart, and no one was in Ytilaer.

Rachelle and Caryn were there, Rachelle without her pitchers, and Caryn looking like a suburban mom at a self-acceptance meeting, along with others he didn't know. Quig, Theo, and Edward were absent.

They shifted comfortably in their seats as Gray took his place in front of the lectern. The other Echo sat in the front row, looking up at him with the same admiration the others showed. In his shirt pocket, he found notes for a lecture titled "Dream Symbolism and Consciousness."

Racked with shaking, he ran out of the room and into the cave again, where he vomited onto the damp sand. He sat with his back against the cave wall, shivering and wondering again if this was an option or a preview. He went into his esuoh and checked to make sure the death key he had received from Theo was still there. It was, hidden in his memory cabinet, wrapped in its cloth and undisturbed. He started walking again.

He came to a place where the roof had caved in, and a big orange moon hung in the sky like a balloon. A pile of rocks lay under the hole, and a knotted rope hung down from above. Gray climbed it out to a grassy hillside littered with copses of small, spiky trees, with no ocean in sight. The moon was so bright that visibility was nearly one hundred percent, but the markings on the moon were wrong.

"What are you doing here?" The voice coming from behind him was familiar, but so startling that Gray almost fell backward into the cave again. It was Mitch, in his brown robe and holding his lantern.

Gray stared at him for a few seconds, waiting for him to morph into something else. "Are you you, or am I dreaming you?"

Mitch shrugged and created two boulders suitable for sitting. "Want to talk about it?"

Gray sat gratefully, resting his face on his knees. "I fell asleep in one nightmare and woke up in another." He raised his head to look at Mitch. "The other nightmare wasn't bad—except that's what was so bad about it."

Mitch nodded thoughtfully. "I have no idea what you mean, but we must be here for a reason." He thrust his lantern's pole into the ground and set his elbows on his knees. "So, from nightmare to nightmare. And you've brought me here. Why?"

"You saw Echo at the meeting today?" Gray examined Mitch's face, looking for a clue whether he was really Mitch or a dream creature of Gray's. "And Theo?"

Mitch nodded noncommittally.

"Well, I went to my soul." He was so accustomed to the Srelevart's expressions of shock that he paused a beat for Mitch to react.

Mitch hardly reacted at all. "That's usually frowned on. Why did you do it?"

Gray thought about that. "Echo told me to." It wasn't a satisfactory answer, but it was all he had right now.

That got raised eyebrows from Mitch, then a nod. "I guess she seems the sort. Would you have gone without her telling you?"

Gray sighed. "I don't know. I haven't had time to think about it." He looked off over the landscape; not a sign of human habitation anywhere. "What about you? Why did you go to your soul?"

"I had to know if the things I told my congregation were true."

"And?" Gray tried to wait silently, even though he had been wondering about Mitch for a long time.

"It's hard to tell the truth in Oge. All you can do is skim along the surface of Ytilaer, who hides bigger realities in her depths."

"Is that why you left your family?"

Mitch shook his head. "It's why they left me. They didn't know how to listen, and I didn't know how to tell the truth I knew." A deep sadness crossed his face. He opened his mouth to speak again, but a noise in the brush interrupted him.

Crashing and howling came from somewhere unseen, and then an enormous creature with shaggy fur and a curved horn protruding from its snout blasted from a thicket, followed by brown-skinned men in loincloths chasing it with spears. They whooped and shouted as they ran, throwing their spears with intensity and purpose, and the wooden shafts entered the thick hide and hung from it like flopping toothpicks. The beast entered another thicket, and the men followed it.

Gray and Mitch sat silently on their boulders and watched the men and beast run by.

Gray nodded and stood up.

"Did you get your answer?" Mitch asked, standing up and taking his lantern in hand.

"Not the one I was asking, but the one I wasn't asking."

"What was the answer?"

Gray shook his head. "Sometimes you have to get up and chase the bull."

Mitch looked at Gray with his head tilted slightly, then nodded. "Need any help?"

"All we can get," Gray said.

"Give me a key, and I'll see what I can do," Mitch said.

"What?" For the Srelevart, keys were dangerous, unpredictable, creating vulnerabilities. "I've never made a key before."

"Do you know how?"

*Just make a thing and load it up with meaning*, Echo had said. "I guess."

Mitch waited a few more seconds. "Suit yourself." The boulders disappeared.

"Wait," Gray said. He picked up a rock from the ground. It was red and felt like sandstone. He held it tight and remembered this moment—Mitch and himself in this alien place—with all the surprise, wonder, gratitude, and terror the situation contained. When he opened his hand, the stone was carved into a brick with a spiral etched in it. He held it out to Mitch, who took it with the loose end of one sleeve and disappeared into his esuoh.

Gray climbed down the rope into the cave and started walking again, either miles and miles or only a few yards until the cave opened onto a moonlit beach.

GRAY STOOD FOR A WHILE ON THE BEACH, watching storm clouds roll in from over the ocean and feeling the forerunning winds stirring up sand that flew into his eyes. Aside from the storm, there was no sign of life, only the unbroken seashore in the cold twilight.

He felt more than heard something like what Echo said when she was silent. It was the same magnetic force he felt when he was searching for his own soul. In response, he turned inland.

He waded across the stream that might—or might not—have led to his soul's castle and kept walking over dry sand toward the forest, holding his memory of Echo in his mind. A blacktop path emerged from the sand and grew to a bike path to a service road to a road wide enough for two construction vehicles to pass side by side. At the end of it was an imposing building like a black hole in the starlight until he came close enough for the faint light to illuminate it.

Jeph's prison—for Gray never doubted that was where he had arrived—was laid out in irregular blocks and chunks that had no relation to form or function or the landscape. If it were in the physical world, everyone who walked into it would be reminded at every moment that they were widgets with no purpose of their own, existing only for the benefit of the intelligence that created the building. It gave Gray a deeper sense of dread than Cain's prison, for that at least acknowledged the gravity of evil. Jeph's prison, in its pristine and urban ugliness, denied the existence of evil—and therefore of goodness as well—gaslighting the viewer by its very existence.

Gray's heart quailed before it, but he followed the road he had chosen, and the clarity of Echo's call seemed to fade as he neared the place.

He pressed Cain's key against the door, and he heard a lock click. The door swung open wide enough for him to pass. Apparently, Jeph and Cain's partnership hadn't fully dissolved yet. The door swung shut behind him with a sound like thunder. Gray felt hope stripped away, leaving only the desire to find Echo and die with her if necessary.

Cages, thousands of cages—some empty, most with people in them; some dark, some giving off an insufficient light like a dying flashlight in a dark cave—stood stacked on each other, up to a ridiculous height. When he tried to follow the stack with his eye, the ranks of cages swooped over him as in a surrealistic painting, stretching into a curving aisle. Everywhere he looked, the view changed; the objects themselves didn't move, but he felt himself spinning—or falling—into a different angle on the world. The result was a stomach-churning geometry, with everything folded in upon itself, and the vanishing point everywhere he looked.

How would he find Echo in all this? He reached out and touched a dark cage. The slim metal bars were like a dog crate, but black fog filled it like a conscious thing, both dead and alive, pulsing with desire to fill the world with itself. Gray's hand felt as if it would freeze to the metal.

He jerked his hand away and walked to the next lighted cage. In it, a man in old-fashioned clothes sat on a wooden sidewalk in an empty street. It was mid-afternoon, and he was utterly alone. He waited for someone to come to his shop, the door open behind him, and no one ever did. His expression spoke of boredom on the verge of panic.

Further along, a legless old man with a vertical scar on his face sat on a rolling platform next to a wall on a city street. He had jars of flowers beside him, and legs walked by like a moving forest in a continuous loop—the pattern of shoes and skirts and pants repeating every ten seconds. The old man shook his fist at the passers-by, who neither stopped nor turned in their passage.

There was a black-haired girl driving a yellow Mustang convertible with its top down, through flat fields that never changed. Her lips mouthed "Born to be wild" over and over again. He watched for a while to determine if it was Echo and finally walked away empty.

Gray wandered for days or years, always stopping to look into the next cage before him. An aisle always curved away into the distance, but he never came to a crossroads, never a place where he could make a rational search, just an endless display in a rolling maze. Still, he looked carefully at every cage, doubt growing whether he would recognize Echo in disguise—or even as herself.

And then he saw a woman who made his heart stop. By now, he was so confused that he thought she must be Echo. He looked at her as if she were a museum display. Someone important. But not Echo. He held the bars of the cage—which felt like metal but were not painfully cold as the cage of darkness had been. He stared at her, searching his mind. She wasn't much older than Gray, mid-twenties maybe, sitting at a kitchen table, wearing faded overalls and a sky-blue hoody, looking at a magazine. Her hair was thick and dark, and her face—even in the serenity of the moment—showed strength and intensity. The clock on the wall said five minutes to three. The second hand swept around, and the minute hand clicked forward and then back. The woman looked up at the clock and down at her magazine.

He leaned his head against the bars and stopped thinking. Tears and loneliness rose up within him. Might it be sympathy for the woman, even though she seemed neither sad nor lonely? Water welled up in his eyes, and a mean boy spoke from his distant past, from the first foster home, which he had almost succeeded in forgetting—*You're a big baby*. And then Guaril's voice from within himself, "Mama."

Gray looked up in wonder. She was his mother.

He banged on the bars and looked for a door. She didn't look up.

He shouted, and she didn't hear. He leaned his back against her cage and saw all the others swirling around him, as if they were in a slow-moving blender. He turned back in panic and grabbed the bars, afraid he had lost her. But she was still there, and she turned the page of her magazine.

Then he remembered Cain's key. He pulled it out of his pocket and stared at it. It seemed both possible and impossible that it should work, but he pressed it against the bars. The walls disintegrated, leaving his mother sitting on the floor of her cage.

She woke slowly and looked around. She wrapped her arms around herself as she took in her surroundings—the darkness, the smell of misery, the caged people around her—an old veteran reading the banner headline of a newspaper about war being declared, a woman whose child was running into the path of a car on the street, a child watching his dog die under the knife of a passing sociopath.

Gray stepped forward into the space her cage had been. He held out his hand to her. "Mama."

She looked over at him, her facial expression geared for horror, then surprise and confusion. She looked back to where the room had been, but found only shadows. "I need to get my son from the bus stop. What time is it?"

"It's OK. I am your son."

He led her outside the space where the cage had been. An opening formed around them, and the other cages closed in. She came close and inspected his face. "You have his eyes." She stepped back into a longer view. "Who are you, really? Cain?"

"I really am your son. I'm nineteen now, and we're in the prison of a man named Jeph, who stole Cain's prisoners."

"So I'm dead, then."

Her tone was a simple statement, but he felt it as an accusation. "Not quite. Not all of you. No one knew. I would have come for you."

"Shh." She spoke as if to her small boy waking from a nightmare. "I know. What's past is past. Is Cain dead?"

Gray nodded.

"Did you kill him?"

"I wanted to, but no."

"Did he make you like himself?"

"I had a foster father, a good man."

She sighed and patted his hand. "That's good then." She nodded once, and her eyes gradually went unfocused, and she turned in a circle, taking in everything. Then she turned to him again. "Who are you?"

Anguish rose in Gray. If he could have imagined this moment at any time since his mother's death, it would have been pure joy. Having her beside him, even if only for a few minutes, even if only her ghost, would have been a chance to tell her he still loved and honored her. But she looked at him with nonrecognition in this place of horror.

"Look at me, Mama. I'm the same person, just older."

She looked at him steadily for what felt like a long time, then nodded.

"Come into my esuoh," he said. "It's not so horrible."

Fear came into her face. "Who are you?"

"I'm your son. I love you."

"But I'm waiting for him to come home on the school bus."

"Come wait inside," and he took her hand and led her into his esuoh.

She walked in with her eyes wide. Taking in the painting on the wall, she asked, "Is that Cain? It's been so long—"

"No. That's Douglas. The man who chose to be my father. Here. Sit down." He made the ornate wooden rocking chair she had enjoyed sitting in when she was alive. "Be comfortable."

She didn't sit. "You are not a prisoner here?"

"Not yet."

"You came of your own will, but not for me." Again, not an accusation, but a statement.

"I didn't know." The pain of leaving her here, with her life on hold, her body decaying in the ground, ate at him. How could he not know?

She sat in the chair and made another one right in front of her. "Sit there and look at my eyes as we talk."

He sat.

"Give me your hand."

He did.

She stroked his fingers, and he felt the irony that now his hand contained hers, when the last time they met, it had been the other way around. "So you came for a girl—a very special girl."

Gray sighed. "I don't know how I'll ever find her."

"But you found me. Ytilaer has her ways. You stirred things up by—opening my cage." She walked to his front windows. "Let's see what's coming."

They looked out the window and found a man-sized bird walking toward them. More than man-sized, seven feet tall, with a pink bald head and a gray-on-gray beak that looked capable of ripping flesh. The bird spoke with Jeph's voice. "I've been expecting you."

Gray told his mother to stay in the esuoh and stepped out. The bird covered the distance to him in just a couple of hops. It looked at him with its red eyes, turning its head this way and that. "I don't know how Cain let you in. I should have changed his locks before now, but I've been busy." A noise reverberated through the echoing silence, thousands of clicks not quite in unison.

Cain's key, which Gray had forgotten he was holding, crumbled to dust in his hand.

"I guess you won't need that anymore." The bird flapped its wings, stretched its neck, and by what appeared to be a mighty effort, made itself appear as a man. He was the Jeph who could have been a movie heartthrob, except now he looked like a fading star: a little thin on top, a little thick around the middle, his nose showing the effects of too much alcohol. And even that image glitched occasionally, revealing the vulture with its bald head and hunched neck, its red eyes measuring Gray by its hunger. Gray shivered, knowing there was no place to run even if he wanted to.

Didn't matter. He wasn't going anywhere without Echo.

"I guess you've had a chance to check out my guest house." Jeph looked around appreciatively and spoke with an edge of sarcasm that he could deny if he wanted to, putting the entire burden of anger on Gray, even while provoking Gray's anger, a cycle of malevolence that started working right away.

"Easy," his mother said from inside. "He's working you."

"Did your old man send you over? I suppose my sympathies are due. It must be hard to meet your long-lost father and then have to say goodbye so soon." He looked Gray up and down with an appraising eye. "I can see he's done something with you. Your years with the Srelevart made you weak and pathetic. Now you're only weak, not as pathetic, so you owe him that."

Gray watched Jeph's mouth move, the muscles of his face creating gestures that were supposed to have an effect on him. All the time, he was wondering how he would find Echo in this maze.

"Did you expect to find your mother here?" Jeph looked this way and that. "Somewhere. I guess you found her before I did." He smiled. "Cain was proud of her, but never showed her to me. I might—you know—take her out, do something with her. She could decorate my esuoh."

Gray's anger grew. He didn't even know if the threat was a possibility, but he wouldn't put anything past Jeph.

"That seems to disturb you. Maybe I should ask your permission. But you did leave her to rot in Cain's prison all these years. No one could expect you to care."

Gray's blood thrummed in his head. But his mother spoke from within. "We're together now."

"Where's Echo?" Gray asked.

The question jarred loose a fault in Jeph's attention, and before the silence of the waiting darkness filled the hall again, Gray felt the magnetic call of Echo's presence.

"Oh, right. Echo. I thought you had forgotten about her the way you forgot your mom. I should tell you that she and I— You know that syzygy thing you Srelevart do? For you it's one person forever, which seems—limiting. Anyway, Echo loved it. Asked me to tell you never mind. She's happier sharing the consciousness of a real man than a pathetic boy—her words, not mine. I told you I don't think you're as pathetic as you were, but you know women—oh, wait, you don't. Well, trust me. They're quite opinionated."

The words were having their effect. Gray's panic increased under the influence of images of Jeph and Echo—merging in syzygy, lost to Gray forever.

Jeph stood there, smiling his malicious smile, holding a bloody knife blade-forward in his hand. "Wouldn't you like . . . ?"

Yes, he would like, but his mother's shouting finally came through the miasma of anger. "Stop. You came to rescue the princess from the dragon."

"I came to rescue the princess from the dragon," Gray said.

Jeph smiled. "Don't you need to kill the dragon?"

Gray shook his head. "Not with that knife." The words grounded him, and he realized the knife was a key—why else would Jeph be offering it? "I've got a different key. I'm saving it for you." He shocked himself with those words. He had intended to use the death key only on himself, at the direst emergency, but now he was thinking how he could get Jeph to take it. It frightened him to realize how much this place, this interaction, was infecting him.

Jeph flipped the knife in the air, and it disappeared. "OK. I'll bring her here, so you can see for yourself." A girl stepped out of the shadows. Superficially like Echo, she was dressed in an outfit like the one Echo wore in Ytilaer, but was ripped as if in a fit of passion. It was tight around the waist, and a breast was exposed, and one leg of the leggings was ripped away. She had a glamorous beauty that tempted him, but it wasn't Echo's beauty. She hung on Jeph like a starlet on a handsome billionaire, giving only one glance to Gray with a dismissive grimace.

"That's not Echo. It's not even a good fake. Do you even have her here?"

But Jeph's attention had turned elsewhere. Echo disappeared as suddenly as the knife had, and now Jeph was muttering and doing a sort of dance that involved liquid movements of the arms, high stepping, and sudden turns. He spoke softly in a guttural foreign language, and gradually shining golden cords extruded from his fingers.

"Gray, look out!" his mother called from within.

The cords whipped like string in the wind and snapped like whips, covering the distance to Gray like snakes.

Where had Gray seen this before? *Echo's display: the attack on Lazar.*

"Gray, move!" his mother shouted.

But the track of the cords fascinated him. He knew they were dangerous, but they were so beautiful. He knew Jeph meant evil for him, but the dance was hypnotic.

The cords fell on him and then fell away. He remembered with relief he was still wearing Lazar's armor. The bindings dissolved into a spray of sparks that bounced back onto Jeph, who staggered back, looking older than ever, bending over like a man about to vomit. In Jeph's moment of weakness, Gray heard Echo's cry again, reverberating among the cages, seeming nearer this time. Then the hideous bird emerged from the man Jeph and, flapping its enormous wings, flew away into the swirling maze of corridors.

CHAPTER 25

# Larceny

GRAY RACED TOWARD ECHO'S CRY, which grew fainter as he approached. Before the last reverberation died in his mind and soul, he had come to a dark cage lit only by the faint light of a woman who ordinarily blazed light everywhere she went.

She lay like one sleeping on the floor of her cage, as still as death. Gray called to her, shouted her name, pulled at the cage walls, tried to reach through even though the bars were barely wide enough for his fingers.

He went into her esuoh and found it dark and abandoned. He produced a candle and caught glimpses of destruction: a burned streak on the wall behind her stove, a flood of termites running across every surface, shutters over her windows. Peeking out her front door, he saw only the cage and no ladder to the memories upstairs. With growing dread, he moved the rug that hid the trapdoor to her basement. The door was gone, and the rug covered only a scuffed and dirty area of floor.

Echo lay with her head on the table among deteriorating sketchbooks. He touched her and felt only a faint spark, but also felt power flowing into her. He held her close to his heart, feeling his strength draining into her. Weakness came into him, as when Cain took his energy. At the same time, Echo became more substantial, and soon she could sit upright. He arranged her arms so that she could sit comfortably and sat beside her holding her hand.

She came to herself gradually and rubbed her eyes with the clumsy gesture of a baby. "Who are you?"

How he hated that question. He held her close again and whispered to her. "I'm Gray, and I've always loved you."

She didn't return the hug, just sat there with her arms at her sides. "I'm Echo." She spoke like a child who has just learned that piece of information and is proud to share it.

"Yes, you're Echo. I've been searching for you."

"I was calling someone. Gray, I think. Was that you?"

"I came as soon as I could."

"I don't remember why."

"Because we need to get out of here."

She turned to the table. "I was—" She moved the books around, speaking sleepily. "I was looking at these. They told a story, but I couldn't find the end. And then the lights went out." She brought one closer to her. "I want the lights on."

Gray set a lit candle on the table. "Is this enough? This place"—he shivered— "siphons light away."

A knock on the door, and his mother asked, "May I come into your house?"

"Who's that?"

"My mother. Sylviana. She's a friend. Tell her to come in."

"Did I call her?"

"No. But you called me, and I brought her."

"What color is she?"

"What?"

"There were blue and green women at the party."

"She's light brown, not blue or green."

"I want to go back to the party."

Gray sat across from her, trying to look into her eyes. They were darting in every direction. "Please tell her to come in."

"Who?"

"My mother. She's at the door. She can help us."

"I want to go to the party."

"I don't know where the party is, but my mother might know. Let's bring her in and ask her." He hated lying that way, but he felt more and more at sea with this new Echo.

"OK. If she'll help us find the party, she can come in."

The word was all it took, and his mother entered and stood beside them. She looked at Echo, and Gray looked to his mother for some understanding of who this person was.

"Is this Echo?" his mother asked.

"I'm Echo." The same triumphant tone.

"I'm not sure," Gray said. "She's so—different."

"Are you going to take us to the party? I want to go to the party." Echo's tone was petulant and demanding.

Gray felt he had come too late, and despair crept into him. His mother touched his hand, and power flowed into him. He felt a little better. He pulled his hand away. "Thanks, but you're going to need that."

"You said she was going to take us to the party," Echo said.

Sylviana sat beside her. "Tell us about the party. We'll take you there if we can."

"It was fun! Fun! Fun! There were girls and music. And a fancy man in a funny jacket. He gave me a key."

She jumped up and ran outside her esuoh. Before Gray could follow, she was back, carrying a bloody knife with the tail of her tunic. "Don't touch it. It's dirty." She wrapped it in a towel and set it on the table. Then she started crawling around on the floor reaching under cabinets, looking under the stove. "I want my dinosaur."

Gray and Sylviana exchanged a look.

Sylviana spoke gently. "You were telling us about the party."

Echo squealed in toddler frustration. "I need my dinosaur!" She pulled cushions off the bench and books and knickknacks off the shelves. "Did you take my dinosaur?"

"We'll help you look for it." Sylviana started searching.

Gray raised his eyebrows at her, and she lowered hers at him. He started looking around under the table. There was a plastic T-Rex about three inches tall. "Here it is." He reached for it.

Echo came running over. "Don't touch it!" she screamed. "It's mine!" She brought a towel. "Get out of the way."

He stepped aside, and she lunged for it. She picked it up with the towel and wrapped it and held it like a baby doll. "It's mine."

Gray looked at his mother. "This isn't Echo," he whispered. He pictured a future with this child. Was this the purpose of the death key? He had to consider the possibility, but rejected the idea immediately. Better Echo the child in Ytilaer than soulless Echo locked out forever. He wouldn't abandon her, but she was not the woman he had expected to give his life to.

Sylviana shook her head at him, then turned to Echo, who was still cradling the dinosaur. "Echo, where's your soul?"

Echo looked up with tears running down her cheeks. "She's sleeping and can't wake up. I've been a bad girl, and the fancy man took my treasure." She put the dinosaur on the table and wailed, "I want my walnut!"

Sylviana enfolded Echo in a motherly embrace and spoke to Gray. "Listen to her. She's dying, and she's telling you how to rescue her."

"But she's so strange. Why aren't you—?"

"Like her? Think with your soul. She broke the illusion by herself, somehow. How much energy does she have left to maintain her existence?"

Gray stared at the two of them for a second, and then everything clicked into place.

They stood here together—Gray, his mother, and Echo. Gray was fully alive and in Jeph's prison voluntarily, his body entranced where his journey began. He could leave at any time and presumably find his way back. His soul was safe on its island. Sylviana had been Cain's prisoner, taken among many others into Jeph's prison, and freed from her cage by Cain's key. But it was only her persona, the aspect of herself that faced the world, who could walk with him among these cages. Her body was dead, and her soul still captive. She was not whole. And then there was Echo. Her body was still alive, just barely, but her soul, like all the others in this place, was locked away somewhere. Jeph had underestimated her, again, placing her in a comfortable illusion to give himself a slow and steady energy source. Echo would never be satisfied with a comfortable illusion. By an extreme exertion, her persona had broken free of that illusion, but she would not be liberated from Jeph's prison until she was reunited with her soul. The energy she had spent to break the illusion had left her depleted in both resilience and understanding.

He could kick himself, but he would save that for later. "Echo," he said gently, "I'll get the treasure for you, and the walnuts. Tell me how to find them."

"I have to go, too. My friend was there, and Aunt Doris. They wouldn't like it."

"They weren't real." Gray hoped he was telling the truth. "I've seen him make fake people."

She sighed and looked at him as if she hadn't yet seen him. "There was a fake Gray. Are you the real one?"

"Let me prove it. I'll bring back the treasure."

"And the walnuts."

"And the walnuts."

"Pinkie swear."

"I—" He started to protest, but his mother interrupted him with a look. He held out his pinkie. "Pinkie swear." He felt a trickle of power go out and the binding of a promise in Ytilaer.

"Use the dinosaur to get in. And the knife—" Echo shivered.

Of course. It was a clone of the knife that Jeph was going to use to imprison Gray. Who knew how many existed? But they were all keys.

"Jeph made the dinosaur, and the knife got me here." She seemed sleepy but lucid. Gray felt a spark of hope. "They're all I've got and I don't know how they'll work when you need them."

He took the two keys wrapped in their towels and shoved them into a leather shoulder bag that emerged to his attention from the clutter of Echo's esuoh. "Mind if I use this?" She answered with a wave of her hand.

"Tell me about the treasure," he said.

"Pfff. You've seen it before." Her energy seemed to be returning. Gray's mother grew paler.

"Mom—"

She gave him the look again.

"Let me hold her for a while," Gray said. He reached for Echo's hand, but Sylviana pulled it away from him.

"You've got to do this." Her voice was becoming quieter, her words slurring a little. And yet she spoke firmly. "No one wins if all our lights go out. Shut up and listen."

"It's a—" Echo seemed to grope for the word. Her hand went up to pull a light switch on a chain.

"The key to Lazar's esuoh that you made."

She nodded. "The real one. It's in a box. On the wall." Sylviana had fallen asleep with her head on her arms on the table.

"And the walnuts?"

"On the table. The coffee table."

"Got it." He didn't want to waste any more time on unnecessary questions, although he had many.

"Gray."

He turned to her.

"Please come back."

"I will." He hoped he sounded more confident than he felt.

THE DINOSAUR KEY CARRIED GRAY ONTO A HIGH BALCONY, from which, far below, he could see a black velvet ribbon of river lying in the midst of a city whose lights sparkled like many-colored stars.

A sliding glass door opened into Jeph's esuoh. It was calm and quiet, with no sign of the party Echo talked about. Gray closed the door behind him to look back through the window and see what Jeph was seeing. Cages in Jeph's prison flowed past, and the picture zoomed in, now on this prisoner, now that. Then the movement stopped, and the picture expanded to take in a wide view, slowly turning. Gray waited, still and silent, sure he'd been detected and pondering how his life path had led him to burglary.

It was a short moment of regret, if you can call it that, because the answer came as quickly as the question. He had to take the key back to Echo. And the walnuts. He rolled his eyes and shook his head. Walnuts? But he would take them, because Echo said so.

Jeph's esuoh was huge—and a mess. The party was over, it seemed, and the esuoh looked like a rock band's hotel room after a concert. Torn drapes, splintered glass, a broken piano in a far corner. Whatever rage of madness had destroyed this place had left one thing intact: a dark-wood shadow box with a glass cover containing a small silver three-bar cross, exactly like the one Echo had used to enter her display about Lazar. That small, sheltered thing was radically incongruous in this chaos, but by its very presence it also witnessed to the existence of a calm and rational beauty. *Why on earth would Jeph keep it here?* He took the box from the wall and shoved it into the leather bag he had brought from Echo's esuoh.

The walnuts were harder to find, until Gray smacked his shin on a coffee table so covered with clothing and debris that he hadn't seen it. Pushing everything aside, he found a small blue glass bowl that appeared to have about ten walnuts in it.

He picked up one of the rounded, wrinkled shells. It was similar in size and shape to a walnut, but it wasn't that. It was motionless and yet vibrating, blurry like something both there and not there, and it gave off a faint light. As he held it, its vibration became so intense that it felt as if it might fly away. He opened his hand, and it lay on his palm, rocking this way and that.

Echo was right that they weren't ordinary walnuts. But what were they? He pulled on the bowl and discovered he couldn't lift it. He grabbed a handful and then another, and walnuts refilled the bowl like water in a spring. He knew Jeph would come, so he dropped the ten or so he had taken into the bag and turned to leave.

At that moment, something enormous landed on the balcony, shaking the building like a nearby explosion. Holding the bag against his abdomen, Gray made a door into his esuoh, to get out of there before Jeph arrived.

But the door slammed in his face, and he turned in time to see Jeph, tall as a building, distorting reality to fit around him, enter the room. A huge condor sat on Jeph's shoulder like a trained parrot. "Don't leave yet," giant Jeph said, his feet shaking the world as he walked. "I think you have something of mine." When he looked down at Gray, his eyes and mouth displayed the blackness of outer space.

Gray's knees sagged, and his mind quailed. Monster Cain was a cuddly toy compared to this. In his fear, he reached into the bag and grasped a handful of walnuts. "Here," he said, his voice shaking like a willow in a windstorm. "You can have them back." But when his hand brushed the wooden box that held Lazar's key, an image of Echo popped into his head. *A girl?* Giant Jeph's voice spoke inside him. *You think a girl could help you? You are less than nothing. You are deader than dead already, and you just don't know it yet.*

Giant Jeph moved closer, appearing to shrink to a mere ten feet tall as he came, but he continued to be all Gray could see in the room; he seemed to be the only thing in the world. Gray's perception closed in around him, shutting out everything that he had ever believed to be beautiful or joyful. All the love and light in his life appeared as sham and scam, lying deceivers whom he deserved because he was one of them.

He continued to grip the box. What was in it? He had no clue, but it seemed important somehow. He left the walnuts at the bottom of the bag and held the box as if he could crumple it with his fingers. A different voice spoke to him, warmer, a voice of love not fear. *Not just a girl. Echo.* And then he remembered: *Get back to Echo.* Echo seemed infinitely far away, and he despaired of ever seeing her again, but he knew who she was, who he was, and why he was here. The walnuts in the bag buzzed like insects caught in a jar.

The condor, now taller than most men but shorter than the giant Jeph, flew down and hopped over to the bowl of walnuts. It turned and gave Gray a piercing look before picking up one in its beak and tossing it down its gullet. Immediately, the bird took on Jeph's human form, but old and haggard—thick drooling lips, bulbous nose, thin hair, blotchy skin. He picked up another walnut, his head returning to condor form to receive it greedily, and then he was human again, in form at least, Jeph in his prime, with light flowing through him—confident, serene, conventionally attractive. *A fancy man in a funny jacket*, Echo had said.

Echo's laughter sparked through Gray for just an instant, cracking his paralysis of terror. A bubble of laughter formed in him, then popped and escaped as a breath. It opened his darkness to a glimmer of hope-shaped light.

Jeph noticed the change in Gray. The giant Jeph looked down at him with those empty eyes, and the man Jeph gave Gray a look of curiosity that widened to an "Aha."

Human Jeph smiled at Gray, showing shining white human teeth. "You took my trophy—and some of my souls. You thought I wouldn't notice?" He spoke lightly, as if it were a very small thing, a child taking a piece of candy without permission. "Why don't you just hand it back now, and then we can talk. I'm not sure you really want that key; it did kill your father."

The shadow box. The key. Gray jerked his hand away, and the heaviness dropped on him again like a blanket, so fast he almost forgot the remedy. Yes, the key was connected to a dead man, apparently, and the outcomes were unpredictable. But when he dropped contact with it, the terror and despair returned.

Jeph was still watching Gray with a coldly detached and sadistic curiosity. "Did you eat them?"

"Eat what?" Gray asked, but he knew what.

Giant Jeph, who was gradually ditching his human appearance, but had only reached the Uncanny Valley that lay between what he had appeared and what he was, moved around to hem Gray in, as slowly as the movement of the sun through the sky.

"If you did, it's OK," Jeph the man said as the hairs on Gray's neck stood at attention. "I want you to have it." He took two more walnuts from the bowl, held them in his hand, rocking them like dice, with a look of pleasure on his face, and then tossed one to Gray.

Gray caught it and felt its pulsing life. "This is someone's soul?"

Jeph shrugged. "If you believe in that sort of thing. It's a new product of mine. I think it will be a winner."

A chill grabbed Gray's spine that shook him to his fingers and toes.

Jeph nodded. "That's the way I feel when I touch them, too. But think about it. There's, what, seven, eight billion on the planet? Most of them completely useless. The top one percent would pay a considerable amount for this." His head turned into the condor again, and he tossed the walnut down his throat. Again he turned back into Jeph, now looking like

Superman, bulked up, wavy hair so black it shone, probably able to leap tall buildings at a single bound.

"But you don't have to worry about the price," Jeph said. "Take it as a free sample. See what it's like; tell me what you think. If you like it—" and he smiled with a manufactured warmth that was almost persuasive "—and I think you will—you'll have an endless supply for yourself and anyone else you decide to bring in."

Gray stared at Jeph, then at the small thing pulsing in his hand as if begging for mercy.

"It's easy," Jeph said. "Just toss it in your mouth, and it slides down your throat. Just one. If you don't like it, you can walk away."

Gray felt the monster behind him, by his unfathomable presence pushing Gray toward "human Jeph"—although there was not much left of Jeph's humanity. Jeph's face had grown harder and colder, even more supercilious than the last time Gray had seen him. Jeph and the monster stood at the edges of Gray's field of vision, while between them marched memories of bullies from school, cruel parents and siblings from the foster homes where he'd stayed, even Echo and Sylviana laughing at him, Quig hating him, Theo and Edward throwing up their hands at what a waste of life he was.

In the middle of that, Jeph's hand floated like wreckage from a sunken ship, holding one of the walnuts. It seemed to speak to him: *Just one.* All Gray's weaknesses and insecurities could disappear; all his tormenters, too, leaving Gray the master of his own universe, regaining all that had been stolen from him. To be strong enough to beat Jeph at his own game. Now *that* would be worth it.

But he gripped even tighter the wood and glass of the shadow box. There was no "just one." The first was a step on a path that led to *this*— Jeph getting older and older, but continually going back to the glamor of his youth, which never lasted long enough and made him hungrier for more. He would keep company with such as Cain and *that thing* who stood over them and smiled like a god of the underworld.

"You could be my partner," Jeph said, as if he believed that would influence Gray.

Giant Jeph looked down at the two of them, smiling like a hungry man contemplating a peanut.

Gray nodded slowly and squeezed the shadow box containing Lazar's key. It vibrated now in a way that made the box feel brittle and insubstantial. Lazar had helped him. Echo trusted him. His mother forgave him for abandoning her and now waited for him to return. Goodness existed. His heart leaped in his chest, and the key leaped into his hand.

He pulled the cross out, tight in his fist, with light escaping through his fingers. He grasped the small thing by its chain, and as it swung in the open, its light unmasked all the deceptions.

Jeph was still  a decrepit old man; his esuoh a dry cave in a land with no water. The giant that formerly looked like Jeph was a monster armored in blood-stained black metal with a stained steel arch over his head with skulls impaled on it, whose enormous clawed fist swung to throw Gray into its greedy maw.

The last thing Gray heard from them were screams of rage as he was whisked away back to Echo's esuoh still holding the bag and the cross.

CHAPTER 26

# Echo Opens Her Eyes

Echo dreamed about a diner—carrying empty trays to empty tables in a dirty, ramshackle, and abandoned building—and woke to her decrepit esuoh, with Gray and a dark-haired woman standing over her, looking down with concern on their faces.

Hope and horror smashed together like two waves hitting the beach. She rubbed her face and looked again. Yes, her esuoh was falling apart, but Gray was here, and a woman who looked vaguely like him. Echo felt she should know more, but memory eluded her.

She got up to look out her window and found it boarded over. She kicked aside the rug covering the trap door into her basement and found only scratched and dusty floor.

"Gray?" She tried to manage the panic in her voice. "What's happening? Why can't I see out my window?" She made a door and stepped through it into a cage in a complex of cages, with a smell of fear and death filling the air. She stepped back into her esuoh and slammed the door shut. "What is all this?"

"Sit down." Gently he took her arm and drew her toward the table. She felt warmth and strength flowing from his fingers. "I'll tell you everything I know. What's the last thing you remember?"

She wracked her memory, walking down a long hallway where doors should open into her past, but there were no doors. She shook her head.

Gray opened a leather bag he carried over his shoulder and pulled out something wrapped in cloth. "Do you remember this?" he asked as he opened it.

It was a bloody dagger. She reached to touch it, but he wrapped it up quickly.

"It's a key," he said. "Best not to touch it again."

*Again.* She remembered—something. Like a memory she hadn't accessed in years, more a feeling than a picture. And the feeling was—rage. Over what? She glanced at Gray, but his face held only curiosity and concern. He held out something else in his hand, also wrapped in cloth, then opened it to reveal a small silver cross.

"Hold this," he said, but worry clouded his face. "It's probably safe. It just got me out of trouble, and Lazar gave it to you."

She opened her hand to receive it, wondering who Lazar was, and when anybody gave anything to her. It landed on her palm like a bolt of lightning that flowed through her arms and legs and made her hair stand on end. It all came back to her—Lazar's death, her despair, their conversation at God's Thumb, her quest for help, her rage at Jeph, the diner, and now Gray, the real Gray, here, with—yes, his mother, trapped in Jeph's prison.

She turned to Gray's mother, not sure if they had been introduced. "I'm Echo," she said, holding out the key.

Gray's mother laughed for some reason and said, "I'm Sylviana," and accepted the key on her open palm.

The effect didn't seem to be as dramatic for Sylviana, but color returned to her face, and she looked more alert.

"Where did this come from?" Echo asked. "I mean, after I lost it."

"I've been to Jeph's esuoh," Gray said. "You told me what to do, and you were right." Then he related his visit to Jeph's esuoh, how he had acquired the key—and the walnuts—and the paralyzing horror that Jeph was keeping company with these days. Echo struggled to comprehend his story, even after all the outlandish things she had seen over the past week.

"The giant with Jeph—it's like a demon out of a video game," she said when he had finished. "I thought Jeph was a monster, but this . . . ."

"And I thought Cain was," Gray said. "But this one makes them both seem like toys."

"I didn't mean to get you involved in this," Echo said.

"I know," Gray said.

"Lazar told me to get help." *Am I protesting to him or myself?*

"I'm here." He stood with his shoulders squared and his head held high. She was sitting, but even so, he seemed taller than before.

"But we're not enough by ourselves." She heard despair creeping into her voice.

"Lazar's key seemed to get their attention—"

"And carried you back here, into Jeph's prison," Echo said. "I'm glad to see you again, but I'm stuck here, and nobody's coming for us. You and your mom should go."

"My body died a long time ago," Sylviana said, "and my release will come only through Jeph's defeat."

"I can't help anybody." Echo felt the pressure of tears, but her eyes were dry, and she felt more emptiness than regret. "All I can do is get other people captured or killed." She turned to Gray. "Get *you* captured or killed." She leaned forward, as if that would make her words penetrate. "You need to leave. This isn't your fight."

A look of pain crossed Gray's face, and he doubled over for a few seconds. "It is my fight, and it's bigger than any of us knew." He made a chair and sat to look her in the eye. "Jeph and that—thing—are willing to depopulate the world, and if we wait, they will become stronger, not weaker."

He seemed about to continue, but he stopped, looking as if he had heard something behind him. "Just a second." He opened a door into his esuoh. "Hey," he said to someone there and walked on through. He came back in just a second. "It's Mitch," he said. "Please come into my esuoh." Sylviana followed him, but Echo hit an invisible barrier. Gray looked at her, concerned. "I'll bring him back."

Echo nodded, and the door swung shut behind him.

She went back to the table, where Lazar's key lay like a discarded pearl. She hung the chain around her neck and was assailed by a memory that felt like a presence or a presence as evanescent as memory. Lazar's face with its horizontal scar under his right eye appeared before her. "Are you—" she asked, then stopped and tried again. "Are you Lazar?" And then he was fully present, as real as if she could touch him.

He didn't answer her question but commanded her attention with an expression that conveyed concern wrapped in joy. "You need some light in here." He created a chair and smashed through the boards over her windows, then dusted his hands. "That's better."

He turned and opened a door with blue light shining through the opening.

"Wait!" Echo said. "Won't you stay? I've got questions."

He laughed. "You always do. But this is just a short visit. We're rooting for you." He waved over his shoulder as he slid through the opening and shut the door behind him.

Echo dashed forward, feeling an overpowering urge to follow him, but the door was gone. She sighed heavily, regretting her wish to escape, then turned to the window Lazar had broken open.

There were two windows now, and outside were two scenes. In one, Ytilaer, Gray and Sylviana stood silently in the passageway outside her locked prison cage. In the other window, which looked into Oge, Quig and Theo sat in chairs near the window of Jeph's office, with Cain lying on the floor and Gray sitting cross-legged beside him. They all had the quiet stillness of people traveling in Ytilaer.

A shudder ran through her. She pulled the cross off her neck and spoke to it, as if Lazar could hear. "I don't deserve this." She eyed it for a few seconds, as it swung sparkling in the light coming in. Then she said, "But you gave it to me," and put it back on, hoping she would be willing to release it when the time came.

ECHO STEPPED BACK FROM HER WINDOWS and tried to reconcile the two disorienting realities. A slight movement on the Oge side drew her attention to Edward, looking out the window. *It's easier in sequence*, Lazar had said, so she stepped closer to the Oge window and concentrated on the scene outside.

She became aware that she was sitting in a chair. Her limbs were heavy and unresponsive, but she could turn her eyes side to side, taking in Quig and Theo, Gray and Cain, motionless as statues. Edward turned to her as if he had heard her return to consciousness.

"You're awake?" he asked coming close, bending down to peer into her eyes. He reached down, and she saw her wrist rising in his hand, but couldn't feel it. "No, I don't think you are," he said, more to himself than to her.

She needed to contact him, but how? She tried to blink, but her eyelids didn't respond. With great effort, she managed to stay in her body while at the same time stepping back from the windows of her esuoh, looking from Oge to Ytilaer and back. In that way, she was able to blink several times, and Edward watched with an expression that could almost be called surprise. She blinked again, three times in quick succession, hoping he would read her mind.

"Are you in your esuoh?" he asked.

She blinked again, twice, hoping that was the universal signal for "yes."

"May I come into your house?" he asked, excitement creeping into his voice like an estranged relative visiting for the first time in years.

"Yes," she blinked, remembering how embarrassed she had been at using the wrong answer at the Srelevart meeting. Such a long time ago.

He pulled a rorrim from the inner pocket of his suit jacket, and then he was inside her esuoh, looking around at the chaos and stopping to stare out the windows into different worlds. He turned his attention back to her with his eyebrows lifted in a question.

She shrugged. "A gift from Lazar. I don't know why I received it, but it may be useful."

In the Ytilaer window, he studied Gray and Sylviana standing in the corridor of Jeph's prison, as still as Quig and Theo. "Who's that with Gray?"

"He found his mother. I guess Cain didn't entirely kill her."

He turned to Echo. "Gray's not here with you?"

Echo shook her head. "I can't get out of my esuoh. Gray said Mitch had come to his esuoh. He didn't plan to be long—he hasn't been long, but in the interim Lazar came and broke out the windows, and here you are."

Edward made a chair and sat down, leaning forward with his forearms on his thighs. It was out of character for him; Echo would have expected him to sit with one leg crossed over the other like a professor on a discussion panel. "Where is this place?"

Echo made a three-legged stool and sat facing him. "Jeph killed Cain and brought his prisoners here. I haven't seen much of it—I got caught in Jeph's trap."

Edward's face lost its color, and he covered his eyes with his hand. "We didn't want to believe it."

Echo tried to sympathize, but it wasn't coming easily. "Gray learned more about it. Jeph is a monster, but there's another one with him that makes him look like a doll by comparison. Jeph is willing to use billions of low-value people as a source of power."

Edward's hand slid from his eyes to his mouth.

"I think we're overmatched," she said.

He nodded slowly. "I think you are."

She noticed the pronouns in that sentence. She had thought—hoped—that reaching Edward would help in some way. But how could it? Nothing had changed. Nevertheless, she begged for something. "What do we do?" Maybe there would be at least a strategy.

Now he held her attention with his steady gaze. "I'm afraid I don't know."

"'Afraid' being the significant word," she said.

He shot her a look of fury—eyes wide, jaw and mouth tight—that he quickly converted to unconcern. "It's easy to be courageous when you have no idea what you're dealing with. And it's easy to ask for others' help when you don't know the choices they're making."

Echo sat back on her stool as if she'd been slapped. "I'm sorry. I keep forgetting you don't know what you're doing either."

His expression softened. "Children always think adults are wise and rational—" Echo bristled but didn't interrupt "—when in reality, even someone as old as I am is just muddling through."

"OK," Echo said. "I understand."

Edward shook his head. "I don't think you do. I'm not refusing to help, just trying to get you to realize it's no small thing, and the outcome is uncertain."

Echo sat with that for a moment.

"You could get out," Edward said.

"What?"

"Well, you came out into Oge and communicated with me." He gave an almost imperceptible shrug. "I mean, once you establish consciousness, Oge medicine might be able to get you out of your 'coma.'"

She stared out into Jeph's Oge office, bathed in bright light and empty of meaning. She looked to Edward again. "What are you saying? Leave Gray behind here? His mother? And after all the help I got from Lazar? I made a promise in Ytilaer before I knew anything about all this, and I wouldn't break it if I could."

Edward nodded. "I thought so." He stood up. "Very well." He paused, thinking. "Quig and Theo went out looking for you—" He shook his head. "They didn't have a clue where to start." He looked at them again, standing like statues in Jeph's office. "I will try to contact them."

"You will?" And then another question seemed even more urgent. "You can?"

"There's a sort of beacon," he said, looking sternly into her eyes again. "Theo is not the only one with an ancient history—mine is more ancient and less exciting than hers, but here we are."

"OK," Echo said, choosing not to badger him for details, lest he change his mind. "I'll give you a key to get back here."

"We don't . . . ." But he stopped himself.

"I know. Srelevart don't use keys," she said. "But we're probably beyond that scruple now."

He deflated a little.

Echo held out her hand, and a memory deposited itself there in the form of a small Mason jar with souvenirs of the seaside: tiny seashells, sand dollars, agate rocks, a glass fishing float, a small plastic orca, and other things, buried in the sand and occasionally visible when you turned the jar in your hands. She loaded it up with the invitation to her *esuoh*. She wrapped it in a cloth and offered it to Edward. "This will bring you back here. I hope."

"Keys aren't always predictable—" He gave her a significant look. "Either in the giving or the taking. That's one reason *we Srelevart*"—and he emphasized the phrase in a self-deprecating way—"avoid them." He accepted it, though. "But as you say, dangerous times sometimes require risky measures." He looked down to the jar and back to Echo's face several times before giving an almost imperceptible shake of his head and looking out her window into Oge again. "I'll do what I can." He nodded to her and opened a door into Jeph's office. Once there, he turned away from Echo, walked back over to the window overlooking the city, and then went quiet with the stillness that indicated he was going into Ytilaer.

At that moment, Gray's friend Travis came into Jeph's office, followed by Meghan the receptionist. Her face was puffy from crying, and her makeup was smeared. Travis was carrying a copy-paper box. "I think we got all the mirrors," he said to the room, then stopped and looked around at the motionless, silent travelers. He turned to Meghan. "Let's go put these in my car, then I'll walk you to yours. You don't need to stay any longer."

Echo closed the blinds over her windows and went to her table to wait.

Echo had scarcely sat down at her table again when a door opened in the center of the room and Gray entered. "May we come in?"

She answered yes, expecting him and Sylviana, possibly Mitch, but instead Sylviana, Mitch, Quig, Theo, and Edward followed him, crowding into her little space. The dimensions of the room seemed to shift around them even as they moved in to sit at her table, leaving her trapped in the center at the back with Gray on one side of her and Theo on the other.

As the others slid into place, Gray whispered to her, "Did you bring them?"

She shook her head. "Didn't Edward explain?"

"He said he didn't have time," Gray said. "We just needed to get back here."

Echo looked around the table at the eyebrows drawn together in confusion. The only exceptions were Edward, whose expression was more ironic skepticism, and Sylviana, who didn't seem to expect understanding but was content to be next to her son.

Echo opened a door into the center of the room, and stepped out near her windows, where she opened the blinds a space. Peering through the cracks, she found Jeph's office empty except for the people in her esuoh—and Cain. She opened the blinds wide.

Within seconds the others surrounded her, looking out one window at the dismal prison and out the other at the bright office, then back to Echo.

"How did you do this?" Theo asked, and the others' faces said she was speaking for them as well.

Echo pulled Lazar's key out of her tunic and showed it to them. "Lazar. The windows in his esuoh were like this, which—" and she couldn't resist a dig at their skepticism "—you would know if you had looked at the illusion I prepared for you."

They looked now, their mouths open. In the silence that followed, Echo felt a fleeting embarrassment at continuing to scold them after the fight was over.

Quig said, "I see it now, and I'm appropriately amazed, but does this answer any question or solve any problem?"

"No," Echo said, "and I don't have any answers or plans to fix this. I know this is a lot to ask, maybe too much. When I first came into Ytilaer, everything was exciting and fun, but now I see the darkness, and it looks like the end of the world."

Quig gave a subtle shake of the head. "The world has ended many times, and yet here we are."

"Did you tell them, Gray?" Echo asked. "Tell them."

He did, giving them a play-by-play of his most recent encounter with Jeph—his plans and the shape-shifting behemoth with him.

At the end, all the Srelevart seemed to be holding back nausea, except Mitch, who pointed out that Lazar's key frightened Jeph and his monster. Sylviana said, "My grandmother warned that the elder gods were present at the breaking of the primordial rorrim, and if you venture too deep into Ytilaer, you'll find them."

"Or they'll find you," Theo said.

No one looked at Echo at that moment, but she felt their attention, or maybe the feeling of being examined represented her own questions about who had found whom. Lazar had been waiting for the opportunity to stop Jeph and Cain when Echo arrived to "save" him. The weight of her insertion into this business hung heavy as a stone around her neck. Lazar had tried to prepare her. He had even brought the gift of seeing both worlds. "Mitch is right," she said at last. "Lazar's key is our only weapon."

She was interrupted by a ruckus in Jeph's office. The disturbance was Jeph, staggering like a drunk and shouting at the still and silent Srelevart to get out of his office. Not wanting Jeph to see her eyes open in Oge, Echo quickly closed the blinds on the Oge window, leaving only a crack to peer out of. After a certain amount of stomping and arm-waving, Jeph tilted his head as if hearing something and then stopped to examine the people in his office more closely.

He walked around the room, trying to lift their eyelids with unsteady fingers. He felt for Cain's pulse and a slow smile crawled across his face. And then he turned to Echo. She slid the blinds fully closed and waited. There was a jostling, like a small earthquake that rattled the dishes on the shelves.

Gray said, "I need to go out there."

Edward said, "No. You stay here. I'll go."

"We'll all go," Quig said, and at once four doors opened into four sesuoh, and Gray, Theo, Edward, and Quig exited Echo's esuoh and opened their eyes in Jeph's office, leaving Mitch, Sylviana, and Echo behind.

Distressed by their absence, Echo risked opening the blinds the tiniest bit she could manage and see Jeph's blurry, shadowy figure moving around his office.

Echo turned to Mitch. "I know why Sylviana and I can't go, but why not you?"

She hadn't meant it as an accusation, and he didn't take it that way. "If I went into Oge right now, I'd find myself at the desk in my apartment, so I wouldn't be much help."

Outside the window, Jeph went silent for a moment, then returned to himself more in control. "What are you doing here?" His voice was ragged, as if he'd been shouting for a long time.

Quig gestured toward Echo. "We were concerned about a friend of ours, and we found the office abandoned."

Jeph gave Echo a daggers glance and pointed to the door. "Take her with you then. She's not my problem."

The Srelevart wore stoic expressions, and Gray walked toward Echo's wheelchair. Quig stood his ground. "What happened to your employees?"

Jeph's eyes widened, and his jaw clenched in fury. But again he seemed to hear something and went still for a second or two. "If you're so concerned—" He sauntered to his desk and sat in his chair, speaking pointedly to Quig "—why don't you call the police? Isn't that your realm?"

He opened a desk drawer and pulled out a few envelopes the size of a wedding invitation, then rose and walked among his visitors, handing one to each. He fixed Echo with a penetrating gaze before Gray stepped in front of her.

They all stared at the envelopes as if they contained poison, but Jeph laughed and walked out. "I'm not going to need this place much longer. You can call the cops if you want to."

The four opened their envelopes. Gray showed his to Echo, who fully opened her blinds to read the looping calligraphy:


You are invited
To an evening's entertainment
At the esuoh of Jephthah Blackthorne III
Success Transformation
Reputation Management
(Admit one to the festivities)

As soon as she had finished reading hers, Theo slid her invitation into her purse. "Wrap them up and put them away before we cross over. They're keys."

No one bothered to argue or to tell her they knew it already. Quig and Edward each wrapped his in a handkerchief and put it in his suit pocket.

Gray set his on the desk. They all went silent, and in less than a second they entered Echo's esuoh, Gray holding a huge red bandana wrapped around the envelope.

CHAPTER 27

# An Evening's Entertainment

Gray again used his mother's rorrim to cross over from Oge to Ytilaer. The small square had been as big as the palm of his hand when he took it off the bedroom floor to try to stop his mother's murder. Now, though it seemed smaller, it was heavy with the weight of memory, including the deaths of both his mother and the man who had fathered him. *If we ever get out of this, I'm going to get back the rorrim Douglas gave me.* It was a weird thought for such a time: *When I finish saving the world, I'll go on a lost-and-found mission.* He shook his head at his own folly and created a huge red bandana, wrapped it around the invitation, and entered Echo's esuoh without asking permission. *We're past that,* and the thought was as comforting as the tea he had drunk in the house of his soul.

As he stepped in, Quig and Theo stood near the Ytilaer window, arguing. Gray thought the discussion would be about what to do next. They spoke over each other so that it was hard to get the gist, but a lot of it seemed to be more about ancient history than the future. Edward and Echo sat at the outer seats of Echo's table, like spectators who didn't have a favorite in the match. Gray's mother stood before the Oge window looking out with an expression of longing.

"Is that the rorrim that used to be mine?" she asked.

He held it out to her. "Yes. I found it in Cain's shirt pocket this morning."

She stepped back from it. "I don't have a place out there." She blinked rapidly. "And I don't have a home here either—except with you, and the price of keeping you here with me is more than I would pay." She turned away from him for a moment, then turned back with a determined smile. "You—" she lingered on the word, then, "and your friends—you belong out there, and here, crossing from world to world. But we—prisoners here—are like ghosts, existing but not living, waiting for a resolution to our stories that never comes. You don't have to help us, but here you are. Please send us home." She took his hand, and he felt strength going out of himself and into her, and she dropped it immediately.

"Gray." Theo's imperious tone broke the mood like the shattering of a glass bell. "Are you in this discussion or not?"

"What discussion?" Gray heard irritation creep into his voice. "We take Lazar's key and go to Jeph's little party. There's nothing else to do."

"It's not that simple," Quig said. "What if it doesn't work? What's the backup plan?"

"We don't need a backup plan," Gray said. "They were screaming when . . . ."

Quig finished his sentence for him, "When the key took you back to Echo."

Echo stood up. "If I go with you, that won't be a problem."

"I don't like going without a Plan B," Quig said. "This is a volatile situation, and anything can happen."

"The key *is* Plan B, Plan A through Z, everything we've got and either enough or nothing." Gray's long frustration with the Srelevart suddenly rose in his craw. If only he had been able to bring Echo in sooner, they might not be in this situation. And Jeph—his breath caught in his throat— might be carrying out his plans unopposed. "You'll probably just reason with him until he comes around."

Quig met his gaze with sad eyes and a set jaw. "Reason can keep savagery at bay, if only we would allow it." He pulled the handkerchief-wrapped invitation from the depths of his robe. "But when reason fails, we throw ourselves on the mercy of Ytilaer. And a tender mercy it is."

The others pulled out their invitations as well. Echo and Sylviana stood beside Gray, one on each side, ready to touch the key, and Mitch beside

Theo. Quig counted down from three, and they all touched the keys at once. Gray, Quig, Theo, and Edward disappeared, leaving Echo, Sylviana, and Mitch alone in Echo's esuoh.

"Oh, shit," Echo said. "They don't have Lazar's key." The magnitude of the disaster fell upon her like an avalanche of despair and kept falling and falling. She sank to the floor and cradled her head in her hands. Why didn't she give Gray the key? Why didn't she take the plain language of the invitation seriously: "Admit one"? Why? Why? Why? There were answers but no excuses, and she felt darkness close over her as she realized that her situation was possibly eternal, and she had brought Gray and the Srelevart into the trap.

"When you're finished lamenting your lost hope—" Mitch's voice was calm and patient, yet hard as stone "—we might want to look at our options."

"Maybe you've got options," Echo said bitterly, "but I apparently don't, and I don't think Sylviana does either."

"My option—if there's no other key—is to go back to my desk in my office in Beaverton. The board fired me after my wife accused me of using drugs. I was cleaning out my desk, where my body is sitting with a bottle of pills and a .38 in front of me. I decided to take one last journey of exploration. Now I see that my life can have meaning. What about you?"

Echo stared at him for a second, then took a deep breath and stood up. "OK." She looked slowly around the room, taking every familiar object into her attention, asking, *What about this?* before moving to the next. On the seat at her table was the leather bag Gray had brought back from Jeph's esuoh that morning. Something about it spoke to her, but she couldn't remember what. She picked it up and dumped its contents on the table. Two items wrapped in cloth fell out, along with a powder like fine sawdust and sand. She blew away the dust and carefully unwrapped the two keys. One was the bloody blade that had been the means of her capture. She rewrapped it and left it alone. The second was a small dinosaur, and seeing it, she remembered where it had come from. "Jeph made this himself on my first day in Ytilaer. Gray got to Jeph's esuoh with it. Maybe it will work for us."

Mitch nodded. "Maybe it will."

Echo thought about that for a second. She pulled Lazar's key off her neck. "Take this," she said, holding it out for Mitch. "That way, if you're the only one who gets through, you'll have the most important thing."

He gave her a level look, and then accepted it and put the chain around his own neck. "I'm sure it's important, but not so sure it's the *most* important."

Echo unwrapped the key and held it in the cloth in her hand. "On a count of three?" She counted down, and they all touched the dinosaur at the same time.

Chapter 28

# The Last Battle

Echo, Sylviana, and Mitch stood on the balcony of Jeph's esuoh under a drizzly gray sky, with fog obscuring the city below. Echo stepped across a puddle on the concrete patio floor and walked to the glass door into Jeph's esuoh.

Inside, the scene was less chaotic than when she had seen it last. The room seemed smaller, and some of the furniture, including the piano, was gone. Jeph's back was toward the door, and the Srelevart faced him from across the room. Quig's mouth moved, his face active with persuasion, but she couldn't hear him.

Echo slid open the door and stole inside, with Sylviana and Mitch close behind her. She exchanged a quick glance with Gray, who, along with the rest of the Srelevart, attended urgently to Quig's conversation with Jeph.

"If you care about yourself at all," Quig said, "you need to stop this. There's a path back for you. It's not too late."

An exhalation like a laugh came from Jeph, but Echo couldn't tell from behind whether it was sad or derisive. "The only thing in my past is a bunch of people with their hands out. I'm looking toward the future."

"You can still—"

"Ask for mercy?" That laugh again, definitely derisive. "I can do what I want, get what I want, go where I want. Do you have that, *Judge*?" The way he said "judge" sounded like a devastating insult.

"No one does," Quig said.

"Wrong." Jeph's voice rose now in both pitch and volume. "I do."

"For that kind of freedom you have to give up everything that truly matters," Quig said, as if pronouncing a final judgment.

Jeph reached into his pocket and pulled out something that fit in the palm of his hand. He tossed it toward Quig, and the walnut—Echo identified it en route—flew in a shining bluish-silver arc. Quig stretched out his hand instinctively, without aim, and the walnut flew to it like a magnet to iron. Jeph took another one and tossed it into his condor-mouth, which appeared just long enough to catch the soul and was quickly replaced by Jeph's head.

Quig looked at it with wonder. "What is this?"

"It's a soul." Gray spoke softly to Quig, meeting Echo's eyes but looking quickly away.

Quig held it in the palm of his cupped hand, his face showing curiosity, concern, and horror. "What happens to these people when you take their souls?" Quig asked.

"It's not bad," Jeph said. "Right ladies?" He tossed the question lightly over his shoulder to Echo and Sylviana. "It's like Cain said—a nice, quiet source of power. Until—" He tossed another walnut from his pocket into the air, and the condor head emerged, snatched it in flight, and became Jeph's head again. He didn't finish the sentence.

"And then what?" Quig asked, his face contorted with disgust.

"Nothing," Jeph said. "Nothing before, nothing after; from the dust of meaningless nonexistence to the ashes of meaningless nonexistence."

"No," Quig said. "Life has meaning—even yours."

Jeph laughed again, this time turning to include Echo, Sylviana, and Mitch in the joke. "Does it? How about your lover-boy, Lazar, Echo? Does his life still mean anything to you?"

Echo caught the look that ran across Gray's face at the gibe, a look of wonder, fear, mistrust. "No!" she shouted. "Gray! Listen to me. He gave me a hand getting off the boat. It was just a hand. He's a good man—better than all of us—but there was no electricity. No electricity at all." Then to Jeph: "The difference between you and Lazar is that when you're dead, everyone will be glad."

He turned to her, rage distorting his features. Echo was glad she had left the knife key in her esuoh, because if she had it now, she would probably try to use it. Instead, Gray came racing toward Jeph, grabbed him from behind, and shoved him to the ground. Jeph lay there, shaking and raging, and Gray kept his knee on Jeph's back, shouting, "What can we do with him?"

Quig, Edward, and Mitch looked at each other in helpless confusion.

Theo shouted, "Get the key!"

"Then help me!" Gray said to her.

*What key?* Echo wondered. Jeph turned into a condor, and with a mighty effort of wings, legs, and neck, flipped himself over and nearly stood up. Gray kept hold somehow, despite the iron beak pecking at him and the great claws slashing. Echo ran to try to help contain him, but she couldn't get past the flying beak and talons. Gray shouted to his mother, "You know how to hold him; I know you do!"

Sylviana opened her mouth in a soundless sobbing wail, wrapping her arms around herself. Then she looked at Gray, riding the condor like a cowboy on a bucking bronco, if a bronco could peck or slash his eyes out. The other Srelevart men tried to reach in to catch the bird's foot or grasp the neck, but their only help to Gray was to provide a distraction. Sylviana mastered herself and began to do the soul-capture dance around the fallen Jeph. Golden cords formed around him, and Jeph screamed in pain and fear.

The cords tightened around Jeph, and he returned to his human form—old, decrepit, insane, gibbering obscenities from his drooling mouth.

"What can we do with him?" Gray asked Sylviana.

"I can't hold him like this for long, unless I take his soul—" She shivered. "And if I do that, I'll be just like him."

"If he even has a soul," Gray said. "Can we put him in one of his cages?"

Echo watched helplessly; the only means of defeating Jeph seemed to be Jeph's ways. *What would Lazar do?* She didn't get an answer to that question, but it reminded her of a solution they hadn't tried yet. "Give me the key," she said to Mitch, practically snatching it off his neck herself. "If

I can free the souls, maybe Jeph will lose his power." She ran to the bowl of walnuts and started tossing them out into the room. They rolled around on the floor, defenseless and vibrating. She picked up one of the souls and held it close to her face to look for some way to set it free. Lazar's key vibrated in time with it, and the two objects pulled toward each other like merging galaxies. She held up the tiny cross, and it flew against the walnut, which burst into a ball of light like a distant star and dashed away to crash through a wall of Jeph's esuoh, leaving a tiny hole.

Holding the cross in her hand, Echo thrust it into the glass bowl and watched the tiny stars burst out like a meteor shower, then like a mighty glowing river. The ones lying on the floor leaped up to join them, and they flowed through the wall, breaking an ever-widening hole that revealed a dark cave beyond.

Suddenly, Echo felt something sting her fingers as she grasped the cross. It burned like a fire starting inside her hand and spreading up her arm and through her core and out to her extremities. Like the rush of blood returning after a tourniquet is released, the feeling was unpleasant but good. Her muscles spasmed and she fell to the floor, dropping the cross into the depths of the bowl. The flow of freed souls slowed to a trickle and stopped. When she could control her fingers again, she reached desperately for the lost key, but even with her arm in the bowl up to her biceps, she touched only empty air.

Jeph writhed in anguish under Sylviana's trap, and Gray stood next to her, imitating her actions and holding a couple of faint golden cords extending from his hands. Theo stood beside them and tried her hand at it as well. She was more successful than Gray, and she turned to him. "You've got to get the key."

He gave her a long questioning look, then nodded and went into his esuoh. The cords he had been holding dissipated.

*The key.* Echo didn't know what key Theo was talking about, but she needed to find Lazar's key. Could she get to it in Oge? She abandoned the bowl and went into her esuoh. The door to her front porch was there now, and the small braided rug once again hid the trap door leading Underground. She had reconnected with her soul.

Looking out her Oge windows, she saw Travis leaning against Jeph's desk with his arms crossed, watching and waiting.

Through the Ytilaer window, the ground was shaking. Sylviana and Theo held on to Jeph as if he were wreckage from a sinking ship, while the floor rocked and leaped as if it were breaking up in a hurricane. There was fear on their faces, and cords cracked under the strain, only to be regenerated more slowly than before. Echo wondered how long the women would last.

Echo went out into Oge and surprised both herself and Travis by being able to stand up out of the chair. She started crawling on the floor looking for the lost key.

Travis snapped to attention. "You're back?"

"We're in trouble, and I lost a key." She slid her hands over the carpet. "It's got to be here, but I have no idea where."

Travis began scanning the floor. "Looking for a key?"

"It looks like a tiny cross on a chain." *No, wait. That's what it looked like in Ytilaer. In Oge it was—* "No, it's a chip from a china cup wrapped in yarn. About so big." She showed the measure with her fingers.

Travis began scanning the floor. "Could it be on the furniture?"

"Anywhere," she answered, despairing. She crawled around the room, looking under Jeph's desk, under the chairs and other furniture. She even pushed aside Gray and Cain's body to look there. All the time, she was aware that anything could be happening where she'd left the battle. If Jeph recovered enough to fight back, would Sylviana and Theo be able to overcome him again? What if the monster Gray described arrived? What key was Gray looking for? The search was taking too long, and Echo might be too late to save anybody.

"Is this it?" Travis's voice startled her from her ruminations. She turned and saw a small object swinging on a loop of green yarn.

"Oh, thank you so much." She took Lazar's key from his hand and returned to her esuoh and then into Jeph's esuoh.

GRAY RETRIEVED THE DEATH KEY WITH CARE AND LOATHING. The prospect of using it—on friend or enemy—seemed like blasphemy. Could there possibly be a reason to shut a human being off from Ytilaer forever?

When he crossed back from his own esuoh into Jeph's, Echo was gone. Suddenly the idea of using the death key on Jeph—or even himself if it came to that—seemed entirely justified.

Jeph jerked under the golden cords held by Sylviana and Theo. Sylviana was translucent, her energy nearly spent, and even Theo looked tired and much older than she had before. Jeph's gyrations were having an effect. Because the women didn't take his soul, the cords of light kept breaking, and in their weariness Sylviana and Theo struggled to create more. There were only a few of the golden cords left, more from Theo now than from Sylviana. Gray subtly gestured to Theo with the hand that held the key, and she nodded gratefully and looked significantly at Jeph.

But Jeph wriggled free and stood up. With a wave of his arm he created a sphere around himself like a glass globe, and he half-shouted, half-sang:

> Abaddon, Destroyer, Dweller in Darkness,
> Come from the abyss I created for you
> And join me here at the meeting of matter and spirit.
> I have brought you food: Come and feast.

A gargantuan monstrosity appeared in their midst, warping reality around itself. Its center was a mouth lined with pointed teeth stretching backward into a hole of unimaginable darkness, and that center was held aloft by six black, leathery wings, each covered with eyes facing every direction.

It turned to Jeph with its mouth open wide, and words poured from the abyss at its center. "You promised me a feast. Where is it?"

Jeph looked at the thing as if he had never seen it before, his fear no less than that on any other face in the room. "My—my entire storehouse is yours," he said, "and these—" he gestured weakly around himself and stumbled over his words "—are the most powerful travelers—"

The demon floated on its hideous wings, and Jeph came closer step by step as if pulled by invisible ropes. "Your storehouse is nearly empty," the demon said, "and these pathetic creatures have the nutritional value of a fart. You promised to be my conduit to the world of flesh, and now you shrink away like a frightened child."

Jeph looked terrified, and Gray was torn between pity for him and fear for the rest of them. Theo signaled to him again, raising and lowering an eyebrow and looking pointedly at Jeph. *Throw the key.*

Gray didn't trust himself to throw it accurately. He carried it to Jeph, unwrapping it as if it were a gift of mercy. He still wasn't quite sure what the key would do. It was a death key because it meant death to Ytilaer; but excising Jeph from Ytilaer could be a kindness for all of them. He said softly to Jeph, "This will get you out of here."

Without even asking what it was, Jeph grabbed the key and disappeared.

Gray heard cries of surprise from around the room. Quig asked, "Where is he?" Even Abaddon seemed shocked, mouth and eyes open wide. Theo's answer flowed through the room. "He's gone."

In response to Jeph's disappearance, an earthquake shook the floor, and the flow of souls from the blue bowl became a mighty flood, pouring into the cavity like a mineshaft at the back of what had been Jeph's esuoh.

Jeph's esuoh was gone: everything—walls, furniture, the night sky, the patio, and the sparkling city; all that was left was a wind-blown cave like a toothless mouth in bare rock.

Abaddon remained. Its mouth turned toward Gray, and it floated toward him. "You owe me my passage to flesh." Gray watched mesmerized as the teeth came close to him, feeling like a bird being hypnotized by a snake. The darkness in its mouth became his whole reality, and he realized the futility of everything. *Pain and sorrow,* it said without speaking. *Pain and sorrow, regret and death. And when death comes, it is a blessing of nothingness.* The mouth opened wider, and a second jaw came from its throat with grasping pinchers. *After the suffering,* the voice didn't say, *you will not be.* Just as it struck, he felt himself pushed aside and Quig was taken into the monster's jaw instead of him.

At that moment a door appeared, and Echo came into the room holding Lazar's key swinging from a chain in her hand. She stood in open-mouthed horror as Quig writhed and screamed in the monster's mouth.

Theo screamed as well, and only then did Gray notice that he himself was screaming, too.

Echo glanced once at the silver cross, once at Quig, and then threw it. "Quig," she shouted, "catch!" But the demon's second jaw grasped Quig around his chest and abdomen and pulled him into the maw of darkness. Quig disappeared, and the cross flew into the monster's mouth.

A moment later, a sudden silence, and Abaddon shrank to the size of a tiny black marble, which expanded into the blue-fire portal. Quig was gone.

CHAPTER 29

# Aftermath

Echo and Gray, Sylviana, Theo, Edward, and Mitch stood staring at each other and at the emptiness around them in the cave that had once been Jeph's esuoh. Jeph was gone, along with his esuoh. The demon was gone. Quig was gone. The blue portal remained like a window into another world. Prisoners emerged from the tunnel that had been Jeph's prison and ran, walked, or stumbled toward the portal. Echo turned to Theo and Gray, who were standing near each other, and asked, "What the hell happened?"

"Hell happened," Theo said. She looked meaningfully toward the open portal. "And now it's gone."

The last of the captured souls trickled from the hole in the floor like a swarm of lightning bugs and flew to meet the personalities that had been taken from them. Echo watched in awe, but a question pulled her away from the scene. "Where did Jeph go? Did that—*thing*—get him?"

Theo shook her head—regretfully?—and Gray looked nauseated. "No," Theo said. She gave Gray that look again.

Gray answered. "He's separated from Ytilaer, forever."

"Lost his mirror?" Echo asked.

Gray shook his head, looking back to Theo.

"Separated," Theo said. "No contact with the inner world."

"What? How?" Echo had been in Ytilaer for only a few days, but it felt like a reality she had always known. If she were locked out, it would be there in her dreams, shaping her life in ways her Oge self might not understand. "Lost contact?" she asked. "What does that even mean? No dreams? No memories? No sparks of insight?"

"I made the key in an emotional state," Theo said, "more instinct than will. I had intended to use it on myself, because I saw where my life in Ytilaer was taking me. Overkill, looking back. But while I know my intentions, I'm not sure of the true function. So, no dreams, certainly; memories? I'm not sure. Sparks of insight? The muse is a creature of Ytilaer. Personal connection? Dubious. I never used it but gave it to Gray in case he needed it."

"And Jeph took it with him." Gray shook his head. "I wonder what he'll do with it."

A burst of light bumped into Sylviana, and her return to opacity started from the place where it hit her arm. It spread outward; first her color was ghostly, then lightened to merely pale. She stood with her hand on her arm where her soul entered, her other hand holding her forehead. Gray walked over to her and put his arm around her. She turned and hugged him as if he were a small child who happened to be taller than she was, and then she turned toward the portal. Openly weeping, Gray held her hand as she walked away, and she turned back with one last smile, releasing his hand to enter the blue fire as if it were a park on a spring day.

She was only one of a procession of people flowing from the cave toward the portal. Some trudged as if through soft sand; others sprinted joyfully; some screamed and cried and begged for mercy; others marched singing.

Pushing against the flow of the inbound crowd, Quig stepped out of the blue light of the portal. Gray ran to him and reached for his shoulders, but Quig signaled him to stay back. Echo didn't hear their conversation, but Quig spoke, and Gray nodded, sometimes hiding his eyes. Echo wanted to go up and say something, but what? An apology would be inadequate; an acknowledgment that she was wrong about him would be true but irrelevant. She watched the two men share last words until Quig nodded with a sad smile to Gray and returned into the portal.

Echo would have gone to Gray, but Theo was calling her. A collection of people had gathered around Theo and Mitch. Just a handful, really, they were the ones who had not died and who needed to be guided back to their sesuoh to continue their lives. Mitch opened a door and walked out with a man in a tattered red velvet coat of a fallen king just as Edward opened a door and returned from somewhere else.

Standing beside Theo were Aunt Doris and Galynn.

Aunt Doris was dressed in her pink and purple track suit. Her hair was messed up, and she looked around as if she could do something with this place if she had the time.

Standing beside Aunt Doris was a tall raven in heavy boots and her eyes taking in everything around her. Passing Aunt Doris, Echo went to Galynn and said, "Wait with these people. I'll be back in a second and take you home. I'll tell you everything." Galynn, whose silver raven's eyes Echo was seeing for the first time, gave the appraising glare that Echo knew so well, then flapped her wings once and settled down to wait.

Echo then went to Aunt Doris, who looked at her in surprise. "This is the craziest dream I ever had. Are you safe?"

"I know. Right? Yes, I got home this afternoon. Let's go back to your house." Echo led Aunt Doris into her esuoh, from which she made a door and opened it into Aunt Doris's esuoh. "Just go through this door, and you'll be at home. Get some rest. These big dreams are tiring. I'll see you later." She took Aunt Doris's hand and felt a slow outflow of energy as the older woman walked through into her own esuoh. The door closed behind her and disappeared.

Echo went back to Galynn. "Are you ready?"

"Not really. I'd like to look around. What's the blue thing?"

"It's the door out. I've never seen anybody except the dead go through it. The light feels like a severe mercy."

Galynn had gone to look over the edge of the cave; Echo followed her. "What do you see?"

"Nothing. Totally dark." Galynn turned to look at her. "I don't want to leave."

"There's no place to go from here. Go back to yourself, your life, so you can come back."

"Why should I trust you?"

Echo sighed. "I get it. I didn't mean to dump you. But I was beginning to see where this journey was going and didn't want to be responsible for what might happen to you."

"Why didn't you tell me?"

"I tried, but if I had been in your place, I wouldn't have believed it either. I didn't know then what I know now." She touched Galynn's elbow. "Come into my esuoh."

Galynn followed her in. "This is kind of a disaster." She gave Echo a side glance. "But cute."

Echo laughed. "That's what I said about somebody else's, but his isn't cute anymore."

"Is this what it looks like inside my head?"

"The same, but different. The parts are there—short-term memory, a passage to long-term memory, a passage to the Underground, a front porch, and windows to the outside."

Galynn stood up and looked out the windows. "Wait a second. That's Jeph's office. Who are all those people?"

"It's a long story. I'll introduce you to them later," Echo said. *The ones who are still alive*, she didn't say. "I'm sorry. I've got to help get the others home. I'll give you my phone number, and we can talk."

"You threw your phone away. Remember?"

"Give me yours, then." She handed Galynn a sketchbook, and Galynn wrote her phone number in a strong, bold hand.

Echo made a door into Galynn's esuoh.

Galynn preceded her in but turned to look back. "Don't forget me."

"I won't. If you hadn't been with me, I wouldn't have made it. It's obvious that Ytilaer has called you, but be sure you're ready. It will save you heartache."

"You sound like you mean it."

"You have no idea how much."

"You'll tell me about it?"

"I'll tell you everything." She opened the door to her own esuoh. "You've got parents who love you. Don't waste it." She closed the door and went back to the cave to help walk the rest of the living to their homes.

When the last of the dead passed through the portal and all the living had gone to their own sesuoh, Echo sat alone with her legs dangling over the ledge of what had been Jeph's esuoh. The dark of the night had passed, and the first rays of dawn touched high desert and distant blue mountains. Jeph was gone, and the cave from which the prisoners came had closed. Now it was a windswept shelf with rock above and below, ten feet deep, maybe twice that long. The wind carried away the last of the stench, and it looked as if no human had ever been here.

The rising sun illuminated outcrops of rock and forests, some ravaged by fire. A flashing river snaked below her, and overhead she heard the cry of an eagle.

ECHO WENT BACK INTO HER ESUOH. It seemed larger now, more streamlined and orderly, with fewer knickknacks and more empty space. The trap door to the Underground opened at her touch, and she closed it again. The door to her front porch also opened easily, and she pulled down the ladder to see that her hall of memories was the same as before. Only one Adirondack chair sat on her front porch, and only one eagle soared over the windswept canyon. She felt a heavy loneliness fall upon her, but she put it aside and went back inside her esuoh.

Through the Oge window looking into Jeph's office, Echo saw Theo and Marlo in deep conversation. Jeph's employees—Jack, carrying a backpack, and Chris with a messenger bag—stopped for a word with Marlo and left. Travis, Gray, and Edward crouched next to Quig, who was pale as death with his legs extended and his arms across his chest, and Cain lay in the middle of the floor like a disassembled piece of furniture. Out the Ytilaer window, the fog was so thick she couldn't see anything. She chose to enter Oge.

She lifted herself from the wheelchair and walked over to Gray. She put her hand on his shoulder. "If there's anything—"

He looked up at her, his eyes closed, and said in a cold voice she had never heard from him before, "I think you've done enough, don't you?"

Her eyes stung from the slap of his words. "Yes. I have." She got up and turned to walk out of the office, but Theo called to her. Echo looked over her shoulder, tempted to leave without waiting, but she went to where Theo and Marlo were standing.

"This isn't over," Theo said, looking at her with cool confidence.

Echo glanced back at Gray. "My part is."

Theo looked at Gray as well. "Give him time. He's lost a lot and gained a lot. It will take time to find the balance."

Echo sighed. "Me too." She turned toward the door, then back again. "Did we kill it?"

Theo looked at her solemnly. "Unlikely."

Rage leaped within her, stronger than her anger against Jeph. "Then what was it all for? All the people who died—Lazar, Quig, even Cain, who was better than Jeph, but that's not saying much— They're all dead and Jeph's alive? Where's the justice in that?"

"The justice of Ytilaer doesn't operate on our timeline," Theo said. "Or according to our definitions." She gave Echo a penetrating gaze that seemed to reach into her soul.

"I was supposed to finish it—" Her eyes burned with unshed tears.

"You were supposed to play the Fool's part, and you did."

"And now?" Echo asked.

Theo shrugged and turned back to Marlo. "What will you do now?"

"I'll see my lawyer first thing Monday to divide up the assets," Marlo said. "Jeph will find that he's been very generous to me in our contracts." She turned to Echo with a sad, stern gaze. "I know you didn't mean for all this to happen."

Echo waited for the "but."

"You were just trying to get a job," Marlo said.

Echo blinked rapidly.

"I'll give you a recommendation." She held out a card, and Echo took it reluctantly. "It's not one of Jeph's special cards," Marlo said. "Just my contact information. Call me directly."

Echo didn't have a bag anymore, so she put it into her pocket. "Could I come to work for you?" The words represented the triumph of desperation over judgment, but, still the fool, she said them anyway.

Marlo shivered and shook her head as if bees were flying around her eyes. "I'm offering a reference, not a job."

Echo took a deep breath and let it out quietly. Back to the job search, without Gray to talk to about it. "Thanks." She turned to leave.

"I'll walk you to the door," Theo said. She held the wooden box with Jeph's rorrim in it, the one Echo had used to enter Ytilaer for the first time.

"You should take this."

"I don't need it."

"Ytilaer called you, and you stopped them."

Echo shook her head. "I ran into the path of a car and got other people killed trying to rescue me." She looked back at Gray. His head was bowed, and for all she knew he was crying. She wanted to cry with him, but she would cry alone, later.

"Give him time to grieve." Theo touched her shoulder. "He's had some big changes in the past few days, but I don't believe his love for you has changed."

Echo nodded, doubting it but not needing to argue the point.

Theo held out the box again. "Somebody needs to keep this, and it should be you. It's valuable—not just in money, but in history."

"I don't need it," Echo said again.

"I think you do."

It was sitting there in Theo's hand, as if hanging in the air. Echo took it and left the office. It was only a couple of hours' walk home.

CHAPTER 30

# Saturday Morning

ECHO GOT UP LATER THAN HER USUAL 7 A.M. and went to the kitchen. It almost felt like a normal Saturday.

But Aunt Doris wasn't up, and nobody would be waiting to meet Echo at Ugly Mug, so she sat at the table and watched the morning light creep across the empty kitchen. Out the windows over the backyard, Aunt Doris's garden glowed like a scene from Ytilaer. She got up from her chair, feeling the cold floor against her bare feet, smelling the coffee as she measured it into the pot. Nothing in Ytilaer was small or trivial, nor in Oge. She hadn't realized how much she had missed Oge—nor, truth be told, how little she had taken the trouble to experience it when she had a chance.

Aunt Doris came downstairs in blouse and slacks in flower print and periwinkle blue.

"You look nice," Echo said.

Aunt Doris gave a strained attempt to smile but couldn't quite pull it off. "What day is it?" She sat heavily at the kitchen table.

"Saturday morning." Echo tried to maintain her cheery manner, but Aunt Doris worried her. "Do you feel OK?"

Aunt Doris sighed. "I slept the whole day yesterday—didn't even hear you come home, although I was scared to death about you—and now here you are making coffee instead of going to see that boy of yours." She shook her head. "And what a dream I had."

Echo went over and put her arm around her shoulder. "I'm sorry I worried you. I was trying out for that job I told you about and just didn't call."

"And how did the job go?"

Echo shook her head. "Not a good fit. I'll keep looking."

"Did that boy find you?"

"Gray?"

"Of course Gray. How many boys are willing to chase you to the end of the earth?"

*How many indeed?* "Yes, he did." She tried to keep her voice casual.

"You'd better hang on to that one. There aren't many like him anymore."

A sound escaped from Echo's throat, somewhere between a laugh and a sob, which she covered by a cough. She brought down mugs from the cupboard and poured coffee into them. She brought out the half and half for Aunt Doris and sat at the table with her.

"His foster-brother died suddenly yesterday." Echo handed over the mug, holding her hand and face steady, working for a neutral tone. "I think he's going to take some time for himself."

Aunt Doris nodded. "Different people grieve differently. Don't take it personally if it takes a while."

Echo nodded, observing that wisdom doesn't all come from Ytilaer. "What do you have planned for today?"

"Got someone coming over to see the house."

"Oh? What time? I'll spiff things up and then go for a walk. I lost my phone. I'll have to see about replacing it. And I'll keep an eye out for help-wanted signs."

Aside from those useful tasks, she sat by the duck pond in Eastmoreland Park, and in the quiet of a summer afternoon, she paid a visit to her soul.

CHAPTER 31

# The Ugly Mug Again

ECHO PUSHED OPEN THE DOOR OF THE UGLY MUG CAFE. The August morning already promised to be hot, and she chose an iced drink this morning.

She came because she always did, counting the days since she last saw Gray, and on the fortieth day, she still felt his presence in the dark wood and comforting familiarity of the place. A "For Lease" sign now hung in the window, and the owner told the regulars he was planning to retire. Echo had concluded that Gray must have left Sellwood because she never saw him on the street, on the bus, in the park—anywhere.

Today the thought of sitting across the table from Gray and catching up with him after all that happened brought a seesaw of ache and fear.

The table she and Gray had thought of as theirs was empty this morning, and she sat in the seat he usually occupied, where he waited facing the door because she was always late.

She wrapped her hands around the tall glass, feeling the condensation dampen her fingers, and went into her esuoh and out onto her front porch.

She sensed movement outside and went to her windows. In Ytilaer, she saw a coffee shop, but it was drab gray and beige with a robotic drink dispenser and mannequins at the other tables.

Out the Oge window, she saw that the noise had been a dumpy, down-trodden man pulling out a chair at the next table over and sitting in it. The man looked vaguely familiar but she couldn't quite place him. She looked out the Ytilaer window again, and he wasn't there at all. She entered Oge and recognized Jeph, no longer handsome as a movie star, just a tired old man hunched over a glass of water.

He looked at Echo as if he had something to say. "You."

She looked steadily at him and didn't answer.

"You think you won," he said. A drip of drool fell out the corner of his mouth.

Echo, remembering the deaths of Lazar, Chandler, and Quig and her loss of Gray's companionship, shook her head, choosing not to speak.

"That woman took everything."

"Marlo?" she asked before thinking.

"You helped her."

*No*, she didn't say, *she helped me.* "I would have if I could," she said.

"But you didn't win," he said. "I do what I want, get what I want, go where I want."

"What *do* you want?" she asked.

He sat there, his lips opening and closing, and then he got up again. He shuffled toward the door. Now she saw that his suit—although it resembled the fine blue suit he had worn before—didn't fit right. It was dirty and torn. The pant legs dragged the floor over ratty bedroom slippers. He came back and took the glass of water and threw it in Echo's direction. He threw badly, with a shaking hand, and it was easy for her to dodge it. The glass slammed against the wall and smashed into a thousand pieces.

"Get out," the cafe owner said, "and don't come back."

"I go where I want to go," Jeph said, going out the door.

"Are you OK?" the cafe owner asked, bringing a broom and dustpan over to clean up.

"Yeah, but it looks like some of your artwork got wet." She helped with the cleanup, and just as they were finishing, she looked up and saw a face at the door, both familiar and foreign, with a tentative smile. His eyes were closed in Oge, so she went into her esuoh and came out in Ytilaer, to a sidewalk cafe in the ruins of a beautiful old city.

"I hoped you would be here." He sat in his usual chair and laughed. It was a good sound, like old times.

"It's been a long time." Echo took her usual chair, pulling her drink across the table to herself, noticing that a radio somewhere was playing a sad, sappy song: *You left me crying, and I'll leave you now.* And a frosty voice burbled up from within, *I'll be late for work if I don't leave right now.* It was true that she would be late for work if they covered everything they needed to, but it was also true that this was more important than making lattes. She turned off the radio and sat in silence, watching him.

He spoke after a too-long pause. "Yeah. I'm sorry."

"How are Quig's wife and kids?"

He sighed. "As well as can be expected. Julia sold the house to the Srelevart and moved back to Chicago to be near her parents. I'm living in the house as a caretaker. They left me the dog."

She waited, watching his face and taking in the details of the world. There were tiny green shoots growing in the cracked concrete of the ruined city.

"How about you?" he said finally.

"Aunt Doris moved to Woodburn and I live in the basement of a friend of hers. I work in a coffee shop."

"Do you—" He stopped, flustered. "I mean—" He rubbed his face with his hand. "It's been a long time."

Echo nodded.

He looked at her, his eyes darting away and back. Finally, he spoke again. "What do you do in your spare time?"

"I walk around Ytilaer. I don't go to the city or the carnival. I walk the beach in the other direction."

"Do you see anybody?"

"I saw Mitch once, on top of the bluff. I don't think he saw me."

"Damn it, Echo. Are you as dense as I am? I mean, are you *seeing* anybody?"

She sat back in her chair, flabbergasted. "I suppose if you were to tell me today that you haven't forgiven me and never will, I *might* 'see' somebody, sometime. But who could I ever find who wouldn't look like a bug next to you? When I want company, I visit my soul. She doesn't talk much, but when she does, she tells me to learn patience."

He took a deep breath, and the tension went out of his shoulders. "I've been—waiting . . . ." His voice trailed off. "I couldn't call. It would be too—" He searched for words as if they were insects darting past his eyes. "I hoped you'd be here, even after all this time."

He sat with his hands spread out on the table, fingers dancing as if they were preparing to push him off and away.

*I can't let him go this way.* "Look, I—" she said, and then realized he had said the same words at the same time.

They laughed awkwardly, looking into each other's eyes.

"You go first," Gray said.

"No, you," Echo said, glad for a respite from what she had to say.

He shrugged, then straightened his shoulders. "It wasn't your fault." He looked away to a far corner of the room and then back to her. "It was big and terrible, and we all made mistakes. But you can't take all the blame just because you had the courage to take on every monster you met."

She sighed, half smiling as she blinked back tears. "But it wasn't courage. It was ignorance and stupidity and pride. I dragged Quig into it, and he—" She couldn't finish.

So Gray finished for her. "Died a hero after all. Douglas would have been proud of him."

"Does that soften the loss?"

He looked directly at her and said, "No."

The word hit her like a blow. She covered her face in her hands. "I didn't know him as well as you did, but my part in causing it feels so—" It was like the day she woke up in the hospital after the traffic accident that killed her family and realized she'd lost everything, and it was all her fault. She felt something warm and tingling near her elbow and looked down to find that Gray had put out his hand near but not touching.

"It's not your fault," he said again, emphasizing every word.

"But you said—"

"I know what I said, and I'm sorry. I was angry and sad and guilty, and you were there. I picked up one link in a chain of causality going back to the beginning of time. It's at least as much my fault as yours. Please listen to me now. I don't blame you."

She took a deep breath, wiped her face, and asked, "Where do we go from here?"

He smiled, and a bouquet of red roses appeared next to him on the table.

"Where did those come from?" she asked.

"You brought them. You did the first time, too."

"The first time?" She was confused.

"When you thought I was going to ask you to marry me."

A laugh burst out of her. "That's so embarrassing."

"You laughed the first time, too."

"Not at you, either time. But so much has changed. We're different from who we were before."

"I know. I still want you to share my life with me." He pulled something small from his pocket and slid it across the table. "Let's explore together."

She shook her head. "I don't need a rorrim anymore."

He lifted his hand, revealing a gold band and a small spark of light. "You don't have to answer. I know I—"

She laughed again. "I'm always wrong." She took his hand, feeling the electricity flowing through it.

He turned red, a lovely color, and she leaned across the tiny table to kiss him. It was a mistake. They were like two waves crashing together, joining, separating, their worlds merging. He didn't push her away this time, and she saw why he had been reticent before. Not here. *Not now.* She pushed away, breathing hard. The other people in the cafe were looking at them. She slipped the ring on her finger and held it up. "We're engaged."

Gray laughed, and the other customers applauded. "We'd better get out of here," he said.

They went out, not daring to hold hands, but allowing their arms to lightly brush in the hot summer morning, an intensity of pain and pleasure, a promise of more.

"The Srelevart have a ritual for syzygy—marriage in Ytilaer." Gray's voice was as warm as the sunlight.

"Of course they do. But let's also have an Oge wedding so that Aunt Doris can be there."

THE END

9 798987 751428